Praise for Steven Axelrod

Nantucket Sawbuck
The First Henry Kennis Nantucket Mystery

"Axelrod has a gift for characterization and a strong lead in Kennis. Nantucketers might bristle at the cynical portrait of their home, but his mystery debut gives the island as much personality as its varied inhabitants."

—Kirkus Reviews

"Axelrod's promising debut introduces a protagonist who will remind readers of Robert Parker's sleuths. The two-part story structure ('Premeditation' and 'Post Mortem') also gives readers an Ellery Queen type of opportunity to 'help solve' the crime."

—Library Journal

"Kennis is an honorable small-town cop whom readers will root for."

—Booklist

"This is a promising start for a new author."

—Publishers Weekly

"A well-written small-town mystery that feels like life, complete with suspects who are the sort of people who commit murders and a police chief who's capable of catching them at it. Read this book."

—Thomas Perry

"Axelrod is a full-speed powerhouse of a writer."

—Domenic Stansberry, Edgar
Award–winning author of *Naked Moon*

Nantucket Five-Spot
The Second Henry Kennis Nantucket Mystery

"Axelrod crafts an enjoyable, fast-paced read."

—*Publishers Weekly*

"In the second Henry Kennis mystery, the summer tourist season on Nantucket is under way when a threat to bomb the Boston Pops concert disrupts the holiday feeling, although the poetry-writing police chief suspects this may be a distraction to cover up a much bigger and more dangerous conspiracy."

—*Library Journal*

Nantucket Grand
The Third Henry Kennis Nantucket Mystery

"*Nantucket Grand* has everything I look for in a crime novel—tight, vivid prose; a sharply drawn setting; an intricate plot with lots of unexpected twists; well-crafted characters; and an appealing protagonist in the person of Police Chief Henry Kennis, a dogged investigator you're going to enjoy following on all of his adventures."

—Bruce DeSilva, Edgar Award–winning author

"Using his screenwriting background to good advantage, Axelrod packs plenty of layers and surprises into this intelligent, twisty tale. Henry's wry humor as well as his affection for the residents he serves exudes warmth and will appeal to fans of Bill Crider's Sheriff Dan Rhodes."

—*Booklist*

"Axelrod's characters span the spectrum from homey and nice to proudly nasty. Fans of Spencer-Fleming's Russ Van Alstyne and Frederick Ramsay's Ike Schwartz will enjoy Henry's literary leanings and dogged determination to protect his island and its residents."

—*Publishers Weekly*

"A beautiful island made ugly by class warfare makes a convincing backdrop for Chief Kennis's third case."

—*Kirkus Reviews*

Nantucket Red Tickets
The Fourth Henry Kennis Nantucket Mystery

"Nantucket's many charms fill the pages…"

—*Publishers Weekly*

"Axelrod and his protagonist bring an amused, judicious, and ultimately tolerant eye to the foibles large and small of a mixed Santa's bag of characters."

—*Kirkus Reviews*

Nantucket Counterfeit
The Fifth Henry Kennis Nantucket Mystery

"The fifth in Axelrod's clever series casts a cynical eye on Nantucket's decidedly diverse denizens. Only the most careful readers, undistracted by his satire, will figure out whodunit."

—*Kirkus Reviews*

"The narrative flows along at a good clip, with eddies of philosophy and humor. The witty dialogue perfectly matches the multifaceted characters. That Henry believes in an 'old school low-tech version of police work' allows the reader to readily follow the clues."

—*Publishers Weekly*

Also by Steven Axelrod

The Henry Kennis Nantucket Mysteries
Nantucket Sawbuck
Nantucket Five-Spot
Nantucket Grand
Nantucket Red Tickets
Nantucket Counterfeit

Other Books
One-Man Show
Hollywood Parking
The Rats in the Palm Trees
Heat of the Moment

NANTUCKET
PENNY

NANTUCKET PENNY

A HENRY KENNIS NANTUCKET MYSTERY

STEVEN AXELROD

Poisoned Pen
PRESS

Published by Poisoned Pen Press, an imprint of Sourcebooks
P.O. Box 4410, Naperville, Illinois 60567-4410
(630) 961-3900
sourcebooks.com

Library of Congress Cataloging-in-Publication Data

Names: Axelrod, Steven, author.
Title: Nantucket penny / Steven Axelrod.
Description: Naperville, Illinois : Poisoned Pen Press, [2021] | Series: A
   Henry Kennis Nantucket Mystery ; book 6
Identifiers: LCCN 2020040150 (print) | LCCN
2020040151 (ebook) | (paperback) | (epub)
Classification: LCC PS3601.X45 N348 2017 (print) | LCC PS3601.X45 (ebook)
   | DDC 813.6--dc23
LC record available at https://lccn.loc.gov/2020040150
LC ebook record available at https://lccn.loc.gov/2020040151

Printed and bound in the United States of America.
SB 10 9 8 7 6 5 4 3 2 1

To Jim Berkley, who got me started on the road to this book when I was sixteen years old.

Thirty miles out is a world away
Of the many who go there, all long to stay
Toss a penny as your ship sails round the bend
All good wishes come true, in time, my friend
You'll come back again
To that Faraway Island
— **LISA WENDELKEN**

We should forgive our enemies, but not before they are hanged.
— **HEINRICH HEINE**

THE WHALE ON THE BEACH

FOR DAVID KENNIS AND HIS GRANDSON

Walking on another beach
On another ocean, in another time
You asked me what I meant
When I said
"The ocean has sea gull eyes."
I wasn't really sure.
But your undivided interest
Was a challenge and a dare.
"It's not human," I said. "It doesn't care."
You nodded.
"You have a spark," you said.
And I felt the ember glowing
With your breath.
Feeling death in the dark water,
We stopped to stare into the moonlit Pacific
Standing together on the cold sand
Under the crust of stars
As the surf rumbled beyond us
In the dark
We walked the beach often that summer
Sand flicking from our toes
At the water's edge,
Walking to the pier and back,
Cheating the tide.
One day we watched a stunt man
Parachute into the ocean
He was working on some movie
We found out that night he had died

Tangled in his nylon straps
Drowning before help could arrive
And I thought of Sarah
Loved across the tragic gulf of a decade
(She was in her twenties; I was fifteen)
Who had nearly drowned,
Swimming in the storm surf
A few weeks before—
Fighting the rip tides
Finally crawling onto the beach
On her hands and knees
Gasping
You went to help her
You held her in your arms
Battered but safe
I take my son's hand, thirty years later
On the wide Atlantic shore
Just him and me
Without the glamour
Of a rare anointed moment:
Just another walk on the beach
The familiar small hand in mine.
Today we came to see the whale
That washed ashore to die last weekend
A hulking mystery
An Easter Island statue
Pecked at by the gulls,
Finally carted away
My son asks me, why did he do it?
I cannot say
But these shoals are famous for shipwrecks.
I tried to call you tonight

The number is still in my phone
As if you were still stalking the deck at dawn
Sipping the first drink of the day
As if the house had not been sold to strangers
Real estate brokers mingling with mourners
At the wake.
My mistake—
The number has been disconnected.
I dial it anyway, now and then,
As if you might pick up and say
"Dear boy, it's after ten
No one civilized calls at this hour."
And my son, calling me
Years from now
Just to chat,
"Are you keeping warm?
Did you lose power in the last big storm?
Did you hear Vampire Weekend's new song?"
I'll keep him on the phone too long.
Maybe he'll remember that,
Some decades still further on
Hiking some other beach
Feeling a little boy clasping his hand
As if he'll never let go,
Feeling his own heart lift and fall
Knowing there's no one left he can call
To describe it.

From *The Whale on the Beach and Other Poems*
Push-rake Press, 2020

CONTENTS

Chapter One

THE WHALE ON THE BEACH

The Nuremberg trials were officially referred to as an international military tribunal. They gathered evidence of Nazi war crimes and put the criminals to justice. The cruelties of a middle-class American adolescence, inflicted during the four-year ordeal of high school, are much more common, far less terrible, and hold no historical significance. But some incidents rise above the level of routine hazing and do profound damage. They ruin lives. They create psychic wounds that never heal. And they require their own tribunal.

—From Todd Fraker's deleted blog

For me, the fall wedding season on Nantucket, with its ostentatious celebration of the present and its sunny hopes for the future, began with a disturbing telephone call from my children's school.

"Chief Kennis? This is Alan Bissell."

I couldn't imagine what news the superintendent had decided to bring me on this squalling September morning, but it couldn't be good—Bissell sounded far too pleased with himself.

I set my take-out cup of Fast Forward coffee on my desk blotter, swiveled my chair to watch the milling gray sky and the rain lashing the big picture window. "Is there a problem?"

"I should certainly say so. A very serious problem. I need to see both you and your ex-wife in my office as soon as possible."

"Okay—talk to Barnaby Toll. He can set up something for later in the week."

"Not later in the week. Not later today. Now. Your ex-wife is on her way to the school as we speak, and this matter needs to be addressed by both parents...especially in a divorce situation, where a broken home is actively destabilizing the child's mental state and behavior."

"The child? Which child?"

"We can discuss the matter in detail when we meet."

And then he hung up.

Bissell and my ex-wife, Miranda, were waiting for me when I got to the school. Alice Damaso, Bissell's lovely and long-suffering secretary, gave me a small smile and a sympathetic lift of the eyebrows as I passed her desk.

Bissell looked up from a sheaf of papers as I stepped into the office. "Come in. Shut the door, and sit down."

Miranda, in full real estate attire—black pantsuit with red ruffled blouse, matching red handbag and sandals—sat in one of a pair of armchairs angled toward the desk. She turned, glaring at me with a look I remembered all too well from my marriage. It said something terrible had happened, and it was all my fault.

I ignored her and took the other chair. "What's going on?"

Bissell cleared his throat. "At the start of the new semester, our new creative writing instructor, Dylan Farrell, gave his students the assignment of writing a long story, between forty and eighty pages. This would be a first draft, composed quickly, with the students to spend the remainder of the unit revising their first drafts. I had no objection to this course of study, and it was duly implemented for Advanced Placement candidates. The manuscripts were turned in on Friday. This is what your son, Timothy, presented as an answer to the assignment." He lifted the sheaf of papers on his desk and dropped them again as if they were contaminated. As if to verify my observation, he squirted some hand sanitizer onto his palm and rubbed his hands together.

"That stuff only kills the weak germs," I couldn't resist pointing out. "The hardy ones survive and multiply. It's like a little course in evolutionary theory. The result is you're creating a colony of supergerms. With the best intentions, of course."

"Is that supposed to be some sort of veiled comment on Nantucket High School policy merit guidelines?"

I shrugged. "Just trying to be helpful."

He pushed the plastic bottle away.

"Could you let the man talk, please, Henry?" Miranda said, her voice clipped and irritated. "I have a showing this morning."

"Sorry."

Bissell took a breath and squared his shoulders. "I have referred this matter to this institution's BTAM—the Behavioral Threat and Management Team, which, as you know, is our multidisciplinary group that includes a trained psychiatric social worker; my assistant principal, Craig Rezendez; and, in extreme cases, a member of your own department."

I sat forward. "What are you talking about? How does my son's story constitute any kind of threat to anyone?"

A thin, smug smile. "Why don't we let the material speak for itself, Chief Kennis? I think I've said enough." He extracted several sheets from the pile on his blotter and sorted through them for a second or two. "Here's how it begins. 'Let there be no mistake. This is a confession. A confession before the fact, so to speak, but a confession nonetheless.' A little later he writes, 'I am a murderer. A murderer of seven men, by my hand seven men will die, seven men I haven't laid eyes on for thirty-five years. My only consolation—and it is the reason for my actions, as well—is that these seven men deserve to die. But who am I to make such a judgment, you may ask. If you do, then it is you, whoever you may be, who are at fault. The entire history of the human race has been a story of one man, or a group of men, deciding that a different group of men should die, from the caves to Genghis Khan to Hitler, who exterminated six million Jews during the Second World War. But then came the Nuremberg trials. They tried war criminals there. And hung them.'"

Bissell set the papers down and pushed them aside, nudging the sanitizer bottle. "The title of the story is 'Nuremberg II.' The narrator proceeds to assemble these 'war criminals' of his youth, those who tormented him in high school. The means he uses are contrived and preposterous. The whole tone reeks of adolescent bombast, the desperate effort to seem worldly and sophisticated. The glimpses he offers into the adult lives of his malefactors are predictably puerile and naive. But none of that concerns us here. It is the events themselves that provoked this intervention. The narrator indeed puts his old schoolmates on trial. He finds them all guilty, and he hangs them. Then he hangs himself."

"Oh, my God," said Miranda.

"It's just a story," I said.

"It is the product of a troubled, even deeply disturbed, mind."

"Or a creative one."

"Your son has been bullied."

"That was a long time ago."

"These wounds heal slowly."

"He's healing his wounds. That's a good thing. Writing well is the best revenge."

Miranda sat up straight suddenly. "It's that book! *Beyond Brant Point Light*! By your girlfriend."

"My fiancée."

"The mistreated girl comes back to the island for revenge! Jesus Christ, Henry. Tim is sitting around reading that trash all day. And listening to your True Crime anecdotes every night at dinner. No wonder he's writing these creepy stories. The sick atmosphere in that house! It's perverse. I've said it a thousand times. I've begged you to change. You are warping his mind. You and that hack writer with her sick imagination and her murder porn."

"They're cozy mysteries, Miranda. No sex allowed. And the crimes happen off-stage."

"You know what I mean."

"No, I really don't."

"The question is, how do we proceed from here?" Bissell broke in, obviously irked and embarrassed by our family quarrel. "Mr. Rezendez suggested a two-week suspension."

"For writing a story? What is this, North Korea?"

"No, for confessing in advance, as he clearly states on page one."

That struck me speechless for a moment, but Miranda leapt into the fray, proving once again that whatever our disagreements, and however absurd and annoying she could be, as a mother she was a peerless defender of her young, roughly on par with the polar bear or the African elephant. Forget the mother tiger cliché. She made tigers look tame.

Her voice was soft and level when she spoke.

"If you take any action against our son because of a creative work of fiction he composed as an assignment for one of the classes at this high school, we will contact the school board, file an administrative complaint with the district, and sue you and Rezendez and the teacher involved for harassment, unconstitutional conduct, violation of First Amendment free speech protections, and failure to properly address negligent supervision of student activities. I will personally make sure that the story is the front-page lead on both Nantucket newspapers every week until you lose the five-million-dollar judgment and are fired and blackballed from your chosen profession for life. If you hurt my son, I will come for you, Mr. Bissell. I will hurt you every way I can think of and some ways that I haven't thought of yet. And, rest assured, I'll be thinking hard."

"Is that a threat?"

"It's a fact. It's a hurricane warning. Board up your windows and evacuate if you start this storm."

"Did you hear that, Kennis? She threatened me! I know the assault and battery laws in this state. Threats constitute assault!"

I stared him down. "I heard no threat. I heard one party to a lawsuit giving due notice of pending litigation to another. And speculating on the outcome."

The silence sizzled and shrieked between us for a few seconds. Finally, Bissell pressed a knuckle to his mouth. "Fine. But this school has been on high alert for violence and dangerous behavior for more than a year. If your son acts out because proper school intervention was blocked by his parents, you will become pariahs on this island. You will be shunned and despised, and you will have no one to blame but yourselves. You will have to live with that horrific failure of judgment for the rest of your lives."

"Fair enough," I said, standing up. "Because that's never going to happen." I turned to Miranda. "Let's go."

Outside in the windy drizzle, she gave me a hug and a kiss on the cheek. "Thank you, Henry."

"You were great in there."

She pulled away a little to show me her smile. "We make a pretty good team. Now grab Tim and find out what the hell is going on with that crazy story."

I gave her a small, ironic salute. "Yes, ma'am."

"Seriously?"

"Seriously."

"Okay. Let me know what he says."

"Of course."

"I do actually have a showing."

"Go. I'll take it from here."

She gave me another quick peck on the cheek and trotted back to her car.

I didn't talk to Tim until after school that day. A whale had washed up on the beach over the weekend, and he wanted to see it. My daughter, Caroline, was conveniently disgusted by the prospect ("Let's all go gape at a giant, smelly dead fish! I don't think so."), which meant the expedition would give me time alone with Tim to talk about his story and the ruckus it had caused.

"I didn't write it," he said to me as we circled the giant right whale.

I lifted a hand to say *Not now, not here.* There were a dozen other people gawking, along with a photographer from the *Inquirer and Mirror.* We paid our respects to the deceased cetacean and walked on, east toward Madequecham. Soon we were alone on the wide stretch of sand. A south swell was kicking up some good-sized waves, and we could see the riptide running west, like a river below the surging foam. A few surfers bobbed beyond the breakers, but no one seemed to be catching anything.

We were well out of earshot, far from anyone who might have been interested, when I reopened the discussion. "I don't understand."

"I found that story in the attic, in a box of junk."

"What were you doing up there?"

"Just snooping. There was all sorts of weird stuff—pictures we could put on that 'Nantucket Days of Yore' Facebook page that Jane likes so much. And lots of other stuff—some gold coins. I couldn't tell if they were real or not."

"So—you read the story."

"I thought it was cool. I've been bullied—I could relate. And then I got that assignment and I had no ideas, and I totally forgot about it, and then it was due—"

"So you took the story from the box."

"I'm sorry, Dad. I shouldn't have done it. It was dumb. But I, it's—I never thought anyone would get so upset. I mean, it's just a story."

We walked along.

"Am I in trouble?"

"Well…first of all, I'm glad you didn't write the thing. That's the most important fact. I'm no fan of Alan Bissell, but he had a point today. That story is creepy. But you're not."

"Thanks, Dad."

"I mean…just on the most obvious level—you made friends with your bully."

"Sort of. Because of Hector."

Carrie's boyfriend, Hector Cruz, was the star running back for the Nantucket Whalers football team, and that gave him authority over a second-string right tackle far beyond that of any teacher, parent, or coach. Hector had negotiated the peace, but it had stuck. Tim and Jake Sauter might never be friends, and they had developed an easygoing camaraderie that impressed me. And Tim would certainly not be carrying bizarre grudges into a twisted adulthood like the character in 'Nuremberg II.'

"I shouldn't have ever turned it in, though." Tim watched the sand. "It's plagiarism."

"I'm glad to hear you say that."

"They'd, like, expel me or something if they ever found out."

"But they won't."

"Dad—"

"Kids make mistakes. If they were born grown-up, they wouldn't need parents. I plagiarized something once. To impress a girl. But then the kid who really wrote it wound up dating the girl and gave her the poem for Valentine's Day. I got busted, and everybody found out."

"That must have sucked."

"The weird thing is my dad figured it out before anything happened, when I showed it to him. He said, 'Whoever wrote this is a better writer than you are now, Hank. But he won't be forever. You'll catch up. You'll leave him in the dust. But not until you start really doing the work, and not doing it to get laid. Doing it for…it. For the work itself. Doing it to make your own small, particular noise.' I always remembered that phrase. My own noise. I never took credit for anybody's work again."

"Yeah, but also you didn't listen to him at first and did it anyway, right? And got caught and totally owned in front of your friend and that girl and everybody else in the whole school."

I nodded. "There was that."

"I won't do it again either."

"Good."

We walked along. The tide was coming in, and we had to scamper up into the soft sand ahead of a sluice of cold water.

"That whale makes me sad," Tim said finally.

"Me too."

"Why would he beach himself like that?"

"I don't know."

"I don't get death."

That startled me into a laugh. "Me neither."

I looked out to the hazy horizon and it sparked a memory. "I was walking with my dad on the beach in Malibu—I must have been a little younger than you are now. We saw someone parachuting into the water about a mile out. It was a stuntman. They were shooting a film. He got tangled in the cords of his chute and drowned. We found out later on, watching the news that night. I felt like we should have helped somehow, but there was nothing we could have done. The ocean is so—I don't know—merciless? An older girl I had a terrible crush on had almost drowned the week before, swimming in the storm surf. She was a strong swimmer and she got lucky. But it was terrifying. We stood on the beach for two hours, trying to catch sight of her. It was getting dark, and you could feel death right next to you."

"Like with that poor whale."

"Yeah. It seems so cruel, but it's not even that. More like—indifferent."

He nodded. He understood. "You can't fight the ocean. But people do things to each other, and you can stop them. You can catch them, and you can make a difference."

"That's true."

"Maybe that's why you became a policeman."

I nodded. "And not a surfer. Or a stuntman."

We trudged up the beach to a set of wooden stairs, cut through some summer person's backyard, and walked back to the car along the road.

We couldn't see the ocean, but we could still hear the waves. Feeling crowded by the generations and oddly lost in time, I sat down at our unsteady kitchen table when we got home and wrote a poem about fate and death and the generations—all the big stuff. It was a strange poem to write at the start of that dark season, when so much of the past would repeat itself in terrible ways and every miscalculation felt like destiny. Much later, my friend Pat Folger, the grizzled old-school Nantucket contractor, would sum it up with his usual down-east brevity:

"What goes around comes around, buddy. And this time it came for you."

Chapter Two

MATCH WITS WITH INSPECTOR KENNIS

The first time I saw her I was throwing up in the women's bathroom on the slow boat from Hyannis. I was seasick, and I couldn't make it to the men's room. I couldn't even make it to the toilet. The seas were so rough, the boat almost turned back. I had tried to talk to her as we shuffled along boarding the boat. "Pretty windy, huh?" She laughed and said, "I love a rough ride." That laugh. It knocked me off my foundations. And an hour later I'm retching my guts out in front of her and can see the shock and disgust on her face. Then she was gone, and the door slammed shut behind her. I wanted to call out to her, but I didn't even know her name.

—From Todd Fraker's deleted blog

Hours before the first disappearance, on the day after I brought my ailing mother home to Nantucket, I got a frantic call from Mike Henderson.

He'd been accused of robbery again.

"It's some sort of jug and bowl set," he said. "I literally have no idea what they're talking about. But they're going to fire me unless I can find it for them, and they owe me almost fifteen thousand dollars. You probably know this, Chief, but just for the record? Cindy and I don't exactly have a give-or-take-fifteen-thousand-dollars lifestyle. This will ruin me."

He gave me the address, on Almanack Pond Road. I recognized it instantly as the sprawling estate of Marge and Walter Callahan. I'd had dealings with them the previous summer. From what I'd seen of Walter Callahan, I was surprised he hadn't already assembled a posse of Range Rovers and hunted Mike down for a dose of leather-trimmed frontier justice. But the Callahans, along with most of the other potential billionaire vigilantes, had vacated the island after the Labor Day weekend. They had whipped Mike into a state of panic with one long-distance phone call.

"You go on and take care of it, honey," my mother told me. "Jane and I will be fine here." It was true. They were already best friends, and Mom had actually hugged Jane, not me, when we arrived in California two days before.

I pulled and chewed at the decision to bring my mother to the island as I drove out to Polpis that afternoon, fraying the edges of my resolve. She had Parkinson's disease. She was never going to get better, despite her heroic eating and exercise regimens. With Parkinson's you only get worse. Having her in the house would be a burden on Jane, and though she cheerfully accepted the situation now, I worried for the long run. Still, the alternative was untenable.

Ten years into the disease, still relentlessly ambulatory in her midseventies, my mother had been living in a "retirement community" in Long Beach, California, on the fifth floor of a beautifully restored hotel from the golden era of Hollywood, called The Shingle.

The ceiling of the lobby floated twenty feet above the marble floor with intricately worked plaster panels that put the tin ceilings of Greenwich Village cafés to shame. The peaked red tile of its roofs and turrets lent it a Mission Revival feeling, and the top-floor restaurant, the Panorama Room, earned its name with a spectacular view of the harbor while retaining a heady whisper of old-time movie glamour. The staff was charming and helpful, the suites themselves spacious and sunny, sparked with period detail in the moldings and baseboards, with high ceilings and water views. The resident dining room was spacious and congenial, the other residents friendly and patient. You couldn't ask for a more pleasant and professional assisted living arrangement.

And I hated it, with every fiber of my being.

I hated the way the impeccably courteous and hard-working staff treated my mother and the other residents as a separate, feeble race, inferior but privileged like hemophiliac dwarf royalty, simultaneously catered to and patronized, deferred to and dismissed. I hated the smell in the hallways, some tragic perfume of disinfectant and decay—the sense, so much like the sense you get in a hospital, of a world where human volition and dignity have been sacrificed to the mechanisms of medical technology and routine.

I also hated the dining hall food, tasteless and generic as if the management actually calibrated how many of the residents had no working taste buds left and arranged the meal preparations accordingly. I hated the weak coffee, the fuzzy sausages, and the cardboard pancakes—the sense that the particular texture of life, the look and feel and taste of things, didn't really matter anymore.

Most of all, I hated the resignation of the people there, the heartbreaking schedule of activities posted in the elevator—exercise classes at noon, crafts at three, casino night on Thursdays—and the stigma that seemed to hang over them. To be there was to be forgotten.

It was a world of decay and extinction. It wore me down, made me feel half-dead already, padding through an upholstered necropolis infinitely removed from a child's embrace or a home-cooked meal.

Those smog-bound early September days, wandering the husk of the old hotel, so long past its glory, as forlorn as its inhabitants, sitting in the empty bar where Clark Gable and Greta Garbo had once eaten caviar and toasted the New Year, inventorying the unused walkers and wheelchairs, and the coffee dispensers on the sideboard, made all of this uncompromisingly clear, both to me and to my brother, Phil. When Mom said she wanted to get out of there and spend whatever time she had left with people she loved, with people who missed her and wanted to be with her, we scarcely had to discuss it. We just breathed a sigh of relief, grabbed each other for a group hug, and started planning her escape.

Of course, with Phil always on the move, long divorced and living out of a suitcase, chasing sex crimes cases from San Mateo to Ogunquit, Maine, Mom would be living with us. That was fine with me. The worst part of leaving Los Angeles had always been losing our day-to-day contact.

Tim and Carrie would get to know her now. That was a great thing. But the house was small, and it was already packed with two busy grown-ups, three rowdy kids, and a dog.

"We can handle it," Jane said to me after a solemn kiss to seal the deal. "We'll be fine."

I had to hope she was right.

I took the right turn onto the dirt track of Almanack Pond Road, turning my mind back to Mike Henderson. He had his own problems, and, as I was about to find out, the Callahans' absurd accusation was the least of them.

The Callahans' Nantucket estate was called "High Meadow," and the tiny guest cottage behind the stables featured a quarter board like the one above the main-house front door but with the name "Sod Square" cut into the wood and painted gold, bracketed by golden clamshells. A little too cute for me, but accurate enough. The place was tiny, a glorified shed with barely enough room inside for two single beds, the end table between them, and a narrow armchair with a floor lamp. The walls displayed a wraparound mural of the harbor with the Brant Point lighthouse looming above the headboards. The lamp on the table was a miniature lighthouse, and the theme carried over onto the bedspreads and pillowcases.

This preening, proprietary obsession with island iconography turned simple affection for the place into a tacky collector's mania. These billionaires felt the need to physically connect themselves to the mystique of the island, from the Tervis tumblers printed with local town names to the ACK stickers and vanity Connecticut license plates (SRFSYD, ACK NICE), to the new lightship-basket toilet bowls that local designer Julia Copenhaver had started selling, complete with ivory scrimshaw lids. It reminded me of a teenager tattooing a girlfriend's name on his bicep.

Mike was inside Sod Square when I arrived, and I squeezed beside him.

"The jug and bowl were on this little table, supposedly," he said. "Though I don't really get why you need a jug and bowl, when there's no water in the place."

I glanced around the cramped, over-decorated little shrine. "And they say you took this stuff?"

"Not exactly. They never quite say it. You get a phone call

and it goes like this—'Uh, Mike, we have a little problem out at the house? Apparently, our lovely little jug and bowl set has gone missing. You were the last person out there, so...we're not saying you stole it! But we'd really like it back.'"

"Jesus."

"Walter accused me of stealing some books last year—because, according to them, I'm the only tradesman who reads. Turns out Marge had donated them to the Hospital Thrift Shop when she got her Kindle. And now this."

I noticed a string with a plastic tip hanging from the ceiling and inclined my head toward it. "What's that?"

"Just the pull-down for the attic."

"Did you look up there?"

"Who'd stash a jug and bowl set in an attic?"

I shrugged. "House cleaners? To get it out of the way? And then they forgot about it."

"Worth a shot." He pulled the string, lowered the hatch, took off his shoes, and climbed up on one of the beds for a look. "Bingo!"

He sounded more annoyed than relieved. He handed down the crockery and let the square batten-board swing shut as he climbed down.

I examined the plunder as he straightened out the bedding. "This is crap."

He took the bowl from me. "I saw something just like it at Kmart last year. On the sale table."

"They have you marked as quite the high-class cat burglar! What's next? The Stop & Shop beach chairs?"

"Good thing they don't know what happened at the main house today."

"Something bad?"

"Take a look, and you tell me."

Mike led me out of the guest shack, around the barn, and across the wide, perfectly manicured lawn, amid the smells of hay, horses, and newly cut grass. I heard nothing but the sluggish breeze moving the high branches of the sycamores and a distant motor of bees idling among the geraniums. The property was serene, Arcadian—and inescapably sinister. This imperial wealth didn't exist in a vacuum. It was part of a world where billions of people were starving to death and drinking contaminated water; part of a community where ill-paid and overworked minions scrambled in a controlled panic to keep everything on properties like this one perfect—the hedges sculpted, the flower beds weeded and raked so no footprint would show a human presence, the bedsheets laundered and ironed daily, the paint trim flawless and glossy.

And all for the likes of Marge and Walter Callahan with their luck-of-the-draw arrogance and preening self-absorption. I thought of my daughter's boyfriend, Hector Cruz, and his father, Sebastian, a landscaper like the one who tended these grounds, but also a strident political playwright whose drama about kidnapping people like the Callahans and interrogating them—in one extreme case, waterboarding them—on the subject of their unearned privilege had scandalized the town just a month before.

I took one last look across the rolling parkland dappled with tree shadow before I stepped inside behind Mike, thinking, "*Con madre, mi cuate. Adelante con los faroles.*"

We moved through the massive, sterile "great room"—with its requisite wooden seabirds, fully rigged clipper ship models, and the grotesque note of a three-foot Queequeg sculpture aiming a harpoon at the giant French doors—and on into the kitchen.

Mike stood by the stove. "So what happened in here?"

I scanned the big room with its mix of modern appliances and antique furniture. "It looks like—nothing?"

"That's the idea. But we know better."

"A round of 'Match Wits with Inspector Kennis'?"

"Something like that. Why did *The Shoals* stop running that column, anyway?"

"Nobody ever won—except Jane Stiles."

"So that's why you're marrying her."

I shrugged. "It's a pretty good reason. Anyway, I wasn't necessarily any smarter than the people who wrote in. But I'd read all the same Agatha Christie and John Dickson Carr novels they did—and I remembered the tricks."

"Well, this is no mystery novel. Just a real-life painting disaster. So have at it."

I studied the room, sniffed the air, got down on my hands and knees. I looked into the translucent plastic "contractor" garbage bag by the side door and examined the furniture, the counters, and the glass-top cooking range. I opened the cupboard under the sink and inventoried the cleaning products lined up there. I squeezed and puffed and spritzed like a baffled husband at a perfume counter. Then I stood up, with a plastic bottle in my hand.

"The accident just happened," I said.

"About an hour ago."

"I can still smell the stove-top cleaner."

"That'll dissipate soon."

But there was another odor in the house, much more pungent.

"With the drop cloth, the rosin paper, and the plastic working pot in the trash, along with the water pitcher on the counter and the stink of burnt fabric, it's pretty clear what happened."

His face fell. "Oh, boy."

"First of all, you had two spills, not one."

Mike stared at me. "How could you possibly know that?"

"The first spill was on the stove top." I pointed to the blue-stained antique hutch. "But there's no way the paint would have traveled that far or that direction. The tip-off is that faint little smudge in the side, the color variation where you cleaned it with thinner."

He kneeled down to look. "Shit."

"It's just like forensic blood analysis—the angle of the spatter gives you impact and direction."

"So—the first accident?"

"I'd say you were painting the door casing at the other side of the stove. You had the counter and the stove dropped off, with the paint can on the counter. It's obviously a big tarp. The section covering the stove hid the controls from you, and somehow you turned on one of the burners. Probably just by leaning against it. You smelled smoke, freaked out, filled that pitcher with water to put it out, knocking over the first pot. You doused the drop, pulled it off onto the floor, and started with the glass cleaner on the stove. Charred cotton as well as paint. The burned-on fabric must have been the tough part."

"Yeah."

"Anyway, you did the right thing. Smart move—that stove top would be an expensive item to replace. And it worked. Nice job, by the way. Like it never happened. Problem was...you forgot that your main paint can was sitting on the same drop cloth, and it tipped over when you yanked it. The paint was going down the side of the cabinet while you were putting out the fire. Understandable—you were a little distracted."

"Try panic-stricken."

"But you did good. Glass cleaned, fire out, incriminating material stuffed into the trash. If you'd noticed the main spill sooner, the paint on the hutch would have come off without leaving a mark. Also, you missed a drop of paint—see, down there by the foot? And you left a scrap of rosin paper under one of the legs. So, I can tell most of the paint must have hit the paper, which you pulled up and bagged, along with the ruined drop cloth. Am I missing anything?"

"Nope. Inspector Kennis wins again." He shook his head. "I am so fucked."

"No, you're not. The Callahans are off-island."

"But their caretaker could show up any second."

"No problem. Open the window, clear the air, get that trash bag out of here, put away the water pitcher and the stove-top glass cleaner—you'll be fine. No one the wiser."

"Except you."

"And I'll never tell."

"Yeah, but I mean…"

"No, no, you're missing the point, Mike. The only reason I could piece it all together was that I knew something happened. I was trying to reconstruct an event. No one else will know about the spill, and trust me—if you're not looking for something, you don't see it. That's always been my experience—in police work and regular life, also. People don't notice much. No one will notice this. Not even the caretaker."

I opened the kitchen window. A mild breeze drifted in.

Mike nodded. "As long as he doesn't show up for an hour or two."

"Or see that paint speck on the hutch."

"That I can handle."

He pulled a single-edged razor blade from his toolbox, walked back to the hutch, kneeled down, and scraped off the white speck with a single flick of the blade.

I was impressed. "Looks like you've done that before."

"Don't ask."

"Anyway, your caretaker's not that observant. He never noticed that this storm window is installed upside down."

Mike stepped beside me to look. "Oh, my God, you're right! That's hilarious."

"No one else seems to have noticed either, so…"

"It's like the old-time carpenters used to say when they banged in a bad miter or left an un-set nail—'Good enough for Nantucket'—where all the customers act picky but none of them know shit."

We lugged out the big trash bag and heaved it into the back of his truck. I followed behind him, and we leaned against the tailgate for a minute or two. "I thought you hated working on the weekends," I said.

He expelled a tight little breath, squinting into the dappled sunlight. "Yeah. Cindy always says, show me a painter working seven days a week in the off-season, and I'll show you a guy who's got problems at home. I worked quite a few Sundays during the, uh, the Tanya Kriel business. That was how Cindy knew something was up. Kind of ironic, because it's all about Cindy herself, this time."

"She's having an affair?"

"I don't know. But it's tense and weird at home, and she won't talk to me. Not to mention we have a preschooler crashing around the house. Cindy's someplace else. That's all I know. So I hire a sitter and go to work…and this shit happens. Because I can't fucking focus, man. Seriously. This is bad."

"So—what are you going to do about it?"

"I did it already."

"Mike—"

"I hired a detective. To find out what's going on."

That shocked me. "Really?"

"Totally."

I was about to say that I wasn't aware of any private detectives working on the island, but one had just moved here from Seattle. I'd had dealings with him a few months before, during the Horst Refn murder case. In fact, he'd helped me solve it.

"Rob Roman?" I asked.

Mike nodded. "He's a good guy. And pretty smart. If something's going on, he'll figure it out."

"He fell in love with the last runaway wife he tracked down. FYI. That's why he had to leave Seattle."

"Thanks anyway, Chief, but that's not my main worry right now. Roman's not her type."

"Fair enough." I patted his shoulder. "Let me know what you find out."

Cindy wasn't the first to vanish that autumn, but I barely noticed those early missing persons reports—those that were even filed at all. The island was swarming with friends and relations, bridesmaids and groomsmen, rowdy groups of young men in tuxedoes riding in big open cars, packs of identically dressed young women swirling down Main Street brandishing flowers and champagne. In churches and private mansions overlooking the harbor, on the South Shore beaches, under white tents set up in the moors, dozens of couples were spending hundreds of thousands of dollars on their nuptial revelries.

But the past was hunting some of those people, it turned out. And the festivities provided a perfect cover. People slipping out of a reception or a rehearsal dinner? I had rarely attended one of those shindigs that I didn't want to escape—including my own. For any rational adult, sensibly fatigued with small talk and dreading the next platter of maple bourbon-candied bacon or beet-pickled deviled eggs, fleeing the tent hardly seemed like a criminal matter or even a surprise.

So I ignored those first reports, just like everyone else. These were adults, after all, not lost children. They were free to come and go as they pleased.

Besides, I was distracted—planning my own wedding, settling my mother into the Darling Street house, helping my kids negotiate the first weeks of the new school year. Not to mention trying to prevent one of my friends from being framed by a rogue cop. I understand why I overlooked what should have been as obvious as the paint speck on the Callahans' hutch. I had a full inventory of explanations for that fatal neglect, plenty of excellent reasons.

But no excuse.

Chapter Three

THE LOOK-ALIKE

I followed Sippy into the boy's bathroom after the incident in the dining hall. "I hate those girls," I told him. He shook his head and said, "No, you don't. You just wish you did."

—From Todd Fraker's deleted blog

BONDI BEACH, NEW SOUTH WALES, AUSTRALIA
SEPTEMBER 10TH, 2019

The police departments of three countries along with various inquiries directed to the international law enforcement agencies INTERPOL, EUROGENDFOR, and CLACIP had discovered no connection between the five murdered women.

From different countries—Canada, Ecuador, Belgium, Belarus, and Sri Lanka; from wildly varying economic backgrounds—from trust-fund Uber driver to trophy wife; with diverse criminal records—from pristine to probation to just out of prison—the only common feature was their age. All of them were in their midthirties, but a well-known statistical spike for violent crimes against females in that demographic rendered the fact insignificant.

There was one common feature that all the cross-referenced files and judicial records failed to note. The women all looked alike. They could have been sisters. They could have been quintuplets. And all of them, including this new Australian victim, looked shockingly similar to the face on the dust jacket of the book responding officers found at the scene of the crime.

The book was called *Beyond Brant Point Light*. It was a "cozy" mystery set on the island of Nantucket, thirty miles off the coast of Massachusetts, in the United States of America, ten thousand miles away.

New South Wales Police Commissioner Arthur C. Prelmonte held the book gingerly between surgical-gloved fingers. The crime scene techs fluttered around him, measuring and photographing, poking and prodding, sprinkling and spraying their preferred fluorescent fingerprint powders. He had no idea what evidence the forensic side of the investigation might uncover, and, in any case, he preferred to work the old-fashioned way, the analog way, as his old partner Derek Kilvert had always said. Prelmonte preferred to call it the acoustic way. He had never been much for the electric guitar, either.

The orphaned and ignored item in his hands was all the proof he needed that the old ways were best. It was more than a clue; it was a living thing, throbbing and urgent, trembling against his palm like a wounded bird. He could almost feel the heartbeat.

The woman lying on the carpet in a coagulating lake of her own blood was nothing more than a substitute for the look-alike author of this "Madeline Clark" mystery. She stared back at him from the photograph, a shrewd, pretty woman with a flirtatious half smile that indicated she knew something he didn't. *Not this time, madam,* he thought to himself. *This time the tables are turned. I know something you don't, and that something could be the death of you.*

He studied the corpse. The brutality of the murder suggested an exasperated frustration. The substitutes—even then, Prelmonte suspected there had been others before this one—wouldn't satisfy this madman for much longer. A check through the databases would confirm Prelmonte's intuition, but he didn't plan to wait. The killer was on the prowl, unsatisfied, hungry, looking for the genuine article.

His next victim would be author Jane Stiles herself.

Prelmonte had to send her a warning, soon, now, today. He calculated the time. It was still only eight in the evening yesterday in New England. He despised electronic communications, but they could beat any plane flight if the perpetrator was already on his way. Nevertheless, Prelmonte felt an asthmatic premonition as he stepped out of the sweltering apartment onto the wooden deck. He took a deep breath against the stifling wheeze of apprehension. He was resolutely unsuperstitious. He couldn't see the future, but he was far from helpless in the face of it.

He tasted the ocean air, letting his eyes rest for a moment on the immense opal sea beyond the steep roadway and the beach. Then he climbed down the outside stairs, folded himself into his official car, and drove back to Sydney at top speed, siren blaring.

He had emails to write.

Chapter Four

HOMECOMING

I sprained my ankle when I slipped down the climbing rope. I lost my balance, and I fell—right into Jane's lap. She screamed as I thrashed and pawed at her, trying to get up and get away, and I left bloody handprints on her blouse. But I saw the concern in her eyes. She said, "Are you all right?" and then, to the gym teacher, "I think he's hurt!" After that, I had hope. I had felt the connection between us. I was walking on air. It feels just like flying, until you hit the ground.

—From Todd Fraker's deleted blog

Two days after Mike Henderson's heart-to-heart with Chief Kennis, Mike's wife, Cindy, was having a late Friday lunch at Faregrounds Restaurant with her old friend Vicky Fleishman. The tone was different, but the topic was the same.

"So you're leaving him?" Vicky asked. She had to raise her voice against the clatter of the crowded bar, everyone cheering the Red Sox on the giant TVs. By a small-town miracle, there was no one Cindy knew at any of the surrounding tables. No one was paying attention to them. It was the bottom of the seventh inning, and the bases were loaded. Chris Sale was pitching a two and two count.

Cindy took a sip of her beer. The glass had come frosted, but her Bud Light was tepid now. She didn't usually drink at lunch, and the state of tipsy serenity she had hoped for wasn't materializing. She just felt woozy. "I don't know."

"You have a four-year-old child."

"Really? That must have slipped my mind."

"I'm sorry—I didn't mean... I'm just saying—"

"Maybe she'd be better off without me."

Vicky stared at her. "That is an objectively false statement."

"Mike could be a single dad."

"No, he couldn't! He can barely function as a married dad. He works eighty hours a week. Is he going to put Katie on the crew? Bring Your Daughter to Work Day is *one* day, Cindy."

Cindy knew it was meant as a joke, but she couldn't quite manage a smile. She stared down at her plate and pushed her salad around with her fork. There was too much dressing on it. She should have ordered the oil and vinegar on the side. But somehow mixing her own vinaigrette spoiled the whole idea of going to a restaurant in the first place. Should she help out with the dishes afterward, also? That was the move when you couldn't afford to pay. She inventoried the plastic in her wallet. Having a card declined would be the final humiliation. "I'm just so sad all the time," she said finally.

"And Mark Toland makes you happy?"

"I don't know. Maybe."

Vicky snorted. "Well, that's a stirring endorsement."

"He's fun to be with."

"And he leaves his wet towels on the bed just like every other guy. And gets that same look on his face when he stops listening to you. Plus, if the work thing bugs you? Movie guys never stop. It's twenty-four seven, supposedly."

Cindy looked up. "They make a lot more money than house-painters, though."

"So this is about money?"

"People get rich for a reason. Mark is smart. And talented."

"And lucky. Everyone who ever won an Oscar admitted they were lucky."

"Well, I could use a little luck right now."

They ate quietly for a few minutes. Cindy picked the cherry tomatoes from the slurry of wilted lettuce. What was that old ad her dad loved to quote? "A salad without Wishbone salad dressing is just a bowl of wet vegetables" How true.

"I never liked that guy," Vicky said.

"You never knew him. He was only at NHS for one year, anyway."

"He was stuck-up and lazy and mean."

"He was not!"

"He outed Lonnie Fraker. Remember? He made poor Todd Fraker's life a misery, just because he could. He called them the Others Brothers because he thought they were weird."

"Right. And it was nobody but Mark."

"It wasn't everyone, Cindy. Don't pretend it was. Mitch never—"

"Mitch! The perfect peerless prince of whatever. Who dumped you for boot camp and the chance to kill Muslims in some third-world hellhole."

"Okay, one, he joined the Marines and it wasn't just to kill Muslims. Jesus, Cindy. And Afghanistan isn't a third-world country."

"Yes, it is! Are you kidding me? Of course it is. They don't even have clean drinking water in those cities."

"Unlike Detroit."

"This is stupid."

The silence seethed between them for a few seconds.

"Mitch didn't dump me."

"But he left."

"I said I'd wait for him."

"And you didn't. Which is fine; no one expected you to. No one ever expected him to come back. The smart people get away from this place."

"And the losers stick around."

"It sure seems that way."

Vicky sipped her iced tea. Someone hit a home run. The room erupted. Red Sox Nation. Cindy was a Yankees fan.

"I don't know why he hasn't called me," Vicky said.

Mitchell Stone had been back on-island for more than a month—apparently with a kid in tow.

"Mike could ask him about you. He's working at the same jobsite."

"Banging nails for Pat Folger."

"What's wrong with that?"

"Nothing. It's just…it seems like a long way to go to wind up back at square one again. He worked for Pat, summers in high school. He could have been a GC by now."

"Maybe he didn't want to be a general contractor. He told Mike he's 'retired.'"

"At age thirty-four? From what?"

"I don't know. The military?"

They sat quietly and watched the halftime guys talking, making their points, earning their salaries.

"I've been seeing Mitch everywhere the last few weeks," Vicky said. "I mean—not him. But I'll see some guy and he's got Mitch's walk, or he's wearing that corduroy vest with the jeans and the work boots, or maybe he turns and I catch a glimpse of his profile, and I call out or grab his arm, and it's some stranger looking at me like I'm crazy. Maybe I am crazy."

Cindy reached over and took her hand. "He's back living at the Quidnet house. Drive out and see him."

"No thanks."

"Vicky—"

"If he wants to see me, he will."

The conversation wound down. They had covered the usual topics—Cindy's tyrannical father auditing her entire life when she asked for money to help pay for Katie's Montessori school tuition. "Didn't you mention going out to dinner with Mike last week? That seems awfully extravagant for a woman who can't even pay for her own daughter's education." And Cindy mentioned Katie's most recent wisecrack, countering her mom's refusal to buy her a Mounds bar ("You've had enough sugar today") at the grocery with "Mary Poppins says a spoonful of sugar helps the medicine go down."

As for Vicky, school had begun, and two weeks in she was already half out of her art supplies, forget about getting more Blick watercolors, much less the Sennelier tubes she preferred, and she only had two talented students, anyway. The rest of them took art class as a free period, and half her students couldn't speak English, so lectures on atmospheric perspective seemed exquisitely futile. It was easier to let them doodle and gossip and dance to their Spotify playlists.

Cindy asked about Eli, and the news was good. The second stint in rehab had worked, and though their family had never been particularly observant, Eli had hooked up with a WASP girl named Taylor Pierce who had converted to Judaism, and, like most converted shiksas (at least according to Vicky's dad), had become almost comically fanatical, dragging Eli along with her to Torah studies at the island's only shul. He had recited the Haggadah at Passover. "He's even learning to blow the shofar!" Vicky had laughed. It made sense. The Teshuva had a lot in common with Eli's AA rituals of repentance. And she enjoyed the Rosh Hashanah dinner. "Taylor cooks a mean brisket."

The restaurant banged and clattered around them. Three guys at the bar were laughing way too loud. A waitress dropped a tray of dishes, and five people jumped in to help clean up.

There was nothing left to talk about but the serious stuff. Vicky set her fork down on her plate. "The guys were back again last night."

"After you took their pictures?"

"Well, they threw my phone into the lily pond. I guess they didn't realize I'd uploaded the photographs to the cloud."

"That was stupid of them. They could go to jail for that."

"Yeah, well…they didn't actually steal the phone. There were no witnesses. And the last thing I want is more trouble from those guys."

"Speaking of whom, I called Monica Terwilliger and sent her the photos. She checked them out."

"Isn't that against the rules? She's not even a real cop."

"Forensics has access to all the databases. And she's worried about you."

"That's not the point. She could lose her job."

Cindy stared her down. "Chief Kennis would never fire someone for helping a friend."

"Okay. That's great. That's really nice of her. I have to thank her for this. She was such a bitch in high school."

"Yeah, well…the extra forty pounds seem to have mellowed her out a little."

Vicky sat forward. "So who are they?"

"The tall one is Jimmy Steckler. Moved here two years ago

from Fall River. He signs on to the odd offshore fishing crew in the summer, drove a loader at Marine Home Center until he got fired. No steady income, but he caretakes a house in Tom Nevers. Lives there in the winter. Barely scraping by. The bald kid, Cody Carr, is his roommate. He does handyman work in the winter, drives a cab in the summer. Again—how does this guy make ends meet? The one with the lazy eye is Kip Boynton. He's got a real estate license but no sales in the last eighteen months. Lives in low-income housing—in Norquarta, off Miacomet Road. He had a family when he got the house, but the wife left and took the kid with her. Now here's the good part. The house in Tom Nevers is owned by Ramon Cruz, who runs the Tres Vatos gang. He's a big-time drug dealer, but very clever, supposedly, covering his tracks and laundering his money and all that. Plus there's a lot worse guys than him running around. Another bunch called Malditos Azteca."

"We have two drug gangs on Nantucket?"

"Wake up, Vicky. There may be more. These are just the ones Monica knows about. Anyway, Ramon keeps everyone in line. He settles the disputes and keeps things quiet. He uses Anglo boys to do the street work. I guess he figures racist cops won't profile them."

"Guys like Jimmy and Cody and Kip."

"Yeah."

Vicky nodded. "He's probably right."

"But that makes them a lot more dangerous than they look. Ramon likes to play the kindly old padrone, but Monica told me he's a killer, Vicky. Seriously. They had an informer in Tres Vatos a few years ago, and they found him overdosed, floating in the harbor. It was ruled 'death by misadventure,' but everyone knows Ramon had him killed. Other people have just…disappeared. Don't be one of them."

"Okay, you're scaring me now."

Cindy raised her hands, palms out. "I'm just the messenger. The point is, what Monica was saying basically was just, you know—stay out of their way. It's like…rattlesnakes. They leave you alone if you don't bother them."

"Plus, they have that rattle to warn you away."

Cindy glanced over Vicky's shoulder and her face pulled tight. She stared down at her empty plate. "Speaking of which…"

Jimmy, Cody, and Kip had pushed past a waitress and two guys heading for the restroom to stand over their table. Speak of the devil—or in this case his incubi.

Jimmy smiled, baring nicotine-stained teeth and the gap of a missing molar. "Ladies."

Cindy gritted her teeth. "Shit."

Vicky glared up at him. "What the hell do you want?"

"Nothing, nothing, relax. I just need a quick word. First off, sorry about your cell phone. You should get the waterproof model next time."

"Get lost."

He grinned. "Hard to do on the Rock. When you know every little shortcut and everyone's address."

"Is that a threat?"

"It's a warning."

"A friendly warning," Cody chimed in.

Kip: "You have no idea what you're fuckin' with here."

Cody: "Nosy little girls get hurt in this town."

Jimmy: "They wind up in the harbor, and it ain't for the turkey plunge."

Kip snorted. "Bitch, you called the cops on us!"

"That was fucked up," Cody agreed.

Vicky started to stand. "I'm getting the manager."

Jimmy pushed her back down. "No, you're not. You're not

doing shit until I say so. You can get yourself into big trouble, calling the cops around here. You never know which cop you gonna get. Know what I mean?"

"No. What do you mean?"

"The cop who showed up was a friend of mine, so no harm, no foul, far as that goes. But it could have been a fucked-up situation."

"Yeah," Kip said. "Night in jail, court date, boldface name in the paper. Probation problems, you name it."

"Like going back to jail where you belong," Vicky said.

"We don't belong in jail," Cody said. "We did our time. Paid our debt to society!"

"But you're forgetting the interest," Vicky said. Cindy shot her a look that translated as *For God's sake, shut up.* "Like your maxed-out credit cards," Vicky went on. "Tough to pay down."

"Fuck is she talking about?" Kip snapped.

Jimmy ignored him. "Don't call the cops on me again, bitch."

Vicky stared up at him. "Don't do drug deals under my window."

"She has to make it up to us, Jimmy," Cody whined. "Like you said. Like you told us."

"Yeah. We can think of something for you to do. Prove your contrition, like they say in court. You're getting old, but you're still hot. And experience counts. We'll even let your friend here pitch in."

Cindy felt tears coming. She stared down hard at her empty plate.

Vicky spoke. Her voice was impossibly steady. "Get away from us."

"Gonna call the cops? Like I said, that'll just make things worse."

"Enough."

The voice came from behind them.

Cindy said, "Oh, my God."

It was him.

"Mitch?"

"Hey, Vicky."

"Cindy says you've been on-island for a month. You couldn't call me?"

"Thanks, Cindy."

She looked up into his cold brown eyes. But Vicky answered for her. "Don't look at Cindy—this is Nantucket, remember? Everyone knows everything about everybody."

He shrugged. "It's been a little crazy. I kind of adopted a runaway kid, driving across the country, and we've been getting him into school, signing him up with a doctor, getting him some new clothes, fixing up his room at the house. Shit like that."

"You adopted a kid?"

"Well, Susie and I are trying out the guardianship thing for a while. See what happens."

"It's—how did you—is he...? Are you doing okay?"

Mitch shrugged. "So far, so good."

"Hey, buddy," Jimmy said. "This is a private conversation. You should take off before you get hurt."

Mitch turned to Cody. "Call 911."

"Don't do shit," Jimmy said and grabbed Mitch's wrist. Mitch stepped aside, covered the guy's fingers with his left hand, and rolled his right hand over the wrist, curling around it like a snake. That forced the guy to his knees as Mitch kept the wrist locked with a light grip, moved beside his hapless opponent, pushed against the elbow, and corkscrewed him facedown onto the floor. Apparent effort and exertion, nil. Total elapsed time, two and half seconds.

Mitch released him, and he lurched forward as if he'd been kicked, moaning and clutching at his arm.

Mitch addressed the others. "Time to go."

They pushed their way past a table of customers rising to leave and a pair of waitresses, almost knocking over a tray of drinks. The tall one scrambled to his feet and stumbled after them.

Vicky ignored the retreat. "What the hell did you just do?"

"Nikyo wrist lock. It's easy. I can teach you if you want."

"But can you teach me your gusto for using it?"

Mitch smiled. "This from the girl who pushed Jenny Little down the Atheneum steps because she said she kissed me."

"She bragged about it!"

"She lied."

Vicky lifted one eyebrow in her old sardonic interrogation. "You never looked at another girl back then?"

"Never. Then or now or any time in between."

"So you've been celibate since high school."

"More or less. Emotionally celibate."

"How did that work out?"

"Surprisingly well."

"I got married."

"I know. I follow you on Facebook. It got complicated. Then you got divorced. Now you list yourself as single again."

"Just like Jenny."

"Not quite. You didn't join the LGBT community."

"It's LGBTQ now. Actually it's LGBTQQIAAP."

"You've got to be kidding. What's the rest of it stand for?"

Vicky squinted, thinking. "Hmmm...the whole thing is lesbian, gay, bisexual, transgender, transsexual, queer, questioning, intersex, asexual, ally, pansexual. And some people still feel left out."

"Like who?"

"Trigendered. Aporagendered. Don't ask."

"I won't."

They studied each other for a few seconds, a quiet bubble in the hubbub of the crowded restaurant.

"So you've been saving yourself for me?" Vicky asked, finally.

"It turns out. None of the other women passed the test."

"The test?"

"It was real simple. Would I leave the woman I was seeing with no notice and no suitcase if I got a call from you?"

"And no one passed?"

"No one even came close."

Another measured silence. A waiter brushed past Mitch with a line of burger-laden plates on his arm.

"I may have to change my status back to 'complicated.'"

"Your status was always complicated."

"And you always knew the right thing to say."

"But only to you."

"So, you're back in Quidnet?"

"We'd never sell."

"Same number?"

"You remember it?"

"I use it as my bank card pin number."

That tricked him into a smile. "I'm flattered."

"Don't be. Flattery is fake."

"How about—surprised and pleased?"

"That's a good start."

There wasn't much left to say, standing up, drawing attention, blocking the waiters.

"So you'll call?"

"Maybe I'll just wait until we run into each other again."

"Please don't."

"Hi, Mitch," Cindy said. "Long time no see."

"Hey, Cindy."

"I was starting to feel invisible over here."

"Sorry. Just think of it as—eclipsed. Which isn't all bad. Even the sun gets eclipsed, and by the moon, which, when you think about it, is very comforting for the little guy. There was a total eclipse when we were thirteen years old. I remember thinking— 'Go moon!' It didn't last, but you take what you can get."

"Welcome home, Mitch."

Vicky added, "See, you can talk to other people."

Mitch smiled. "I'm working on it." He tipped his head. "Ladies."

With a final lingering smile, he faded back and eased between the tables away from them, past the bar, through the vestibule, and out the door. Vicky kept staring after him across the tables to the entrance. Did she hope he was coming back in? Cindy could see it—that final smile had gone through her friend like a skewer through a cube of steak. She was ready for the grill. After all this time, she still was ready.

Cindy said, "The return of the prodigal townie."

"Didn't the prodigal son squander his inheritance and return home to a forgiving father?"

"I guess."

"Mitch got nothing, and his father's dead."

"But he returned. That's the only part people remember."

"True."

"Be careful, though, Vicks. There's something about that guy. He's dangerous."

"To Jimmy Steckler. Not to me."

"I guess his time in the military wasn't wasted."

"He didn't need the military. Remember back in high school, when he caught Ham Tyler spray-painting the Star of David on my locker? He dismantled that little turd, just leveled him."

"I heard about that. Ham never pressed charges, though."

"That would have meant admitting that the local weirdo cleaned his clock for him."

"The local weirdo."

"Yeah."

"He turned out okay, for a weirdo. Kind of a hunk, actually."

"Yeah."

They paid their check and left. Lunch had left Cindy feeling restless and sad. She sat in her car and tracked the scuttling emotion until she could crush it under her thumb like a bug on a windowsill. She was jealous of Vicky. That was it. Not because of Mitchell Stone; she didn't care about him one way or the other. It was the thing between them that she missed, the fraught electricity of their conversation, the look in Vicky's eyes as he walked away. For some reason, she recalled the travel poster the teacher had tacked up in her social studies classroom—some sugar-white Greek village perched on a cliff above the Aegean. Sitting bored and miserable while Mr. Felber droned on about pre–Civil War agrarian economies, she had longed to climb into that picture somehow and wander off under that resonant blue sky, away from everything, down some sunlit twisting lane to the music of goat bells.

Mark Toland's Los Angeles lured her the same way.

He had escaped from this place, and he was throwing her a rope. She was trapped in this petty little town, in a puny, unaccomplished life, stumbling toward middle age. Mark Toland was the natural adversary of all that. He could wreck this little world of hers so easily.

And what did he offer in its place? Glamour, excitement, celebrity. Warm winters and ripe oranges. A sunlit world of pale blue swimming pools and cool Mexican tile. An *Architectural Digest* world of dinners on the patio with views of the city lights, brilliant nights of conversation with the people she had read about in *People* magazine, cashmere against the desert chill, palm trees and bougainvillea among the faint smells of cut grass and eucalyptus.

Nantucket would shrink to a crumb of land on the far end of the map, a second-rate film festival, a cage with an unlocked door that she had stepped away from so easily one winter afternoon.

She started the car and felt all the engines inside her kicking to life.

Maybe there was nothing left of her old passion for Mark Toland. Maybe it had never really existed in the first place. Maybe she was just kidding herself. But she deserved a chance to find out. She wanted these stolen days, and she was going to take them. Bliss or disaster, one thing was for certain.

It was going to be a weekend to remember.

Chapter Five

THE DOCKET

I watched my mother die from an overdose, and then the creep who sold her the drugs filmed everything while I was forced to sodomize my best friend at gunpoint. I tried to burn down my shitty school and spent the next twenty years being tortured in a snake pit hellhole loony bin. But the slap is the thing that hurts me the most.

—From Todd Fraker's deleted blog

I had an unusually heavy docket that Monday, above and beyond the DUIs and minor burglaries—three surfboards, two table saws, and a porta-potty.

Most serious was an unnerving email from Australia concerning what looked like a psychotic superfan of my fiancée's mystery novels. Then there was the real mystery of Cindy Henderson's disappearance, with or without her old boyfriend Mark Toland. Neither of them had been seen by anyone since Lina Perry's wedding reception on Saturday afternoon. Most likely they had run off together, but I couldn't be sure.

I bookmarked that problem until my meeting with Rob

Roman, so I could deal with the fracas that had started in the Faregrounds Restaurant last Friday and apparently continued in the parking lot. According to David Trezize, who had been on the scene with his camera, the incident had centered on an old schoolmate called Mitchell Stone, back on Nantucket after almost twenty years in the military.

Despite David's endorsement, and the well-deserved slap down for Jimmy Steckler and his pals, I really couldn't afford to have some ex–Special Forces PTSD-case vigilante cleaning up my town for me. No one was pressing charges, but I still needed to talk to the guy. He might not be so lucky next time.

Haden agreed to get him down to the station, and I pulled the Australian email printout toward me for a second look. Haden, Charlie Boyce, Kyle Donnelly, and Karen Gifford had their own copies.

After the international and interdepartmental formalities, it continued like this:

> …most of the crime in Sydney occurs in the Kings Cross area and the section of town near the Central Railway station, rather in the manner of New York City's Times Square in a different era. But I write today because of a quite unusual crime committed recently in the nearby beach community of Bondi. A woman in her early thirties was beaten and strangled in her home. Her cries alerted a local surfer who followed the alleged perpetrator on foot to another location, apparently the suspect's home. In fact he was renting a single room in an old house in the hills above the beach. The individual apparently realized he was being followed, and a struggle ensued. The young hero was a member of a local surf society, if you will, who refer to themselves as "brah boys." They have

been involved in much petty crime, but I have always held that they are an essentially decent group of young people, and this David Harcourt made my case for me, most emphatically. He was badly injured in the scuffle but managed to alert the police on his mobile.

By the time officers arrived on the scene, the alleged perpetrator had vacated the area and young Harcourt was rushed to hospital, where I am happy to say he is recovering nicely, receiving many good wishes and much praise for his quick wits and stalwart behavior. I believe he has even appeared on the local television news to tell his story. Alas, the alleged perpetrator's room was paid for in cash, and there was no record of the transaction. The landlord described a heavyset but otherwise woefully ordinary individual, and neither the housemates, who worked long hours and rarely crossed paths with him, nor the neighbors and local merchants could contribute very much to a meaningful identification. They all agreed he was an American, and no more overweight than the average tourist from the United States.

The question of his nationality prompts me to contact you now. Fleeing his room, he left only a bar of surf wax, a pair of rather the worse-for-wear athletic shoes, and a book, *Beyond Brant Point Light*, by Jane Stiles, a Nantucket-based author according to the biographical note. Another copy of the book was left at the crime scene, I rather doubt by accident. I was disturbed to observe the very striking resemblance between the murdered young woman and the dust-jacket photograph of Ms. Stiles. One might hope that this is some sort of bizarre coincidence, but I fear not. This man may have some grudge against Ms. Stiles, but I hasten to add that so far as we know, he is ten time zones away from her, across the international dateline in another country, on another continent and a different hemisphere.

He is a stranger in our nation and is currently the subject of a thorough and far-reaching manhunt. If he is still on Australian soil, we hope to find, arrest, and prosecute him to the fullest extent of the law. Nevertheless, the fact that he may have already fled the country for your jurisdiction makes it imperative that I alert you of the potential danger. It's a long plane flight but a small world, and getting smaller all the time. Take the precautions you see fit.

I will personally keep you apprised of our progress in the ongoing investigation. My people gripe about the occasional false alarm. I often tell them that a false alarm is the best one. Hoping for such an outcome here, I remain

Commissioner Arthur C. Prelmonte APM

Haden set his copy aside. "So what do we do about this?"

Charlie said, "Shall we put someone on her for a few days?"

"Well, I live with her. We should put out a BOLO on her landscaping truck—to keep an eye out for her. And an occasional drive by the White Heron Theatre Company's actor's residence on North Water Street couldn't hurt."

Lynne Bolton had given Jane one of the rooms upstairs to use in the off-season after a benefit production of *The View from Altar Rock* a few years ago. Jane's adaptation of the book had gone over well, and they'd been pals ever since.

"Speaking of your friends and relations," Karen said, "there was a break-in at the Cruz house last night. Hector called it in at around two a.m. Dispatch sent a unit over. They found no intruders and nothing was stolen. Not sure what to make of that."

"Bad dream?"

"Sebastian heard it, too. He ran out into the yard with a baseball bat."

I nodded. "We have to figure out what the thieves were looking for."

"Maybe they went to the wrong house," Charlie offered.

"Could be."

"Or some kind of intimidation tactic?" Kyle said. "You know… Immigrants, beware! We know where you live. We can get into your house any time."

I gave him a dubious wince. "Seems a little subtle. Most xenophobes prefer a good beating—or a call to Immigration and Customs Enforcement."

"Yeah."

Haden cleared his throat "We have our own little branch of ICE operating here. And it's starting to be a problem."

"Hamilton Tyler?" I'd had trouble with him before.

"He's pulling over any Hispanic guy he sees in a truck."

"Like every landscaper on the island?"

"Most of them have green cards, and he knows it. We're getting harassment complaints, Chief. I know that's not how you want to present the NPD."

"No, no, it isn't. Leave this one to me."

Hamilton Tyler was the worst kind of small-town rogue cop, from my point of view as a big-city interloper. He was an island kid, from four generations of an island family, embedded in the local trades—his great-grandfather had managed the old ice house on the harbor square, and his grandfather was a plasterer. The uncles on his mother's side were masons, though his father's older brother, Teddy "Toad" Tyler, had broken with family tradition and joined up with the state police. Toad served before my time, but I'd heard the stories. He was notoriously brutal and petty. If you pissed him off, he'd break your taillights with his billy club and use the infraction to search for planted drugs. That was the story, anyway. He also liked to shoot people's dogs when he caught them off the leash.

Lovely guy. Great genes.

Ham's brothers were carpenters working for their father, a general contractor with a reputation for cutting corners. Years before, when an outraged customer had complained that her house leaked, Reg Tyler had famously retorted, "All my houses leak!" It was a tribute to the old man's force of personality that a comment like that could settle the issue. Ham had his father's bullying swagger but none of his shrewd intelligence or work ethic. He was a bully, like his uncle, but difficult to fire. He had a lot of pull in town, and he knew how to use it.

Now it seemed that, for once, young Hamilton Tyler was exhibiting the initiative I encouraged in my officers. In this case it was misplaced and wrongheaded. He had initiated an unauthorized surveillance of the Cruz family—Sebastian and his brother, Ramon. It was odd, but not particularly surprising, that for all his directional microphones and motion-activated infrared camera setups, he had managed to completely miss any sign of the previous night's intruders.

I called Ham into my office that afternoon. Should I have recused myself from the investigation because of my friendship with Sebastian? That cut to the heart of why I had come to Nantucket in the first place. In Los Angeles, the conflict of interest would have been clear, and my boss would have insisted I step down. In this tightly knit small town, knowing someone, taking the measure of their character through dozens of small interactions over weeks and months and years, was actually an asset, not a liability.

"Also," as Jane had pointed out with her usual impish candor, "on Nantucket, you're the boss."

Ham Tyler was also aware of the situation. "Your daughter's dating the guy's kid!" he blurted, leaning across my desk that afternoon.

"Sit down, Ham."

He seemed to realize he'd gotten carried away. "Uh, sorry, Chief." He lowered himself into one of the Chippendale knock-offs Jane had picked up at an antique auction the previous winter. They may have been fake, but they were sturdy and they gave the office a little character. Ham sat clutching the arms as if he were about to launch himself over the desk.

"Sebastian Cruz is not a drug dealer," I said.

"Hell, he isn't."

"He's a landscaper and a playwright."

"Yeah, I seen that play of his. Kill all the rich people. Sell 'em bad drugs, right? Sounds like a plan to me."

I caught my hands under the desk and rolled myself up tight to the edge. "I think you're confusing Sebastian with his brother. It's understandable. They look alike."

"All them spics look alike."

I slammed my hand down. It sounded like a gunshot, and Ham twitched back in his seat. "Never use that word in my office. Never use it in public. In fact—don't use it at home. Don't use it all! Don't even think it."

"You can't tell me what to think."

"No, but I can fire you for cause if I ever hear another ethnic slur come out of your mouth again. I'll fire you if someone reports you. I'll fire you for a fucking rumor."

"Hey, that's not fair! What if—"

"What if someone got you fired by lying about your trash mouth? That would be tough. My advice? Make fewer enemies. Start being nice to people."

"People don't respect a nice cop."

"Actually, they do, Ham. That's the way you earn respect—by having power and not abusing it."

He seethed for a minute or two, and I watched him. Finally: "Why not arrest the brother then?"

"Couple of reasons. Ramon is too well insulated from the day-to-day business, and no one would ever rat him out. We can't touch him. And there's something else. He's actually a moderating influence on the gangs here. There's kids coming up who think you solve every problem with a shotgun or a machete. To them, he's a weak old man, and they'd be dancing in the streets if we arrested him. But he keeps the peace. That's the reality. I don't like it, but I'll take it."

"So you leave them alone, Sebastian Cruz and his greasy little brother."

"That's right."

"Well, you're making a big mistake. I see why they call you 'The LA Dodger' Makes sense, right? Stay out of trouble, duck and cover, pretend everything's fine."

"Who calls me that?"

He coughed out a laugh. "Gotcha, Chief. I just made it up. But, hey, if the shoe fits, why not? The name might catch on."

I stood. "No more traffic stops unless you have a clear violation. And leave Sebastian Cruz alone. I know you pulled him over last week and ran the drug dogs through his van for half an hour. You had traffic backed up from the Union Street duck pond to the rotary."

"I had a tip."

"You had an attitude. And that's all you had. Take a few

minutes to read the Fourth Amendment of the United States Constitution. It applies to you."

"Yes, sir."

"Violate it again, and I will suspend you without pay pending a Board of Inquiry hearing."

The new default setting: "Yes, sir."

He'd give me a "Yes, sir" now no matter what I said. I resisted the temptation to tell him to do something anatomically impossible. "Get out of here and start earning your paycheck."

"Yes, sir."

I waved him out with the flick of my wrist and released a long sigh as the door shut behind him, though his Axe aftershave lingered, and he wasn't the only hater I had to deal with. The island's burgeoning diversity had revealed its long-standing bigotry. It reminded me of the dry rot and powder-post beetles Billy Delavane found while renovating old houses. "Sometimes it's best to leave those places alone," he said to me once. "Or else tear them down."

Neither option was viable for our civic polity, but the hatred and resentment for Nantucket's immigrants were getting worse every year. In fact, the situation was getting worse even as I ruminated on them.

My phone rang.

Haden's nephew, Byron Lovell, was on the other end of the line. "I'm standing in front of Sylvester and Millie Graham's house, Chief. You need to get down here."

I'd known the Grahams for a long time. I'd helped their son practice for his driving test and solved his murder a few years later. They had immigrated from Jamaica a few years before I came "around the point," mostly to avoid the violence there, but it seemed to have followed them north. Sylvester retained a dark sense of humor with a rumbling laugh for the misfortunes of his friends and a honking guffaw for his own calamities. A chum forgetting his wallet after taking ten friends to dinner evoked Sylvester's sharp-eyed schadenfreude chortle. He reserved the big hoot and cackle for the time he rear-ended a cop's cruiser at a stop sign because he was lighting up a joint. Fortunately, the driver of the patrol car was the police chief. I let him go with a warning and took cash for the repair so it wouldn't jack up his insurance premiums.

Sylvester and his wife, Millie, had succeeded on Nantucket the way most immigrants did—by working rings around the locals. A plasterer by trade, he offered unbeatable prices, his stamina was legendary, and his attitude remained stunningly cheerful, even after all the tragedy he'd experienced in his life. Mike Henderson described singing Jimmy Cliff songs with the jovial pot-bellied juggernaut on some jobsite until Millie stopped by with hot lunches for everyone and insisted they stop their "caterwauling."

They launched into a heartfelt version of "Many Rivers to Cross" the minute she was gone.

With steady work as one of Pat Folger's primary subcontractors, and a new house in the Friendship Lane subdivision, life seemed to be turning around for Sylvester and Millie.

But now someone had written *Niger Go Home* across the shingled side of the Graham house and squirted out a giant swastika above the words. The act was vile and heartbreaking but tempered somewhat by the response of Sylvester's neighbors. They had gathered with buckets of soapy water and power sanders to scrub and abrade the graffiti from the cedar shakes, and they stood, a group of twenty people, whole families with kids as young as nine or ten, ready to go to work amid a tangle of power cords and hoses.

Byron was holding them off. "I told them, this is a crime

scene!" he explained as I climbed out of my cruiser. Their presence was primarily good for moral support, anyway—Pat Folger had shown up with Billy Delavane and a crew of five, armed with flat bars and a pallet of new shingles. I suspected the quiet one I didn't recognize was Mitchell Stone, but this was not the right time to talk to him. He and two other guys were spreading a plastic tarp against the foundation as the crowd looked on with the rest of the crew poised to rip the violated siding off the wall. The work would be done in less than an hour. These guys could reshingle a whole roof in less than a day.

Sylvester strode up to me and lifted me off my feet with a hug that knocked the breath out of my chest. "Thanks for coming, mon."

"Who does such a thing?" Millie asked after stretching up on tiptoes to kiss my cheek.

"I'm going to find out."

Millie sighed. "Chicken merry, hawk de near."

I had picked up a little patois over the years, and I knew what she meant. You're never safe, especially when you think you are. I couldn't argue the point—her life was the proof. Instead, I stepped away and approached the side of her house for a closer look.

Byron jogged up to walk beside me. "We got no hard evidence, Chief. No footprints in the dirt, no discarded spray-paint can, no eyewitnesses."

I stopped, studying the dripping scrawl on the cedar siding. Charlie Boyce stopped, too, and we stood there for a few moments, staring at it.

I turned to Byron. "What do you think?"

"Is this a test?"

"Everything's a test."

We stood silently for a minute or two more. "Well, whoever it is, they got the swastika wrong. The Nazi swastika has the arms going left, like—counterclockwise? These go the other way." He must have caught my curious look. "I'm a history buff."

"Okay. That's good. Anything else?"

He shrugged.

Charlie stepped closer. "We started to canvas the neighborhood with a couple of uniforms, and from what I can tell we have some real crazies living around here—survivalists, Second Amendment fanatics, Breitbart tiki-torch types, if you know what I mean."

"And you think they could have done this?"

"Well…Mr. Graham had words with one of them about a week ago. The Grahams threw a big barbecue, and I guess some of the nastier neighbors didn't get invited. There were a lot of cars blocking people's driveways, someone heard this, uh…Pete Hannaford? He said something like 'You people just don't get it. We have rules.' It turned into a shoving match, but friends broke it up before anyone got hurt. I talked to Hannaford just now, and he went into this rant about setting his stuff down at a table on the ferry, and going to the bathroom and coming back to find a whole Jamaican family sitting there. Like they didn't get that his coat and duffel bag reserved his spot. This happened last summer, and he's still pissed about it."

"So you have a suspect?"

"Maybe."

"Describe him for me."

"Uh, okay…" Charlie's face bunched up in thought, then cleared. "About six three, red hair with a bald spot, thin except for a little paunch. Lots of freckles, mean little mouth, blue eyes. Oh, and he had this weird tattoo on his wrist—just numbers. 1488. I figured maybe…his birthday? January fourth? One, four, eighty-eight? He looks about thirty, so 1988 makes sense."

I shook my head. "It's a white supremacist thing. The four-teen stands for 'fourteen words'—some slogan...'we must secure the existence of our people,' blah blah blah. You can look it up. And the eighty-eight...well, *H* is the eighth letter in the alphabet, so..."

"*HH*. Heil Hitler?"

I nodded. "I saw a lot of this stuff in LA. I didn't think I'd ever see it here, though."

"Looks like we have our guy."

"Except for one detail. Something in your description gets him off the hook."

He slumped. "You got me, Chief. What?"

"People generally spray-paint from shoulder height." I lifted my arm in a pantomime. "That would put our perpetrator at around...five five, five six? Way too short. And this is a kid thing anyway, graffiti like this. Hannaford doesn't quite fit the profile."

"So where do we go next?" The answer was obvious, so I let him get there on his own. "School?"

"School."

I called ahead and Superintendent Bissell was waiting for us, blowing hot and loud as a propane space heater when we pushed through the big glass doors.

"I will not have you disrupting the life of this institution."

"That's fine. We just want to—"

"You want to accuse me of harboring some sort of sick, vio-lent, unbalanced vandal in my classrooms! You think you can stride in here on no notice with your guns on your hips and lec-ture me about my own students! Well, let me tell you—"

"First of all, we're unarmed."

"That won't wash here! I will not permit—"

"I don't want to lecture you, Alan. I just want to ask a few questions."

"That's what the brownshirt bully boys always say before the rough stuff begins! 'We just want to ask a few questions.'"

I went back a long way with Alan Bissell. We'd been through a lot together, none of it good. But this seemed like a new low. I didn't bother with his hysterical accusations—taking me from zero to Nazi in five seconds flat. He might have had a worse morning than me. "Someone has defaced a local house with racist graffiti. I think it's probably a kid, and I was wondering if you had noticed anything…"

"What I have or have not noticed within the purview of my authority here does not and should not concern you. We can handle our own problems at Nantucket High School, Chief Kennis. I take pride in that. I don't call the police after every minor scuffle. That's the straight path from school to a life in prison, all because of a childish outburst or a thoughtless infraction of the rules."

"I agree. It's good to hear you say that. But—"

"So, please. Leave this to us."

That was my opening, and I pounced. "This?"

"The incident. We have the situation well in hand."

"What incident?"

"Really, it's a minor matter." I stared at him. "One of our African American students, DeShawn Merriman, found an offensive…epithet…written on his notebook cover. He turned the notebook in to the office, and school security staff have been looking into the circumstances of the property defacement."

"Do they have a suspect?"

"They have several."

"What does DeShawn think?"

"We haven't involved him in the inquiry. That would violate school policy."

"You don't talk to the victim about the crime."

"We don't involve students in the early stages of a disciplinary review. No."

"Can I talk to him?"

"Not on school grounds. Not during school hours. And I would strongly suggest a policy of official law enforcement disengagement until the NHS administration has concluded its internal investigation."

I let the lines of bureaucratic jargon march past and released a breath. "Thanks for your advice. Now I want to see this DeShawn Merriman, a school resource officer, and you in your office in five minutes."

"Or what?"

"Or I will put this whole school under emergency lockdown until I determine whether or not the perpetrator of this hate crime presents an active threat to the safety and well-being of the student body and faculty."

"That is a ludicrous overreaction!"

"I hope you're right, Alan. Five minutes."

I could see some additional bluster churning below the surface of his face, working at his features like fingers. But in the end, he just turned away and stalked off down the hall.

It took ten minutes, but soon enough, Byron and I; along with Bissell; the resource officer, a heavy-set affable woman named Bea; and DeShawn were all gathered in the tight confines of Bissell's book-lined bat cave.

DeShawn was a painfully thin kid with an ostentatious Afro and a manner that indicated he thought he was about to be arrested.

I tried to ease the tension a little. "Hi, DeShawn. I'm Police Chief Kennis, and this is one of my officers, Byron Lovell." Byron nodded at DeShawn. "I wanted to ask you about this crap someone wrote on your notebook."

He looked up, cautiously surprised. "Crap?"

"Okay, shit."

This earned me the flash of a smile. "That shit a'right."

"Do you have any idea who might have done it?"

He shrugged. "Haters be hatin'. They all the same."

"But some hate more than others. For instance, some of them take the trouble to write it down."

"There's always some Cletus clowning on me, you know? But they just frontin'."

I turned to Bea. "Do you have a list of possible suspects?"

"We've gathered ten names, interviewed various students and staff…but it's all just talk, Chief. There's no real evidence against anyone, and I would hate to impugn an innocent young person's reputation on the basis of hearsay and innuendo."

I sniffed. "Yeah, well. How about this? Read the list to DeShawn. We'll see what he thinks. That okay with you, DeShawn?"

"Sure."

Bea glanced over at Bissell, but he had given up. His hands fluttered in a semaphore that said *Do whatever these people want; let's get this over with.*

Bea pulled out her phone, scrolled to the proper file, and started reading names. Tim Honeycutt, Steve Lerner, Andy Boatwright, Kenneth Ames, Chris Contrell.

All white, all local.

I watched DeShawn as Bea ran down the list. DeShawn drew a blank—or so he said. No one wanted to play the rat, even with rats like these. When she was done, I thanked her and Bissell, and apologized to DeShawn for dragging him out of class.

Then we left, taking DeShawn's notebook with us. The vandal had written "eat shit niger" next to the familiar Nazi symbol on the front page.

Sitting in my cruiser in the school parking lot, I said to Charlie, "Any thoughts?"

"Well—it's the same backward swastika."

"And the same spelling problems."

"So probably the same kid?"

"But which one?"

Charlie shrugged.

"DeShawn tensed up and looked sideways down at the floor for a second when she said Chris Contrell's name. That's classic recognition behavior. They must have had some kind of run-in."

"It's not much to go on, boss."

"True."

But I'd watched my mentor on the LAPD, Chuck Obremski, get a full confession on a lot less.

I showed up at the Contrell house on Essex Road at four that afternoon, alone and out of uniform, carrying DeShawn's notebook in my hand. The neighborhood was a dreary subdivision, walking distance from the school, most of the houses broken up into rental rooms—worker barracks, to put it bluntly—with four, five, or six cars crowding every driveway. Not exactly the chamber of commerce view of Nantucket, with a rusting washing machine, cars on blocks, and gaudily colored children's toys cluttering the yards. It occurred to me that long after we go extinct, when there is nothing left but contaminated soil and cockroaches, the Little Tikes Hide & Slide would endure—ugly, indestructible, and mysterious, the last relic of human culture. I could imagine the aliens who found it shaking their heads and saying "Good riddance."

Which made me think of Shakespeare—the phrase actually originated in *Troilus and Cressida*—which led to the despairing certainty that no one on this block or in this house was likely to have seen that play or any Shakespeare play, or any other play, for that matter. This brought to mind Winston Churchill's cold, casually brutal and dismissive response to a newspaperman's question, after his campaign for prime minister took him to London's East End slums for the first time. "What did I think?" he asked. "I thought how strange it must be living there. Never to see anything beautiful. Never to eat anything delicious. Never to say anything clever."

What a snob! And yet—what would he have made of Essex Road? Apart from the newly renovated Apex Academy buildings at the far end of the street, which the new private school had no doubt picked up for pennies on the dollar at a foreclosure sale, it all looked the same—the brown grass and cracked asphalt, the peeling paint and twisted venetian blinds, the torn screens and missing shingles. It might have rendered Churchill speechless. A lot of people would have paid good money to witness a moment like that.

Mr. Contrell, heavyset with his long hair pulled back into a coarse ponytail and still wearing work clothes—steel-toed boots and Carhartt overalls, grimy Patriots sweatshirt—met me at the door. He had a Bud Light in one hand and an American Spirit jammed between two fingers of the other.

"What?"

"Hello, Mr. Contrell. I'm Police Chief Henry Kennis. I need to speak to Chris for a minute."

"He's not home."

From the back of the house: "Who is it, Dad?"

Contrell's shoulders slumped: busted. "Fuck it. Come on in. We're about to eat dinner, so make it quick."

Dinner was pizza from the Muse, Cokes, and a Greek salad in a plastic box. The salad was a hopeful sign.

Chris was glaring down at the pizza. "Shit, Dad! I said sausage, not pepperoni! Are you going senile or something?"

"Sorry, Chris. I guess I just misunderstood what you—"

"Right. Because sausage sounds just like pepperoni. They don't even have the same letters!"

"Except for *E*," I pointed out.

He turned on me. "Shut up, you clueless freak."

"Clueless? Really? Chris, that's one thing you should never, ever say to a detective. That hurts. And even if it's true, it's never true for long. In fact, I have an excellent clue in my hand right now, thanks to you."

"Huh?"

I handed his father DeShawn's notebook. "Your son wrote this, like he wrote on Sylvester Graham's house last night with a can of spray paint. If he's going to be a good Nazi, he needs to learn how to draw a swastika. And spelling is important, even when committing a hate crime. Niger is a country in Africa— and a river. Not a racial slur."

Mr. Contrell drew himself up. "Hold on there! My son would never—"

"Oh, yeah? What if I did, Dad? Someone's gotta do something around here. We're turning into the minority, and these minorities are taking over! Those fuckin' spics were shingling the house next door at eight o'clock last night, banging away. You couldn't even watch TV."

"So the problem is they work hard?"

"The problem is they don't belong here! They're an army! They're invading us, and we're letting it happen."

"Chris—"

"Come on, Dad. You know I'm right. You can't bid against these people, they charge nothing, they live ten to a room and pay no taxes. They got no insurance! But when they get sick— Jesus Christ, stop by the emergency room sometime. It's like Mexico City in there, except all the Mexicans in Mexico City came here instead."

I wondered if Chris knew that Mexico City was a real place. He made it sound like a generic location, crazyville or toontown, that he might have made up in a xenophobic fugue state.

"So you did spray-paint the Grahams' house."

"And that's not all I'm gonna do. It's still a free country, last time I looked."

I was suddenly on high alert. I watched the boy carefully. "What else are you planning to do, Chris?"

"None of your business."

"But it is my business. It's the definition of my business."

"Leave the kid alone," Mr. Contrell said. "You cops already came sniffing around here, and we got a clean bill of health."

I had never heard about this. "What cops?"

He shrugged. "Some kid at school filed a complaint, like Chris was a bully or something. Maybe he was. What's wrong with that? Bullies teach kids to stand up for themselves. It ain't all sweetness and light when these libtard snowflakes go out in the real world."

"Who came to the house, Mr. Contrell?"

"Just some cop. Who knows? A cop's a cop."

"You've lived here all your life, and you can't tell one policeman from another? You went to school with half of them. I saw you at a Whalers game with one of my officers last year. Big guy, red hair—ring a bell?"

"Nope. Coulda been anybody next to me. I don't pay attention to the bleachers at a football game. I'm watching the field."

"I don't remember reading a report of the incident."

He raised an eyebrow. "Like you read every incident report."

"I proofread every incident report."

"Well maybe he didn't bother writing it up because there was nothing worth writing about."

"Maybe." I glanced around the messy kitchen—dishes in the sink, unopened mail on the counter, crusty microwave containers sticking up out of the trash—and a Carhartt work jacket draped over some sort of green carton on the floor. I took a step and lifted the jacket with the toe of my shoe.

"Hey—!" Contrell shouted.

You might have thought it was a tackle box if you didn't know better. But I'd searched enough suspects' houses to know what that heavy-duty plastic chest was used for.

"Care to open the box for me, Mr. Contrell?"

"You got a warrant?"

"You should listen to the guy who works for you," Chris blurted out. "He didn't have a problem with us! I guess some people still believe in the Second Amendment!"

I ignored him and spoke to his father. "I need to know what type of ammunition you're storing in there, Mr. Contrell."

"Fine. I got nothing to hide." He strode to the box, kneeled down, worked the latches, and opened the top. He pulled out a clear plastic hundred-round ammunition container, stood, and handed it to me. "Remington .223."

I took the heavy plastic square in my hand and looked down past it to the main cache. "Expecting a war?"

"Maybe I am."

"Against the tyrannical federal government that wants to force you to have health care?"

"Force me to pay if I don't, you mean."

"These .223s are ammunition for an AR-15. Assault rifles are banned in the state of Massachusetts, Mr. Contrell."

He snorted. "Typical gun hater! Due respect. None of you know shit about guns. I use this ammo in my hunting rifle, Chief. A Mossberg Patriot. Best in the world. I hunt deer, and I stick to the posted season. You got a problem with that?"

We had strayed off-topic. I had come to observe the Sixth Amendment, not to debate the Second.

"Let me cut this short," I said, turning to the boy. "Chris Contrell, I am placing you under arrest for violation of the Massachusetts hate crimes statute, Mass General Law chapter 265, section 39."

His look of outrage was comical. "You can't do that!"

"You have the right to remain silent. Anything you say can and will be used against you in a court of law. You have the right to an attorney. If you can't afford an attorney, one will be appointed to you by the court. Do you understand these rights as I've explained them to you?"

"This is such bullshit!"

I studied him, waiting.

His father said, "Chris—"

"Yes, fine, okay? I understand them. Jesus!"

I took Chris to the station and booked him, but we had to let him go a few hours later. DeShawn wanted nothing to do with the police, and the Grahams refused to press charges.

"It would just make things worse," Millie explained.

"Wah sweet nanny goat ago run him belly," Sylvester added.

"Excuse me?"

"It's an old Jamaican saying," Millie explained. "You know a goat eats a lot of things. They may be delicious for him right then, but they make him sick later. Things you do come back at you, Chief. That's all. We like to stay quiet."

"Besides, you know—maybe this will teach the boy something," Sylvester added. "He does bad, we forgive."

I sighed. "That's very Christian of you, but I prefer punishment."

We wound up cutting a deal: no formal charges, but Chris had to complete a state-mandated diversity awareness program, complete thirty hours of community service, and attend regular counseling sessions for six months.

It seemed like a reasonable compromise at the time. I should have known it was a mistake, just watching Chris's superior little smirk at the conclusion of his hearing.

I called Bissell to follow up, but he didn't want to hear it.

"Chris is a fine boy from an old island family. A superb athlete and a model student. I wish all our charges were as polite and respectful as Christopher Contrell."

"Not to his father."

"The family dynamics of a pupil's home life do not concern us unless they adversely affect his scholastic performance or behavior. Whatever discord you may have observed, I would say that Lawrence Contrell is doing a superlative job."

I gritted my teeth silently. "I don't know how much more clear I can make this, Alan. The kid is a xenophobic creep. He has an arsenal, and he's talking about going to war."

"No, he's an independent young man who believes in the Second Amendment. And he happens to disagree with you."

After the hearing, Pete Geller, the Barnstable County DA, had remarked that Chris looked happy to be "getting away with murder." I agreed with Geller, despite the hackneyed metaphor. When Chris brought his father's AR-15 into school two days later, he was planning to commit real murder, mass murder.

And he didn't care in the least whether he got away with it or not.

Chapter Six

THE ENEMIES LIST

We were fifty yards out into the dark, choppy water of Tuckernuck Bank and angling toward Madaket Harbor before either one of us spoke again. "That coin Mark used in that strip game…it was a magic show prop, Todd," Jane said finally. "Tails on both sides. You were always going to lose."

—From Todd Fraker's deleted blog

Roy Elkins sat on the hard plastic seat in the Washington, DC, Greyhound bus terminal thinking, "People who say revenge is futile just aren't doing it right."

He smiled, running a hand over his newly bald skull and down his baby-smooth cheeks. He looked the opposite of his old self, with the thick, wavy brown hair and the heavy stubble. He slouched now, too, and walked with a slight limp—a simple disguise of deflected expectations. The Roy Elkins currently on the Most Wanted List stood up straight with his chest puffed out and ran marathons for recreation.

No one had stopped him on the flight from Los Angeles

despite a three-hour delay. He noticed two chumps from the Marshals Service scanning the crowds. One of them he'd worked with back in '06—Kenny something, Rainey or Ranney—big, dumb by-the-book robo-cop. Their eyes had met for a second. No recognition.

It made Roy wonder about Superman—everyone always laughed at the fact that he fooled everyone with a pair of glasses. But Roy could see it working. Probably the suspicion skipped across the surface of people's minds, like a flat stone across a still pond. They might have even thought, "This sounds fucked up, but Clark kind of looks like Superman." Much the same way, Kenny Ignatz might have said to himself, "That limping bald guy reminds me of Roy Elkins." Then: "Naaah. He looked right at me. No way."

It was all so easy. That was the big secret. Escaping from jail, dodging a police dragnet, committing murder in plain sight... If people knew how easy it was to do whatever the fuck you wanted and get away with it, civilization would collapse completely. Roy shrugged—it might be fun to see that.

Lots of opportunities when civilizations collapsed.

Of course, he had needed help. What was that political treacle? It takes a village. To raise a kid, maybe. To bust a killer out of jail, all you need is a neighborhood. Or maybe just the neighborhood watch. Fatso didn't need to spoon-feed him the plan—he'd had a version of the plan cooking away in the back of his mind since the indictment. But it was like boiling water for pasta—eventually the water steams away and the pot scorches. Roy's plan didn't work without money. Like what plan ever did? The Feds had seized all his bank accounts and found all but one of his getaway-stash hiding places. The weapons and passports there would help—he had to get to Zurich, to the Zurich Canton Bank, to that squat, ugly cement-grid-and-glass building at Bahnhofstrasse 9, to reclaim the big money. But the measly five grand stuffed into an ex-girlfriend's old Sony Trinitron TV in an Inglewood basement? That would never do the trick.

So he had waited for fate to step in, and fate finally obliged him.

He had a visitor one rainy spring afternoon—his first one ever. And it was Fatty. He'd never seen the guy before, but he had obviously been studying Roy. He knew what Roy had done, and he knew what Roy was doing, and he seemed to know Roy's plans, also. He knew about Henry Kennis's girlfriend; he knew about Franny Tate and her boyfriend. Fatty knew everything.

Fatty had money, and he wanted to make a deal.

All Roy had to do was use his Boston connections to bust some con out of a jail in western Mass—the same way he was going to use his LA connections to bust his own ass out of Corcoran. He would need to give himself a head start—he had things to do on the way back East, but Fatty seemed to have figured out Roy's itinerary, along with everything else. The convict back East, his name was Ed Delavane. Roy knew Delavane slightly. They had crossed paths years before, and somehow Fatty knew it. The guy had done his homework. You had to give him credit for that. Anyway, the money belonged to Delavane— his secret buried treasure, hidden somewhere on Nantucket Island, where Kennis lived. It all seemed very convenient, but Delavane would be coming for the loot, just like Roy.

The trick was to make sure that when Ed got there, the money was gone.

"Once you're out, get a burner phone, and give me the number. When I know Delavane is free, I'll give you the GPS coordinates for the dough."

Roy had squinted into the wide, guileless face. "What do you get out of it?"

"I get Delavane."

"How do I know you won't take the money?"

Fatty had laughed. "Oh, I don't need money, Roy. Money is the last thing I need."

Roy believed him. Fatty had said he had to catch a ten thirty flight, but their meeting ran long. "Looks like you missed your plane," Roy said, standing up to shake Fatty's hand.

"I think they'll hold it for me, Roy. I own the aircraft."

Fatty's smug "gotcha" smile made the whole thing real.

"Looks like you got a new best friend," the guard said as he led Roy back to his cell.

The three guards at Corcoran had been easy to bribe. The idea there was not using money. You want to bribe someone, find out what they want the money for. These mooks wanted to be cops. The youngest kid had given up after he whiffed the exams; the oldest had taken early retirement and regretted it. Middle bear had been caught lifting a couple of eight balls from the evidence locker. He ratted out his pals and skated, but he still missed the life. They all knew Roy, or at least knew of him the way aspiring military snipers knew of Nick Irving or Chris Kyle. Roy was a legend, a closer, "the terrier," the *LA Times* had called him, because once he got a case in his teeth, he never let go. He still had friends in RHD, and the guards knew it. A word from him to them could change their lives—for better or worse.

So they played along.

Now, two were in lockdown, and one was dead. There was a lesson there for the two saps headed back to Corcoran in orange jumpsuits: If someone wins your confidence by making you feel confident? He's a confidence man.

And you're the mark.

As for the rest of it? His pal in Boston was happy to clear the ledgers, and the guards at Cedar Junction—two punks he'd taught and covered for at the Academy—were just as clueless and hungry as their LA counterparts. Roy's Inglewood DL and passport said Dominick Bardo, and Dom was ten years older than Elkins, clean-shaven and bald.

Done.

As for the murders, Roy's private itinerary, no one expected them, so they didn't know how to react. Roy's first targets: two working moms and a housewife. He'd kept track of them from prison, detectives' wives, spouses of the traitors who'd landed him in jail, the straight arrows, the square shooters.

The enemies list.

The Realtor lady worked from home—early retirement.

The hausfrau was puttering in her garden—now she's fertilizing it.

Three taps each. The third victim was trickier, a schoolteacher. Schools had turned into fortresses since Roy started serving time. So she had to be lured outside. Fake police call, husband in the hospital—Roy knew how to make it convincing. He'd done it for real plenty of times. She ran out, and he tapped her in the parking lot. That made three for three, like trap-shooting clay pigeons.

Hennesy should have been the tough one—NSA big shot, security expert, superspook. The NSA Headquarters in Fort Meade, Maryland—a twenty-minute commute south of the city with two dedicated exits off the Baltimore-Washington Parkway—would have made the job next to impossible with its dozens of watch posts and checkpoints bolstered by state-of-the-art total surveillance technology. No one got in there without a clearance, and no left without a pass. But Hennesy was recovering from a bad case of the flu, working from home this week, and living in DC had made him lazy. He lived by habit—just like everyone else who wasn't waiting for a bullet. Hennesy's crucial habit, the lethal one on this particular day, was his mid-morning dash across the street to Starbucks for a grande latte and a slice of caramelized apple pound cake.

Roy dropped him jaywalking across the street while he waited for a pickup truck to move past. The three-car crash and the angry fanfare of car horns when a taxi braked for the body were all the cover Roy needed for a clean escape. A murder that creates its own diversion?

Sweet.

Roy pulled out his burner Nokia and checked the time. He had another hour before the Boston bus. He stood and stretched. Then he wandered aimlessly out of the Greyhound station into the dense, warm, humid DC afternoon and strolled through President's Park and the Ellipse, lost and invisible in the swarm of tourists.

The next job would be trickier. The first ones were people he knew in big cities where he had connections and anonymity. Now he was headed for a small town where he was a stranger. Still, he had Fatty on his side—a freak with his own crazy agenda, maybe, but their plans dovetailed perfectly, and that was all that mattered.

He sat down on a bench halfway along the reflecting pool between the Washington Monument and the Lincoln Memorial, comfortable with the proximity. They were pragmatists, Lincoln and Washington—and killers, too. You had to be a killer if you wanted to be president. No one had ever served in the White House without getting blood on his hands.

He pulled out his battered spiral notebook and took the luxury of crossing the last name off his list in advance—Henry Kennis, soon to learn the meaning of suffering and loss, a lesson he'd never forget from a teacher who had never forgotten him. Roy liked the sound of that phrase; it was like a little poem.

Kennis would appreciate it. He wrote poems, supposedly. Elkins smiled. Maybe he'd write it down on a card and pin it to Jane Stiles' chest, right next to the bullet hole.

———

Franny Tate sat motionless at her desk on the sixth floor of the Homeland Security complex on Seventh Street SW. She had a fine view from her office across the Potomac and over the leafy suburban streets of Arlington, Virginia. From where she sat, it might as well have been a forest down there, the leaves still dense and green in early September. Normally she loved that serene vista. This morning she saw nothing. She felt nothing. Her grief was sudden and absolute, a bag thrown over her head. She was suffocating. Her hand was on the telephone, but she didn't know who to call. There was no one she could bear to talk to. Still, arrangements had to be made. There was no one else to handle them. Mark's parents lived in Costa Rica, and his brother had been killed in Afghanistan three years ago. There was a sister, Carol, but she was languishing in some high-end rehab resort in Northern California. She couldn't organize a change-of-address card.

Finally, Franny understood how Carol Hennesy must feel all the time—helpless and paralyzed and useless and inept.

Mark was dead. Mark was dead.

If you repeated words often enough, they started to lose their meaning. Franny had read that somewhere. The words started to look like random syllables in another language. Mark was dead.

Mark was dead.

It wasn't working. Her eyes burned, but no tears came. She gripped the phone harder. If she let go, she'd start shaking and keep shaking until she shook herself to pieces. She gasped, try-ing to inhale. It was like breathing through a straw.

This made no sense. They had gone to breakfast this morn-ing at Lincoln's Waffle Shop; he had kissed her on the street less than two hours ago. They had seats for *Turn Me Loose* at the Arena Stage tonight. The tickets were in her purse.

She pulled the air in, forced it out. Someone did this, Dale Briscoe had told her when he called. Mark was shot twice in the chest as he crossed the street, with one more in the head when he was down—a mob hit, an execution.

Just like Chuck Obremski's wife.

And Ted Miner's wife.

And Pete Stambaugh's wife.

She felt her chest clenching with rage. It felt good. Rage, she could deal with. Rage kept you moving. Rage was fuel.

Chuck had called from Los Angeles on Friday afternoon. Franny's secretary had left the message on her desk. The nota-tion was "urgent," but she had found that what was urgent for the LAPD could generally wait until Monday morning, so far as Homeland Security was concerned. Plus Chuck liked to talk, and Franny hated the dreaded "catch-up" chitchat when she had a thousand things to do and no time to do them.

He had texted her on Sunday: Roy Elkins is out. Call me.

It was a little early for parole. Had the President pardoned him?

Eight years ago, working with an LAPD-FBI task force that included Chuck and Henry Kennis, Franny had helped put Roy Elkins away. She had fallen in love with Henry during the course of that investigation, but they were both married. Four years later, she was working for DHS when a series of bomb threats brought her to Nantucket. Both of them were divorced by then, and they rekindled their affair. But Henry was never going to leave his little sandspit, and Franny was a DC lifer. So they moved on. Then Franny met a genius NSA encryption specialist named Mark Hennesy. He had a killer smile, Redskins season tickets, and a degree from Le Cordon Bleu in Paris. They became pals. They fell into bed with each other. Sex was athletic, competitive, impersonal fun. Then it got serious. She fell in love and so did he—more like jumped, he told her. Like base-jumping together off the same cliff.

The parachutes opened, and he gave her a ring. That was six months ago.

But she still kept in touch with Henry. He had found someone, also—a writer named Jane Stiles. Franny had checked out her books, cozy mysteries, and looked at her dust-jacket pictures—attractive woman. Henry and Jane were engaged, due to be married in a couple of weeks.

So, happy endings all around.

Then, the news this morning, finally, a lost weekend late. Roy Elkins had escaped from jail during a routine transport from Corcoran to the federal courthouse on Spring Street in downtown LA for another parole hearing. Three guards had helped with the escape. Two of them were in custody, and a third had been shot trying to escape.

Franny stood and walked to the window, thinking hard about Roy Elkins. He had murdered his girlfriend after a bad breakup, but skated on the 187 rap with smoke and mirrors—and a unified RHD behind him. He was one of their own. Franny had gathered a lot of evidence, but it was all circumstantial. She knew only a slam dunk would work with a high-profile case like his. It turned out Elkins was selling drugs as well as using them. They wound up convicting him on felony drug trafficking and racketeering charges.

No murder rap, no lifetime in solitary confinement. Roy

should have been happy or at least relieved. But he was furious, and he was scared. Winding up in jail is every dirty cop's worst nightmare. And somehow Roy had turned things around so it was the police's fault that he killed his girlfriend. They trapped him. She was going to turn state's evidence against him; they had convinced her he was bad. His own family had wrecked his life—other cops were the only family he had left by that time.

"You're gonna feel what I feel," he had snarled in court that last day after the sentencing. "You're gonna lose the ones you love most. I'm gonna take them away from you. One by one."

She knew it was foolish to feel threatened by a man in chains being led away to prison, but the moment had sliced a chill through her. There was something vicious and feral about Roy Elkins at that moment. He meant what he said.

And now he was doing what he promised.

That thought broke her inertia. There was still one action she could take, one life she could save. She allowed herself a bitter little smile. She was still clutching the phone, as if her hand had known all along what to do.

She let out the breath she'd been holding and started poking in the numbers.

Interlude:
Monica Terwilliger

We had crossed the harbor together, we had spoken as equals and shared our feelings. But she screamed at me when I grabbed her. I kissed her anyway, and she slapped me. She stumbled back, wiping her mouth with the back of her hand as if I had thrown a glass of sour milk in her face. Then she scrambled into the boat and fled back to her party and her fancy friends. I sat on the cold sand and cried like a lost child. All I could think was, this isn't over, this isn't over. And it still isn't. That's what none of them understand. It won't be over until I end it.

—From Todd Fraker's deleted blog

Monica Terwilliger was captured by a single phone call.

It came at ten in the morning, taking her out of the lab where she had been updating her local fingerprint archive for the national database. It was tedious work and she was happy for the break, happier to hear from one of her oldest friends after a long silence.

Pooky Parrish—of course, she was Cindy Henderson now,

but for Monica she'd never grow out of her childhood moniker or lose her family name…Pooky had become more distant over the last few years, basically since the baby. She spent her time with other parents and rarely went out at night. No more wild dancing at the Muse or the Chicken Box with her crazy-drunk gal pals. Now it was all preschool and pediatrician appointments.

It was okay—they had joined two different tribes, Monica understood that. The truth was they had started to bore each other a little—Pooky tuning out the romantic gossip and Monica nodding through the breathless reporting of a first word or a first step. Losing touch had been easy—lazy, in fact—probably inevitable, but still sad.

So the call out of nowhere on a dull gray Tuesday morning came as a pleasant surprise.

She picked up the landline on her office desk. "Hey, girl-friend."

"Hey, Mon. What's happening?"

"You know, the usual, twenty-hour days, using high-tech gear to catch the bad guys. *CSI Nantucket* with no ads. Or glamorous stars. Or neat endings."

"Sounds like real life."

"Yeah. You okay?"

"I'm fine, I'm great…that's actually what I was calling you about."

"Because you sound a little weird. Are you sleeping okay?"

"Like a baby. And my baby really did sleep through the night from, like, the age of six months. Now nothing wakes her up. It's awesome. And speaking of awesome—"

"Oh, God, here it comes."

"No, seriously. Remember you asked how I lost the baby weight and I said—"

"When I feel like eating a cookie—I don't."

"That was my dad's line, actually, when he quit smoking. Iron Dad. I could never do that. But I didn't want to admit I was involved with this crackpot woo-woo weight loss group. I mean…it was a lot of money and time and there was—well, there was prayer involved. But I did it anyway, and it worked, and now they're back on-island. It's a surprise visit, just a one-day seminar. We're allowed to bring a friend, and I want to bring you. There. I said it."

"Is this like fat-shaming?"

"Are you ashamed of being fat?"

Monica had no answer. Her feelings about her body were too complex for a quick comeback. She wasn't exactly ashamed, but she wasn't happy either. She missed the way men used to look at her, but it was also kind of a relief. Mostly she was just physically uncomfortable. Buying clothes was a nightmare. She shopped online now. She'd found a great website called StitchFix.

"No one worries about diabetes-shaming," Pooky said finally, into the fraught, breathing silence. "But I worry about you."

Monica let out a breath. "Where and when?"

"It's at 286 Polpis Road, one p.m. Be there or be square."

"But I can be both."

They laughed at their old joke, then Monica disconnected and got back to work.

She was nervous driving out to the house a few hours later. She was hungry, too—she hadn't eaten lunch, in case they weighed her, as if it would make a difference. She was dreading walking into a crowded room, so she made sure to arrive early. There was only one other car parked in the bluestone driveway—the facilitator, or whatever they called themselves. That was perfect—they could chat, get to know each other a little before the other…clients? patients? suckers?…showed up.

Monica parked and sat in the car for a moment, marshaling

her nerve. Then she climbed out of the Ford Explorer and walked up to the front door. She was going to knock, but it was already ajar.

She pushed the door the rest of the way open and stepped inside. The house smelled stuffy, unlived-in. Someone should open up a few windows!

"Hello?" she called out. "Anybody home?"

She walked into the living room and stopped short, as if at the edge of a cliff. She didn't know it, but she was already falling. She literally could not understand what she was looking at. It made no sense, like climbing into the wrong car at the Stop & Shop parking lot. Except a thousand times worse.

She stupidly closed her eyes and then opened them again.

Todd Fraker was still there, standing on the hooked rug, pointing a tranquilizer dart gun at her.

"Hello, Monica," he said. "Time to atone for your sins."

Then he pulled the trigger.

Chapter Seven

MISTAKEN IDENTITIES

They say however bad things are, one adult who understands you can make all the difference. My mother was that one adult for Lonnie Fraker. For me, she was everything. For him, she was everything else. She gave him a lot of good advice—bullshit other people if you have to, but never bullshit yourself. Never ask permission, people love to say no. You can never go wrong by keeping your mouth shut. Fat is good for you. Keep your vinyl. Dress in layers. Unfortunately, she also gave him one piece of catastrophically bad advice. She told him to come out to Mark Toland.

—From Todd Fraker's deleted blog

The three days before the incident at Nantucket High School were frantic and overworked. By lunch on Tuesday I had dropped Chris Contrell firmly into my out-basket—another mundane scrap of business concluded and filed, like a paid Harbor Fuel bill or the RSVP for Lena Perry's wedding. I had more important things to think about.

It started with a phone call from Franny Tate. For a second or two I didn't recognize her voice. "Mark is dead, Henry. He's dead."

"Wait a second. Hello? Who is this?"

She had called on my private cell, and her number was blocked.

"Elkins shot him. It must have been Elkins."

"Elkins? Roy Elkins? He's in jail. Franny?"

"He escaped."

"Wait, what? How could he possibly—?"

Impatience tightened her voice, like a tug on a clove hitch. But that knot comes loose easily. "Don't you watch the news?"

"No, not in the last few days. So wait a second…you're saying Roy Elkins—"

"He's out. And he's killing the people we love."

"He's—we? What people? I don't exactly—"

"Hank, listen to me. Do you remember at the sentencing? He said he was going to kill the people we loved. And he's doing it. He shot Jill Obremski and Carol Stambaugh and Lucy Miner."

"Jill Obremski? How could that possibly—Chuck would have called me."

"Chuck hasn't called anyone. And his phone goes to voicemail. So don't bother trying to reach him."

I took a moment to breathe, and Franny let me put it together. "There's no other connection between the victims, and that means I'm next," I said.

"Crazy as it sounds."

"Yeah."

"At least you got a warning. That's more than the rest of us got."

"Thanks, Franny."

"Keep your people safe."

I sat still at my desk for a minute or two after we hung up, then opened my computer and googled Elkins. As I scrolled through the various news sites, it became clear that no one but Franny had figured out the connection between Roy's prison break and the various murders. Or if they had, they weren't sharing the information with the news media. I'd assign protection details for Miranda and the kids, though the kids would hate it, and Miranda would assume I was being paranoid. More like overcautious—Elkins seemed to have up-to-date intel on his targets. He had killed Jane's boyfriend, not her ex-husband, and left Chuck Obremski's children alone. Still, it would be foolish to assume a maniac would behave consistently. Elkins could have a special grudge against me, or he could be decompensating, spiraling down into some unknowable level of madness. So they would have round-the-clock guards until the crisis was over—I could easily spare the manpower.

But Jane presented a more difficult problem. She was Elkins's apparent prime target, but without a marriage license to officially certify our connection, I would have to protect her myself. I would have to field my own team of bodyguards.

I thought of David Trezize's old friend Mitchell Stone, who had indeed been the new crew member cleaning up Sylvester Graham's house. I had spoken to him briefly the day before, expecting a crazy vet with anger management issues. Instead, he was calm and charming—and sincerely rueful about the Faregrounds fracas. He alluded to a complex history with various intelligence organizations, none of which he could talk about, and none of which mattered to him anymore.

"I'm retired," he told me.

"Okay. Just try to stay out of trouble, old man."

He laughed. "It's weird, Chief. Trouble seems to follow me. I'm like a crazy magnet."

"So, you get into a lot of fights?"

He shrugged. "Mostly, I break them up."

"Well, feel free to do that."

It occurred to me now that Stone might be a handy body-guard, but it seemed a lot to ask of a virtual stranger, and I had a better idea, anyway.

A few months before, I had found myself confronted by a pair of Bulgarian thugs—brothers named Boiko and Dimo Tabachev. Instead of fighting them and getting pulverized or arresting them, I hired them to work for the NPD as part-time undercover operatives, gofers, delivery men, and liaisons to the Eastern European immigrant community. Basically, they did a little of everything and pretty much anything I asked. I paid them in cash and wound up enjoying their company. They were energetic, jovial, basically good-hearted thugs, and they had proved quite useful in tracking down the culprit when the artis-tic director of the Nantucket Theater Lab had been killed at the start of the summer season.

Dimo was the older brother, and Boiko let him do most of the talking. He was no genius, but he had a street-hustler's shrewd cunning, and he took care of his brother in various ways. He collected my cash payments and gave Boiko an allowance. "Otherwise, he lose it all with Keno and boiler making drinks."

"Hello, boss!" Dimo bellowed into the phone when I called him.

"I need you and Boiko to do some bodyguard work for me."

"I am expert with that! Whose body are we guard?"

"My fiancée—Jane Stiles."

"Oh. Serious."

"I'm afraid so."

He knew our address on Darling Street, and I gave him the information on Jane's little office in the White Heron actor's residence on North Water Street. I texted him links to Elkins's

Wikipedia page and the Google Images catalogue of photographs going back fifteen years.

"Be careful, Dimo. Elkins is dangerous."

A contemptuous grunt. "So is Dimo and Boiko. Ask the GDBOP!"

In fact, I already had. Bulgaria's General Directorate Combating Organized Crime had been chasing the brothers for a decade but had never been able to gather enough evidence for an indictment. I had spoken briefly with Miroslav Pabian, the GDBOP colonel in charge of investigating a large-antiques trafficking ring. He had been convinced Dimo was running the operation and had broken into the Tabachevs' Sofia residence—a town house in Boyana, with a view of Yuzhen Park—fully expecting to find various Roman artifacts, including a stolen gravestone. But the house was empty. The brothers were gone—and the snitch recanted.

Dimo was blithe when I mentioned the raid to him. "Foolish to steal gravestone! Much better with coins and crosses—what we are call *engolpion*—religious items, small, easy to carry. Quick to sell for collectors. Not that I would do! These are terrible crimes, Mr. Police! Nothing sacred in Bulgaria now. Is very bad thing."

I hung up with a smile—no need for Skype; I could actually hear the jaunty little wink in Dimo's voice—and turned back to official police business. Rob Roman was coming in later to discuss his investigation of Cindy Henderson. Meanwhile, I had to check the Selectmen's meeting minutes, review some violations uncovered by the environmental police—people were dumping thinner and old paint in the moors again. And I finally got started on Haden Krakauer's evaluations of the summer community service officers—the "summer specials"—all of whom were wildly ambitious and eager for a spot on the regular police roster and many of whom chafed at their lack of authority.

Reading between the lines—Haden was always impeccably tolerant with the wannabees—I could see that a few of them were a little too ambitious. How many times could one kid on bike patrol claim that some hapless person of color or immigrant had "backed into" his ten-speed without the cycle showing a single scratch? At least he wasn't tasing them, but that was only because I had forbidden the use of tasers. Weeding out the bullies was a big part of my job, and I had more than enough of them on the force as it was.

Shortly after that, finally out of the office and back cruising the street, I picked up the backup call from Hamilton Tyler on my scanner.

My excuse for breathing a little fresh air was taking Haden Krakauer to pick up his civilian ride from Billy Built Automotive near the airport. The "officer requests help" request came from Ham and Jill Swenson, his training partner. I put them together hoping she might teach him some of the fine points of social interaction. She was a kind, thoughtful young woman, fresh out of the Seton Hall Police Graduate Studies program, and though her only authority over Ham was a disapproving look, that could often be enough.

Their six was the vest-pocket park near the airport—a cheerless swath of lawn dotted with bronze sculptures of playing children. They were the liveliest aspect of the place. I had never seen an actual person in that little patch of grass, only brown metal boys and girls playing with brown metal balls and climbing brown metal trees. A real tree or two might have been nice—and might even have attracted some real children. But the statues were donated, and real trees were expensive. Anyway, after it had spent years as a ghost commons, now some sort of incident requiring police backup had happened there.

Which brought up another complaint. We had too many

officers, and we deployed them too freely. I had a standing order against sending more than one extra unit to any disturbance, but I couldn't monitor every call-out, and sheer force of numbers made some officers feel more secure. I understood that. But five squad cars, with sirens howling and flashers flaring, clustered around some Jamaican's pickup truck with a broken turn signal served no purpose and made Nantucket look like a racist police state. Three cruisers had arrived at the airport park already—to corral one scrawny-looking Hispanic kid.

Time for another staff meeting.

Byron Lovell and our first African American patrol officer, Patty Stokes, were leaning against their car, sipping take-out coffee from the Trading Post along with Sam Dixon and Randy Ray. Those two presented as a Laurel-and-Hardy pair of townies, though without the charming accents, physical grace, or comic timing. Familiar types—their families went back five generations on the island, and they would always view me as a glorified tourist. I lifted a hand to them as I climbed out of my cruiser. They nodded back.

Hamilton Tyler and Jill Swenson were dealing with the kid.

As we crossed the lawn toward them, passing a bronze fisherman with a bronze toddler on his shoulders, David Trezize pulled up in his new Honda Fit. We had new police band transmitters that used a closed wavelength, but David had managed to hack them somehow. I let it go. Our local alternative newspaper editor was incorrigible, but I liked him for it—and he often proved helpful with my investigations. He loved research, and he never forgot a name or a court case.

Today was a good example.

He trotted up to us, pudgy and disheveled in khakis, an untucked blue shirt, and a flapping cardigan. "Hey, Chief!" He slowed down to a walk beside us. "That's Armando Morales— new kid on the block. Trying to make his bones with the Tres Vatos gang. He's *hermanos de frontera* with Ramon Cruz— second cousin or something. But he's fallen in with Miguel Alfaro, the young Turk who's trying to take over. Nasty little punk. He dropped by the paper to tell me not to write anything about them."

"Did you agree?"

"Fuck, no."

"I haven't seen anything in the paper so far."

David's face clenched for a second. "I'm waiting until I have the whole story. There's two groups here that I know about— the Tres Vatos and the Malditos Azteca. The Malditos are new. Supposedly they're trying to corner the opioid market, and they're nasty—just like the young Vatos kids. So far, Ramon Cruz has kept the peace, but he's on the way out, and they're sick of his old-school rules—not selling to kids, no unnecessary violence, treaties with the other gangs, that kind of stuff. Old man stuff. They'd all love to get rid of him. My guess is they were trying to scare Ramon off today. Send a new kid to rough him up. Some kind of initiation, maybe? I can't think of any other reason to use a punk like Armando Morales for a job like this."

I knew most of what David was telling us, but I let him talk. He always knew a few extra details—like the facts about this Morales kid—and I didn't want to miss anything.

Haden said, "How did you know Ramon was here?"

David shrugged. "The 911 call described a tussle with a middle-aged Hispanic dude. He knocked the kid down, walked over to the gas station, and drove off in a Nissan Murano. Sounds like Ramon to me. That's his ride."

I could see Haden starting a slow burn. "How do you know about our 911 calls?"

"Contacts in the department, Assistant Chief Krakauer. Friends of the free press."

"I want those names."

"I never reveal my sources."

He grabbed at David, who danced away with surprising agility.

"Haden."

He heard the warning in my voice and dropped his arms to his sides with a tight exhale and bitter head shake. I knew he disapproved of my professional relationship with David and his scrappy little newspaper, *The Nantucket Shoals*, but I didn't care. It was true I gave the chubby little reporter special privileges, but he'd earned them, and he never abused my trust.

We reached the threesome in the middle of the lawn.

I nodded at the junior partner. "Jill." Then I turned to Ham. "Break it down for me, Officer Tyler. What happened here?"

"We took the call—"

Jill stepped forward. "Actually, Patty and Byron were closer. They grabbed it, but Ham—"

"We were ranking patrol, and I wanted to check it out for myself. Maybe teach Jill something about dealing with the illegal population. The others showed up anyway. Plenty of backup now that you're here, Chief."

As he spoke, a big black Ford F150 jumped the curb and rolled across the grass toward us, digging up the turf when it stopped. State Police Captain Lonnie Fraker, my longtime frenemy, colleague, rival, and now landlord, bounded out onto the field. A big man with a small head and a high-pitched voice, he moved with an athlete's easy grace. He'd been a star tight end on the Whalers football team back in the day, or so he liked to boast— seventeen catches and two hundred sixty-five yards in his best season. He had the stats and would gladly show you the pictures.

"Everything under control here, Chief?" he squeaked.

"We're good, Lonnie."

Haden was looking past him, pulling his phone from his pocket, scrolling to the camera app. I followed his gaze. A long green snake was slithering down from the tailgate of Lonnie's truck, along the tire and into the grass. Haden got a few good pictures before it undulated away. He shook his head, slipping the phone back in his pocket. "A smooth green snake! Amazing. Guess we know where you've been today, Lonnie."

"I was fishing at Sesachacha Pond."

"Right."

"I was! Caught some gorgeous perch. Looked like record-breakers."

"Can I see?"

"Catch and release, buddy. That's my philosophy."

They stared at each other. This afternoon was going off the rails. I turned back to Ham Tyler. "Lay this situation out for us."

"Well, so, when we got here the scuffle was over. The second individual was running toward the gas station. Jill stayed to question this kid." He tilted his head at Morales. "I pursued the perp on foot. He drove off before I got out of the park. Gray Nissan Murano, license plate NJL249, registered to Ramon Cruz."

"Uh, I think it was a white Murano," Jill put in tentatively.

"It was dusty."

"I don't know…"

"You have to learn to look at what you're seeing, Officer Swenson! A gray car is a gray car. A white car that's dirty is a dirty white car."

"Sorry, sir."

Somehow it irked me to have her calling Hamilton Tyler "sir." In fact, her mistake had confirmed my own theory of what had actually occurred in the airport park. But that was none of anyone else's business. Right now, I needed to break the tension and get things moving again.

I turned back to Ham. "Good catch on the plate number."

"Thanks, Chief." The praise emboldened him a little. He stood up straighter. "The way I see it, the kid was threatening Ramon over some internecine gang dispute. This is a good place to meet—kind of in plain sight but still invisible? Word on the street is, the newer members of the Tres Vatos gang are trying to push Ramon out. But whatever the argument was about, it ended with Ramon knocking the kid on his ass and taking off. It could have been worse."

David Trezize cleared his throat skeptically. It had something to do with the cocked angle of his head, but he looked like a baffled dog. "I don't see what Ramon was doing here in the first place."

"This is police business, Trezize," Ham snapped. Then to me: "What is this hack even doing here?"

"Well, for one thing—asking smart questions. Go on, David."

"I just meant...Ramon is super careful, always was, but especially now, with everyone gunning for him—not just his own upstart members but also the Maltidos Azteca—mostly, he stays home. He makes his living buying and selling Mexican collectibles on eBay—"

Ham snorted. "Launders his drug money, you mean."

"Whatever. Anyway, he's supposedly on the computer all the time bidding for Saltillo blankets or Talavera pottery. Which suits him because the outside world has gotten kind of scary for aging gangbangers. So why come to the airport park today and put himself in the crosshairs? It doesn't make any sense."

"Maybe we should ask him," Ham said.

I nodded. "I'll follow up with Ramon. You talk to the gas station people. Maybe they saw something helpful." I took a step toward young Armando Morales. "Anything to add?" I asked him.

"Who, me?"

"You were here. You have the bashed-in face to prove it."

"I want a lawyer."

"You didn't commit a crime, Armando. It is Armando?" He nodded. "You're the victim here, as far as I can see."

"I still want a lawyer. *Quiero un abogado.*"

"So you did commit a crime?"

"I dint do nothing. But when the cops put you in the shit you gotta have the big boots, *comprende*?"

I nodded. *"Lo entiende. Quién te golpeó?"* Who hit you?

"Cómo dijo—Ramon Cruz. Ese es un viejo hombre malo, si?"

I laughed. *"Si."* Ramon was a mean old man. So was his brother. "What was the fight about?"

"You tell me. He was pissed, though. Tell you that much."

I took Armando's cell number and let him go. We could reach him easily that way if we needed to. Ham and Jill were still hovering. "You two go back to the station and write this up. Everyone else needs to be out on patrol. Let the others know. Coffee break's over."

Back in my cruiser, Haden said, "What?"

"What do you mean 'what'?"

"Come on, Chief. I know you."

I had to smile. Haden's intuitions were on target, as usual. I wished his small-arms results were half as good. He had failed to requalify on the range this year—his hands were shaking too hard for an accurate shot. Whether it was a bad hangover or the aftereffect of a cold-turkey dry-out, I couldn't guess—and didn't want to. Haden's demons were his own problem, and as long as he didn't bring them to work, I let him alone. He was a good cop. He had joined AA—he had told me so, and a friend confirmed it. That wasn't supposed to happen, of course, but it always did. Some wag had called Alcoholics Anonymous on Nantucket "Alcoholics Notorious." Sad, but true.

Haden continued to study me as I drove. "You didn't buy a word of that bullshit back there, did you?"

"What makes you say it was bullshit?"

"Your face, Chief. Not a great poker face. Go Fish, maybe."

"Naaa. I was the worst at Go Fish. Everybody always knew exactly what cards I was holding."

"So give."

"Okay. Armando's injuries were all on the right side of his face. That implies a left-handed hitter. Sebastian is left-handed."

"Sorry, but how would you know that?"

"He wrote a play a couple of years ago—*Sinistromanual*. Ever see it?"

"I'm not sure what—"

"The word means left-handed. It was a satire about all the left-handed people being rounded up and put into camps. 'I love your *jodido* language,' he told me."

"Jodido?"

"It means—fucked up. He said, 'English! You manage to get sinister in there somehow, in case we lefties wondered what you really thought about us.' And it's not just the left-handed thing. The brothers look alike. And Sebastian drives a gray Murano."

"Not a dirty white Murano?"

"Those boys keep their cars immaculate."

"So maybe it was a mistaken identity thing. The kid thought he was confronting Ramon."

"Yeah."

We drove along quietly. I turned off onto Tomahawk Road

and wound my way through Nantucket's newest and ugliest industrial park to the Billy Built garage. We sat in the car and let it idle. "Still," Haden said, "Ham saw the license plate number."

"From that distance? You're the bird-watcher."

"You're saying he knew the number off the top of his head?"

"I'm saying he knew it."

"So…"

"So Ham knew it was Sebastian and covered for him. I can't help wondering if all this has anything to do with the break-in at Sebastian's house last week."

"Why would it?"

"I don't know. But things work that way. Incidents close together tend to get tangled up—like power cords in a closet. It reminds me of something that happened in LA about a year before I left. My boss, Chuck Obremski, was using this low-life movie producer, Dale Phillips, to gather evidence on the Russian mobsters who were financing his movies, using them to launder their drug profits. Phillips managed to get himself arrested for cocaine possession the day before a crucial meeting to which he had agreed to wear a wire. So Chuck took him out of jail, tore up the arrest report, and had the GND detectives who made the arrest transferred out of the Guns and Narcotics Division and attached to Customs Enforcement in San Pedro, a lousy job and a punitive commute. He told them maybe they'd think twice next time before they crapped all over someone else's sting."

Haden frowned. "I'm not really following this."

"Chuck wanted Dale Phillips on the street, free and clear. It's the same thing today. Ham Tyler wants Sebastian Cruz on the street. But why? What does he want Sebastian for? That's what I don't get."

I went to see Sebastian later that day, but he had no answers for me. He had gone to the airport park to pace it out for a bid. He was hoping to secure the town landscaping contract for various public spaces, and he liked to walk the land before he agreed to work on it. Of course, he had never set foot in the park before.

"Armando must have followed me," he said. It had to be a case of mistaken identity—both car and person. "We do look alike. And those Muranos…"

Why had Ham Tyler let him go and then covered for him? No idea. As for Ham, I already knew his views on the interchangeability of Hispanic faces.

As for Ramon, he had time-stamped eBay bids plus conversations with the carpentry crew that was patching his deck to verify his whereabouts. He was dismissive about Armando. "Lucky for him he braced my brother."

"Lucky for you, too. You could have wound up in jail for felony assault. I might not be able to keep ICE off you again. I might not even try."

I ended the day with suspicions and misgivings, and not much else. I put off Rob Roman and his investigation until Wednesday and went home.

My mom was sitting at the kitchen table, having a cup of her chamomile tea with Jane.

"It's always been the same in this country," she was saying. "Socialism for the rich—free market capitalism for the poor."

I stepped over, kissed the top of her head. "Are you trying to radicalize my fiancée?"

Jane smiled up at me. "Too late."

"I'm just so angry about everything that's happening now," Mom said. "And people are losing their outrage. That's the worst part. You have to keep your sense of outrage."

I nodded, pulling out a chair and sitting down. "But it's so exhausting."

Jane said, "The plumber came today, but the sink is still dripping. It's like Billy Delavane always says, 'There's never time to do it right, but there's always time to do it twice.'"

I moved to the sink and twiddled the faucet. One drip bulged out and then another. I shrugged. "Good enough for Nantucket."

Jane laughed. "You're finally starting to sound like a local."

Mom said, "There was beautiful catfish at 167 today. Bill saved me a piece. I thought I'd make it for dinner."

This was odd and yet typical. My mom had been on-island for less than a week, but she'd already discovered Nantucket's best fish store—Bill Sandole's, at 167 Hummock Pond Road—and somehow become good enough friends with the proprietor to get special treatment. Apparently, one of the women who worked there was having trouble with her brother-in-law—there were constant arguments in the small house they shared over everything from politics to house-cleaning.

"I told her, don't say 'You're wrong, you're bad.' Tell him how you feel, instead. He can say, 'I'm not bad, I'm not wrong.' But if you say 'What you did hurt my feelings,' he can't really say no, it didn't. It opens up the conversation. It's non-threatening. So many things people say make the other person stop listening. They don't hear a thing after you say some terrible thing that makes you feel better."

"So what happened?"

"I guess they sorted things out."

"And you get the special catfish."

"Well, we all do. And Bill's going to show me the best places to get mussels. Remember that wonderful mussel chowder we made at Sands Point that summer?"

I nodded. "That was great."

"Well, Bill says the best mussels are under the rocks at the jetties. He said he'd take me."

"Mom. You have Parkinson's! You're not going to go scrambling around the jetties with Bill Sandole!"

"Maybe when I feel better."

"Maybe."

She had recently launched into an exercise program that put my own sporadic calisthenics to shame. If a person could beat back an incurable illness with optimism and sheer force of will, she would be the one to do it. She liked to say "The crazy thing is, I'm in perfect health except for this stupid disease."

Coming from her, it almost made sense.

We were in the middle of making dinner, and Jane was pitching a crazy new story idea, when I got the call from Dr. Conrad Parrish, Cindy's father.

"My publisher is giving me a stand-alone book," Jane was saying. "Kind of a break from Maddie Clark—and I woke up this morning with the wildest high-concept premise ever."

I looked up from chopping onions. "Tell us."

"Okay. Here it is. What if…" She seemed to think better of it.

"Go on," Mom urged her.

"Maybe it's too crazy."

"We'll be the judge of that," I said with a stern finger wag.

"Okay, okay. So—what if every rock-and-roll death since the late fifties was the work of one serial killer?"

"Too crazy," I agreed.

Mom laughed out loud. "I love it!"

"How would that even work?" I asked.

"I don't know…maybe some retired detective sees the same weird face in too many photographs. Or it's a writer, and he's doing, like, a history-of-rock coffee-table book. This weird guy was on the ground crew next to Buddy Holly's plane—and delivering room service to Elvis's hotel room."

Before I could answer, my phone rang. I picked up, opened

the line, and heard an angry bellow. "My son is dead! What are you going to do about it?"

"Excuse me?"

"You put him in jail. You painted the target on his back! Now the shot has found its mark, and his blood is on your hands."

"Who am I speaking with?"

"Conrad Parrish. Dr. Conrad Parrish. Nathan Parrish's father."

"How did you get this number?"

"I'm the chief of thoracic surgery at Lenox Hill. I've donated hundreds of thousands of dollars to the Nantucket Cottage Hospital renovation and operated on most of the other donors. I get what I want."

That jogged my memory. Mike Henderson had been complaining about his father-in-law's raving God complex and his tyrannical behavior for years. Still, I'd never met the man myself.

"Wait a second," I told him. "Nathan Parrish is dead?"

I had arrested Nathan in connection with my first Nantucket murder case. He had paid some local thugs—including Billy Delavane's brother, Ed—to kill swindler and faux billion-aire Preston Lomax before he could run out on a massive real estate deal that would have transformed a hundred acres of pristine island brambles and ponds into The Moorlands Mall. With Lomax dead, the deal reverted to his company's control, and Parrish had an ironclad arrangement with the LoGran Corporation. Or so he thought. A murder conviction tends to be a deal breaker, even in today's America.

"These people have long memories, Kennis."

"Which people?"

"You tell me."

"Listen, I'm sorry, Dr. Parrish, but I've had a long day and—"

"So you've decided it was just some random hit-and-run incident?"

"I haven't really—I wasn't even—"

"Some total stranger texting with his girlfriend happens to plow into a group of low-security work-release prisoners cleaning up the roadside. No one else is even injured, but one prisoner is killed. Pure happenstance! According to you."

"I'm not saying that, but—"

"And on the *very same day,* his accomplice in crime miraculously escapes from prison. Coincidence?"

"Well…"

"I thought policemen didn't believe in coincidence."

"Wait a second. You're saying Ed Delavane—"

"He's gone! He was being taken into Boston for some kind of hearing. He overpowered the guards and took off. Both of the guards are in custody, which makes sense. I don't see how he could have done it without their help!"

"I haven't heard anything about this, Dr. Parrish."

"Then you should start paying attention! I would say that was your job description. I would say that's the minimum requirement."

"I can talk to the people at Cedar Junction in the morning, Dr. Parrish. They may have some idea of what's going on if the incidents are connected. But it's not my jurisdiction, and—"

"Of course it's not your 'jurisdiction'! Don't hide behind that bureaucratic mumbo jumbo. You have a moral responsibility here, Kennis. Nathan's killing reeks of malice! It reeks of bitterness and rage and retribution—and all of that ripened and festered on your little island. Nantucket! The place makes me sick. So putrid and petty and ingrown. I've told Cindy this for years. All the little feuds and grudges. It's like a fire without a screen, Kennis. Everything's fine until a spark jumps the hearth and sets the rug ablaze. Then your cozy little hideout turns into a living hell."

"I'll look into it, Dr. Parrish."

"You better! Or everything that happens will be on your head."

"Wait a second. What are you trying to—?"

But he had already hung up.

"What's going on?" Jane asked.

"Nathan Parrish was killed by a hit-and-run driver yesterday. He was on work release, picking up trash. And Ed Delavane broke out of prison."

Mom looked up. "The doctor thinks the two incidents are related?"

"Yeah, but I don't see how. They're in different jails for the same crime, and if someone wanted to kill them both, busting Ed out of jail doesn't seem like an ideal strategy."

"Death by police?"

"I guess that's possible. But a toothbrush shiv in the shower seems a lot less complicated."

"And someone else from your past is stalking Jane now."

"Yeah."

"But not Ed Delavane," Jane put in. "I never had that kind of problem with Ed. I mean, he was a bully and a psycho, but I was dating his brother, and he never seemed interested. He had no grudge against me, and I don't see him carrying a grudge for twenty years, brooding, anyway. That's not his style. I really like Dimo and Boiko, by the way. I thought I'd hate having them around, but Boiko is very polite and quiet, and Dimo...he found out I'm a writer, and now he wants me to put him in a book. 'I am immigrant success story! With big funny adventures. We make big bestseller and share monies!'" She mimicked him perfectly.

"He might be onto something there," I said.

"I just don't see why I need them around."

"You don't know Roy Elkins. He's a stone killer with scores

to settle and nothing to lose. If Franny Tate is scared, you should be, too. Seriously. I posted a BOLO on Elkins, the FBI put out an APB on him from Maine to New Jersey, and every one of my people has his picture. He can't board a plane or rent a car. He can't use his credit cards. Which is all great, but it might not be enough. Hence, Dimo and Boiko. They're your insurance policy."

Jane studied the tabletop. "Okay, now I'm scared."

Mom was frowning. "What about that crazy fan with Jane's book—the one who killed that girl in Australia? That wasn't Roy Elkins, Hanky."

"I love it that she calls you Hanky," Jane said.

"I'm not really worried about some Australian whack job," I said. Clearly, Jane wasn't either. "There's crazy people all over the world, and you can't get much farther from Nantucket than Sydney, Australia." I was starting to regret telling Mom the Australian story.

She shook her head. "It is a long plane flight. But not that long. It's actually a little bit shocking how quickly you can get places now. Remember that wonderful old movie *Around the World in 80 Days?*"

Jane smiled. "David Niven and Shirley MacLaine."

"And Cantinflas! No one remembers Cantinflas anymore."

"Such is fame," I said. It was one of my mother's pet phrases.

She shot me an irritated squint. "That was my world. Around the world in eighty days. Not in one day! That's what it takes now—less than twenty-four hours."

"Plus the jet lag," Jane added. "That adds a day or two. Or ten, on the way back."

"So the killer will be jet-lagged," Mom said. "That's a plus."

"Mom! This is crazy."

"I guess so, Hanky, but I keep thinking about the book they found in Australia, next to that poor girl's body."

"What about it?"

"Well, have you read *Beyond Brant Point Light*? It's all about a local girl who was so horribly mistreated in high school that she comes back to ruin the mean girl's wedding and winds up getting killed for her trouble."

"Don't mess with the mean girls," Jane said. "Unless you're Maddie Clark."

"I read the book, Mom."

"Well, there you go—it's the same thing—the past coming back to get you. Like Faulkner said, 'The past is never dead—'"

"'—it's never even past,'" I finished for her. She was one of the few people I'd ever met who had actually read *Requiem for a Nun*. But then again, she thought *Ulysses* was a "page turner." She could swallow one of Jane's books whole in an afternoon like a shark gulping a guppy.

"So, this loony in Sydney is someone from Jane's past?"

"Could be."

"And what does that have to do with Roy Elkins?"

"I don't know—maybe nothing. Sometimes events just kind of…harmonize, you know? Like that wonderful girl in the program, Lakeisha Taylor, who sang "The First Time Ever I Saw Your Face" so beautifully and then had a stroke, just like Roberta Flack. Or the way I suddenly saw pregnant women everywhere when I was carrying your brother."

My mom had run the Upward Bound program at Connecticut College for many years, with a short, wide, spiky, hilarious African American woman named Josephine White. They got hundreds of inner-city kids from New London into college, and my mom still corresponded with many of them. It didn't surprise me that she remembered Lakeisha's name. She remembered all their names. They all adored her, but they didn't have to put up with her irritating habit of scraping and scraping across the grain of their thinking with her stubborn, half-baked theories and harebrained ideas.

The problem was, in my experience, the more she annoyed me, the more likely she was to be right.

That had been true since seventh grade. I still remember complaining about some annoying girl in my class and Mom saying, "I don't think you dislike Abby. It's just the opposite, sweetie. I think you like her too much." God, that was infuriating! And she didn't even say I-told-you-so when I came home dizzy from the group excursion at Wollman Rink in Central Park, where I kissed Abby, my first kiss ever, and knocked us both down, and she leaned over while we sat on the ice and kissed me back.

But this was different. This was serious. Speculating about mysteriously connected killers on different continents and conjuring twenty-year-old grudges out of obscure cozy mystery novels (sorry, Jane) was pointless and scary and rude.

It was annoying!

I should have paid more attention to that.

Interlude: David Trezize

Lonnie went out for some air and saw Mark Toland in the
hospital parking lot talking to Dr. Field, otherwise known
as Dr. Feelgood because of his easy hand with the pre-
scription drugs. But this wasn't just a few Tylenol -codeine
or Percocets for a broken finger—Toland slipped him a
wad of bills, and he gave Toland a big package wrapped
in brown paper from the trunk of his Audi. That was when
Lonnie understood. My mom died that afternoon, and
Toland sold my mom the drugs that killed her.

—From Todd Fraker's deleted blog

On the afternoon David Trezize was taken, he was driving his
new car, and no one recognized him. Four acquaintances passed
him on the way up Milestone Road; two others saw the little car
turn off onto the dirt road that led through the moors to Altar
Rock.

None of them noticed.

The only person who had paid attention to the new vehicle was Chief Kennis, and in this claustrophobic small-town

ant farm, that had seemed like an unexpected luxury and a relief, though David had known it wouldn't last. Soon, people would see him with his new Honda Fit and start to identify him with it as they had identified him for years with his old VW bus. Then the drive-by socializing would resume. People would wave as their cars approached his on Milestone Road. If he failed to see them—and he often did, as he was in his own world when he drove, looking out for deer crossing in front of him or cops in his rearview mirror, but pretty much oblivious to the faces behind the oncoming windshields—he would inevitably have to explain the lapse a day or two later, in the canned soup aisle of the Stop & Shop, or the Fast Forward parking lot. People actually got insulted. It was like "cutting them dead" on the street in some nineteenth-century English village.

But that was only the most superficial level of the ritual. You adjusted your responses according to how you felt about the other driver. There was the full wave, lifting the arm and flopping it around. That was reserved for your real friends. Acquaintances got a descending scale of gestures: the raised arm, the partial raise, the fingers extended from the steering wheel, the nod, and, finally—the most minimal of all, reserved for people you really didn't like but couldn't afford to ignore—the chin lift. You could start a round of gossip just by stretching your neck a little when the wrong car was going by on the way into town. It was a finely calibrated machine.

"You having problems with Bob Liddell?" someone might ask. "He says you gave him the chin lift on Polpis Road last week."

David had actually lost an advertiser for *The Shoals* that way last winter. The guy had been truly offended. And on top of that, a few days later, David had failed to stop his car in the middle of Broad Street and have a brief chat with him while traffic piled up both ways. That was a serious lapse, almost as bad as refusing to flash your headlights when a cop was giving out speeding tickets. It was an exhaustingly complex web of automotive courtesies and protocols, and David was glad to be out of it for a while.

Anonymity was precious.

Or so it seemed. On this day, flying under the small-town radar toward his imminent death, he would have given up his newspaper to be recognized. He remembered griping about all the new development on the island one autumn evening several years before, even as he was getting lost in the moors and couldn't see a house or a person in any direction. The island could trick you that way sometimes—turn its back on you, leave you out in the cold.

Today's reversal had begun with an irresistible message on his voicemail. "People are disappearing. I know why. If you want the scoop, meet me at Altar Rock tomorrow at five."

The message touched a nerve. David had noticed a couple of ominous wrong notes—Cindy Henderson, his friend and crush since high school, ghosting him. And Monica Terwilliger, with her perfect phone manners, refusing to return his calls. Coincidence? Maybe. But coincidences didn't make good newspaper stories, and they cut across the grain of village life where narratives crossed and people's lives tangled up with each other like the root systems of the elm trees on Main Street.

So David gathered up his pen and pad, set his phone to record, and set off with half an hour to spare. His girlfriend, Kathleen, was off-island, so there was no one who could establish a marker for his disappearance—*"I haven't seen him since he left the house—it must have been around four thirty? He had some top-secret appointment out in the moors."* He hadn't even seen a

Chapter Eight

MOUSETRAP CITY

Finally, Sippy grabbed my wrist. "Here's what I've learned living my short crummy life on this fucking island," he said. "When someone does something crazy, and you can't understand why, the reason is money. Whenever you have a question about how fucked up things are, the answer is money. When you have a problem, the solution is money. And, most of all, when you want to hurt someone, the weapon is money." Lonnie gave him a worried squint. "You—want to hurt someone?"

"Fucking right. And so do you."

I figured it out. "You're going to rob Mark Toland."

—From Todd Fraker's deleted blog

Jane left to pick up Sam from Apex Academy when Mom finished detailing her conspiracy idea, and my kids tumbled in ten minutes later. I was glad they missed hearing her theory. Nantucket was one of the safest places in the world to raise children, and I didn't want them absorbing any big-city paranoia and feeling scared to walk freely in their own hometown.

I needn't have worried. Some spooky criminal lurking in the shadows was the last thing on their minds.

The school bus had let them off at the corner of Pleasant and Silver streets, and they had been haranguing each other, happily oblivious, for the length of the ten-minute walk home. They were still arguing, rabid as demonstrators on opposite sides of an NRA rally. Sam sulked by the window, clutching a social studies test with a prominent C at the top of the paper, and kept his distance.

"You are such a bitch!" Tim shouted, throwing his books down on the kitchen counter.

"I'm a bitch? Are you fucking kidding me?"

"You and all your stupid bitch friends."

"Kids—!" I broke in. "Watch the language! Please!"

Caroline put her books down next to Sam's. "Sorry, Dad. But this squinchy little puke puddle is trying to—"

"All I'm trying to do is get you to act like a regular, nice, basic human being!"

"Oh, sorry I can't pretend to like some lame, pizza-faced tick-bite retard who doesn't even—"

"That's what I'm talking about! Did you hear that, Dad? She's talking about a human being."

Carrie sniffed. "Technically."

"You suck. There's nothing wrong with Judy Gobeler."

"The lacrosse team coach agrees with you. I can't believe they even let her on the team. Maybe she'll win the participant trophy."

"At least she was brave enough to try out."

"I didn't want to try out! Check out the paper this week! There's a picture of the whole team on the front page. It's a total losers gallery! The caption should have been 'Too lame for the basketball squad.'"

"You have to be fit to play lacrosse. There's lots of running."

"And she can barely walk! Gobeler the gobbler. She walks like a turkey! The way she moves her head. It's pathetic. Like those guinea hens crossing Polpis Road."

"That's just stupid!"

"If you love her so much, why don't you marry her? Break up with Debbie and marry the gobbler!"

"Maybe I will!"

"Just don't let her sit on you."

"She's not that fat."

"Save the whales! They make us look thin!"

"I broke up with Debbie anyway. Today! After math class. Because of this. The way all of you are. You're like—a pack of dogs. African wild dogs! I saw a video—they're vicious. But they're nice compared to you. They hunt to survive. You do it to feel good about yourself because you can't feel good unless you make someone else feel shitty."

"Oooh, that's savage. I have homework to do." Her parting shot: "Debbie's interested in that new kid, anyway. Ricky Muller. He's cute."

She turned to go, but her grandmother stopped her with a word. "Carrie?"

"What? Sorry, Gramma... I mean, what is it?"

"Have you read Jane's book *Beyond Brant Point Light*?"

"I started it. I'm kind of busy with school right now? And we had assigned reading in the summer."

"Which you didn't start until August," Tim put in smugly.

"Shut up!" Back to Gramma: "What about Jane's book?"

"Well, it had a girl in it who sounds a lot like you, and another girl who sounds a lot like this Judy Gobeler. I guess things don't change much over the years. But, anyway, in the book the Gobeler girl comes back just as the other girl is about to get married. She wants revenge. And it doesn't end well for anyone. Revenge stories rarely do. I think revenge is like scratching a poison ivy rash. It feels good for a second, but you wind up making things worse. Anyway…I guess the point is, people remember when you make them feel bad."

Carrie let out a tight little breath. "Well, I didn't make anybody feel anything, and I'm not some character in some cheesy mystery novel. I'm a real person, and I don't appreciate being ganged up on after a really bad day!"

She stalked out of the room, and Mom said, "She'll be all right. It's hard being sixteen."

Tim snorted. "It's easy for her. She makes it hard for everyone else."

"So Debbie's part of her gang now?" Jane asked.

"They used to hate each other. Now they're besties. I can't keep up."

"Are you going to patch things up with her?" I asked. I always liked Debbie Garrison.

"I don't know. Maybe. If she's interested in someone else, that's fine. She's gotten so awful lately. I don't even know what to say to her. All she cares about is stupid stuff and what brand of jeans to wear and who's following who on Instagram or whatever. Maybe I should ask Judy out. Or at least have lunch with her. She always eats by herself."

Mom said, "You might start a trend!"

Tim's doleful look doused the optimism. "Let's not go crazy, Gramma."

Meanwhile, Sam had come over to sit on Jane's lap. He seemed younger and smaller than his eleven years this afternoon.

"What is it, honey?" Jane asked him.

"Nothing."

She ruffled his hair. "Everything is something."

She gently lifted the test paper from his hand. "You studied so hard for this!"

"Ms. Fox hates me."

"No, I don't think she really—"

"She does! She hates me! I always get detention for no reason, and she said I was stupid yesterday!"

"She what?"

"She said I was stupid, and I could never learn anything, and I ought to be in some special school and ride the short bus."

"Sam!"

"She did!"

"What about that English paper we worked on together?" She turned to me. "Fox is obsessed with trivial shit like indentation and the Oxford comma. So I went over Sam's last assignment—he had to write a story about a pet—"

"I wrote about how Dervish chases everything, even the moon!"

Dervish was Billy Delavane's beloved pug whom Sam had known since he was a baby, long before I met Jane or we adopted Bailey, our Portuguese water dog, currently circling the table, always hopeful for a scrap of food.

"Sam wrote the piece all by himself," Jane added hastily. "I just line-edited it, the spelling and punctuation, made sure every paragraph was indented exactly six spaces. And only one space after every period." She sniffed. "All the important stuff."

"What did Ms. Fox say about it?" I asked.

Sam started to answer, but a pulse of tears silenced him.

Jane smoothed his cheek dry with her thumb. "Sam! What did she say?"

"She's so mean, Mommy."

"Tell me what she said."

Sam sat up a little straighter, bunched up his face, and

lowered his voice. Despite his upset, some part of him obviously enjoyed imitating his teacher. "'So! You finally did *something* right! Amazing.'"

Jane held him away a little to look in his eyes. "She said that?"

"She hates me."

"That's it. It's time for me to have a little talk with Diana Fox."

"Don't get me in trouble, Mom."

She smoothed his forehead. "You're not in trouble, honey. Ms. Fox is in trouble."

He sighed. "She didn't even like my riddles."

I sat forward. I liked riddles. "What riddles?"

"I found an old joke book at take-leave-it, and I thought the puzzles and stuff were so cool. Ms. Fox said they were dumb and took away the book."

"Do you remember any of them?" my mom asked. She'd been listening to the conversation carefully, though she hadn't said anything.

Sam grinned at her. "Sure! Here's one! Ready? Two girls are born to the same mother on the same day and the same hour in the same hospital, but they're not twins! How can that possibly be? Wanta hear? Wanta hear?"

Ms. Fox was forgotten for the moment.

"Wait a second," I said. "Let us think."

Mom got it first: "Triplets! They're two girls in a set of triplets."

Sam raised an arm and slapped her five. "Nice one, Mrs. Kennis."

"Call me Hope, sweetie. Everyone else does."

"Okay, Hope. Try this one! What gets wetter the more it dries?"

"I know this one," Tim offered.

"Then shhhhhh!!" The urgency of Sam's frown made me smile.

"Okay, okay," Tim said.

The rest of us were stumped. "A towel!" Sam crowed. "Here's the last one. What word is always spelled incorrectly in the dictionary?"

I got that one. "The word 'incorrectly.'"

His face fell for a second. "Yeah." Then he brightened. "Good one, Henry!"

"Great riddles," I said. "You know the best thing about them? For me? They teach you how to be a better detective. Like the first one. So often you look at a problem the way it was presented, and all you see are the terms you were given—twins who can't be twins, like a suspect with a perfect alibi. You have to move outside of those rules you make for yourself—to imagine triplets or to figure out that the suspect was standing in front of a clock where he'd shifted the hands back forty minutes."

Sam's eyes widened. "Wow."

"Or the second one. The trick there is making us misread the word 'dries' as something that happens to the towel instead of something it's doing. Like the time I arrested someone for framing someone else—making it look like someone else had committed the crime? And, in fact, someone was doing the same thing to him—making it look like he was setting someone else up…actually framing him for framing someone else. Just like one of your riddles—tricking me into seeing things the wrong way. Those riddles really make you think. They'd be a fantastic teaching tool. Too bad Ms. Fox couldn't figure that out."

Sam nodded solemnly. "Yeah."

It turned out that the third riddle, and the easiest one to solve, was the most germane to my life and to the case I didn't even know I was working on.

The lesson: see the obvious—before it's too late.

———

Rob Roman, our island's newest private investigator, came into my office on Thursday morning with his newest client, Mike Henderson, slouching behind him. Mike's face was drawn down with worry and lack of sleep, his long hair was unruly, and it looked like he hadn't changed his painting clothes since the day before. By contrast, Roman, short and bulky, wearing a crew-neck cotton sweater, khakis, and horn-rimmed glasses, looked like a college adjunct who'd been grading papers all morning.

"Mike," I said. "I wasn't expecting you."

"Well, I had to come, Chief. Rob and I are having kind of a disagreement, and I wanted to make my case in person. We need another pair of eyes on this."

I stood up behind my desk and reached across it to shake Roman's hand. "Rob, good to see you. How can I help?"

He pulled up a chair next to Mike's, let himself down heavily, and shook his head. "Well, Chief, I gotta tell you, this is one crazy little island you got here."

"I've noticed."

"Kind of a plantation police state, ghetto gulag, moated elite resort, high-crime, pill-popping, post-preppie playground, am I right?"

I had to smile. "Let me take a second to process all that." I gave it maybe five seconds, then shrugged. "Pretty much."

"And don't take it wrong, I'm new to the place, so what the fuck do I know? But it's getting crazier all the time."

"How so?"

"People ditching, people breaking up, people taking off, people disappearing. The disappeared! It's starting to look like Argentina around here! Without the junta."

He had my attention now. "I'm not sure what you're talking about, Rob."

"Sure. Makes sense—someone goes missing, most people

would rather hire a PI than bring the cops into it. Especially small-town people. Nobody likes the gossip machine, am I right? When it's probably nothing. But, see…everybody I talk to? They're just dealing with their own problems. They don't see the big picture."

"Who exactly are we talking about?"

"Well, take David Trezize, for instance. Local newspaper editor?"

I nodded.

"Okay, let's start with him. He texts his girlfriend he was working on a big immigration story, supposed to run in *The Shoals* this week. She was in Boston at the time. See the paper yet? No story."

"I don't really see why that would—"

Rob held up his hand. "The girlfriend, Kathleen Lomax? You know her, right? She gets back home and there's a note. Says he's going off-island, following up another big scoop. Some lead in Brewster."

"Go on."

"Well, I looked into it. I found no trail at all. No record of plane or boat tickets. Did he swim?"

"He could have a commuter book."

"I'm hearing that a lot lately. The all-purpose commuter book. How many people really buy those things, Chief? And Trezize went off-island, like, once a year, that's what Ms. Lomax says. The two of them fly JetBlue to New York and see plays in the summer, but they always go together. Then there's the whole texting thing. Trezize hates texting, always griping about it. And he never told his ex-wife anything about this trip. He was supposed to have the kids last night, but he never said a word. Total no-show. Which isn't like him. He's a good father, even the ex admits that. But now, all of a sudden, he turns into Mr.

Deadbeat Dad. His phone goes dark. Calls go straight to voice-mail, no more texts, no email. No message on Facebook. I tell Kathleen, 'He'll turn up. Relax.'"

"Which is just what I would have said."

"But I don't like it."

"Me neither."

"And now Cindy is gone," Mike put in. "I knew Mark Toland was coming to the island for Lena Perry's wedding, and Cindy told me she wanted to see him and settle things, and I said fine, but then I freaked out."

"He asked me to keep an eye on them," Rob finished.

"Mike mentioned that he'd hired you."

"Right, well, this was just part of the job. I checked the hospital first, then the steamship and the airport. No one dead or injured or traveling. I picked them up at Toland's house—"

"—and lost them at the wedding."

"Hey, Mike—"

I sat forward. "How did that happen?"

Rob frowned. "If I knew that, I wouldn't have lost them. They separated. She went off with the bridesmaids, he went to the can. I didn't want to follow him in there. Turns out there was another door, led into some kind of service area and the rear exit. The bridesmaids wouldn't say a word, and that's that. Cindy and this Toland guy are both in the wind. Looked to me like they had it planned."

"Tell him the rest."

"It's just a theory."

I set my elbows on my desk and rested my chin on my clasped fist. "Let's hear it."

"You see as much crime as I do, maybe you start looking for it."

"Go on."

"What if they didn't run off together? What if they were kidnapped? You know—first this David Trezize, then Toland and Cindy. Makes you wonder—who's next?"

"Unless that's not happening at all." I thought for a second, rummaging, then pulled out a loose fact from the junk drawer of my memory, like a stray triple-A battery. "There is an actual connection between the three of them, you know."

Mike shrugged. "Vampire Weekend fans?"

"Maybe. But also—Dalton."

"Dalton?"

"Cindy and David both spent at least one year of high school in New York, attending the Dalton School. One of the first times I spoke to her, she was trying to decide whether or not to go to her reunion. The main draw was a guy named Mark Toland. It was a classic high-school sad-sack love triangle: David crushing on Cindy, Cindy crushing on Mark, and Mark paying no attention while he dated the cool girls. And Toland wound up here for his senior year. She never mentioned this to you?"

Mike studied his lap. "We don't talk about Mark Toland a lot. Cindy and I didn't get together until college. If she was mooning over that prick in high school, I wouldn't have known about it."

Rob pushed his glasses up on the bridge of his nose. "So, this is some kind of Dalton reunion?"

"Could be."

He grunted. "Some kind of long-delayed three-way? The fantasy hookup that never happened?"

Mike winced like Rob had just spilled something on him. "Please."

"It could be a normal reunion. Or a fundraising session. One way or another, David and Cindy know quite a few of the local billionaires. Toland is probably the head of the alumni association."

"I guess."

"Or it could be a get-together for some teen organization, something that would connect the cool kids and the geeks—the AV club or the drama department. David writes, Mark's a director—"

"—and Cindy played Alma in the school production of *Summer and Smoke*."

I lifted my hands, palms up. "There you go."

Mike sighed. "Well, maybe, but I think it's a lot simpler than that, Chief. No bizarro high school reunions or impromptu fund drives. No serial kidnappers haunting the Nantucket wedding receptions. Just a confused woman and an old flame."

"What about David?"

"I can see him in Brewster following up some crazy lead. And he forgets his phone all the time. He came to some jobsite a few years ago where the people had built their house two inches over the property line and the neighbors were suing. David wanted to interview the contractor and the homeowner. Anyway, he left his phone on a sawhorse, and some kid who worked for me knocked it into a bucket of paint. Kind of a perfect Nantucket story in so many ways. The point is, David gets oblivious when he's working. Kathy should have figured that out by now. But that has nothing to do with Cindy and Mark Toland. Or what's going on in my marriage. I did some snooping on my own, and I found this."

He pulled out his phone, located a screen grab, and handed it over to me. I caught Rob Roman's long-suffering, save-us-from-the-amateurs eyebrow lift.

"What?"

Rob shrugged. "Read it."

"It's from Cindy's diary," Mike added.

"Not a great idea, reading your wife's diary."

"I know, I know. But this particular entry made me feel a lot better."

Rob said, "You might need your glasses. The text is small, and her handwriting doesn't help."

"I don't wear glasses."

"Not even for reading?"

"I know—it's annoying. Drives Jane crazy. She has six pairs of drugstore glasses, and she can't hold on to any of them. I found one pair in the vegetable drawer of the fridge last week. They must have fallen off while she was looking for the spinach."

"Sounds Freudian to me. She hates wearing them, so her unconscious mind keeps sabotaging her."

I looked up at him. "Probably true. But stunningly unhelpful."

I tilted the phone for the best angle.

> I don't know I don't know I don't know
> I can't sleep
> Everything I think is wrong everything I want
> is bad everything I write is lie. And all the things
> I don't write, why do I leave them out? That's a
> bigger lie, sins of omission. That drive out to Snake
> Hollow, why would I hide that? No one's going to read
> this. And why would I even want to go back there,
> especially with Mark? It was perfect, we almost
> got stuck in the sand just like the old days. Flat
> cactus souvenirs, quoting Eliot, Hollow Men in their
> local habitat. All the echoes. Mark said remember
> rowing against the tide? He was laughing but it was
> one of the scariest days of my life. So many awful
> scary bad days with Mark Toland. Why do crimi-
> nals revisit the scene of the crime? Why do they
> want to? Maybe—to feel it again, to know it really

happened, not to feel better but to feel worse, to keep the wound open.

But those are just—thoughts. I can control my own thoughts. I can stop this. I can say no. Turn around and walk away. Never look back, finally stop looking back.

I can end it and I will.

I handed the phone back.

Mike slipped it into his pocket. "Is that a woman heading off for a romantic tryst with the long-lost love of her life?"

"She's conflicted, Mike. But if it was easy to close things down with Toland, she would have done it already. She wouldn't be fretting about it in her diary."

"I'll email you the file, so you can look it over if you want. Read it over, you'll see what I'm talking about. When I read it, I thought of that poem of yours, the one that got honorable mention in that *Glimmer Train* contest. Yeah, yeah—I googled you. And I thought—wow, the Chief has been there! Your wife was cheating on you with some long-lost lover, right? And you said it perfectly—what was that line? 'The fire has to burn to burn out.' That's it. That's what's going on here. She'll be back. The proof is, she left a penny on our pillow. It slipped off, but I found it when I made the bed."

I nodded. "Just like Jane's book."

Rob said, "Right, your fiancée. She used the tradition in one of her mysteries. If you throw a penny off the ferry when it's passing Brant Point, it means you'll come back."

"Jane says old-timers used to wait until they got to the end of the breakwater."

Mike jumped in. "You see? She's coming back—that's the message! Maybe this will even the score. I fucked up a few times myself, Chief. We both know it. And this makes sense for Toland, too. He probably thinks he can sweep in and whisk her away. I mean…the guy's in the movie business. He likes big gestures and happy endings. They're his bread and butter."

"So you're firing Rob?"

"Well…I mean…"

Rob was shaking his head. "Mike thinks I'm nuts, but that penny thing gives me the creeps. I say someone came back already. Someone who should have stayed away."

"That's what happens in Jane's book—someone comes back for revenge."

"Yeah."

I backtracked a little. "How about David? Any pennies there?"

He frowned. "No. Not that Kathleen mentioned. But no one really looked too hard, either. Far as I know."

"Cindy's coming back," Mike said. "She may be home already. We understand each other. We both have baggage…"

Rob puffed out a breath. "Women with baggage! I tell my girlfriends—carry-on only."

I knew a little of his history. "Including the married woman in Seattle? The one you tracked down and fell in love with? Who trashed your life and turned you into unemployable pariah?"

He shrugged. "The exception proves the rule."

"Not in my business. For cops, the exception disproves the rule. Exceptions are the weak spots where your slipups get you in trouble."

"I learned from my mistakes. I hope you're not making one here."

We ended our meeting on that ominous note. I agreed with Mike, but I could sense the faint, puzzling tang of trouble in the air, just as Rob Roman did. It was like that moment before you hear the sirens, when you sniff the cozy scent of woodsmoke riding the winter breeze.

And you think: *That could be a house on fire.*

Karen Gifford passed them on the way out, nodding to Rob Roman and smiling at Mike. She looked fresh and well rested, dressed in khaki pants and cream silk blazer over a pale-blue open-collared shirt, black hair pulled tight behind her head in a short ponytail. My long marriage to an Imelda Marcos-level shoe obsessive allowed me to identify her Italian leather wedge sandals as vintage Pappagallos from the seventies. But the shoes were her only vanity; she wore no watch, no jewelry, no earrings and, as far as I could see, no makeup. Pretty but stern, she could have been a bank officer or the executive director of some high-end nonprofit organization if not for the badge clipped to her belt.

But that was the one item in her wardrobe she really cared about.

I half stood and gestured her to a chair. "Hey, Karen. What's up?"

"Nothing good." She pulled a file from her shoulder bag and handed it across to me. "I just printed this stuff out. It's from Chris Contrell's blog—MousetrapCity dot blogspot dot com. It was easy to find; I just googled him. He's not hiding anything—in fact, he's pissed off that he doesn't get enough hits and comments and shares and likes. His little videos don't go viral. Maybe if they were shot in focus and the sound was audible...on the other hand, best not."

I was paging through the file. I picked a post at random:

At first I was going to call this blog Fortress Island becus
I belived that the illegal immigrants were an invading
army. We were being invaded and we needed to defend

ourselfs. Now I kno better. I realized the truth a few days ago when I was riding my bike to school and I saw this Mexican woman with three kids waiting for the bus. She had a baby in her arms and she was pregnint. This is not invasion, this is infestation. Arrive, steal jobs, pay no tax or insurance and prokreate prokreate prokreate. They say if you see one roach in your sink at night there are thousands in the drane. You don't crush the one bug, you call the exterminater you tent the house and gas them all at once. Same with rats and mice or skwirruls in the house. Just kill them. The opposite of a sanktuary city— mousetrap city. Cum on in and taste the cheese!

   When to do it was my question and then I red about Constitution Day. It has a fake name like all these illegals who get alieses when they get here. Even our own Police Chief. I looked it up. His real name is Kenisovsky. They changed it, like that made them real Americans. So we're going to celebrate the fake holiday this year and make it real.

I set the page aside. "Jesus Christ."

"Constitution Day is also called Citizenship Day," Karen said. "That's the 'alias' Contrell is talking about."

"September 17. That's today."

Karen paled. "What do we do?"

"Close down the school."

"Can we do that? On the basis of one blog post? Bissell won't like it."

"I'm calling him."

But he was already calling me.

Bissell's voice was pitched high, wavering and panicky. "There's a shooter in the school, you have to help us, he's got an

automatic rifle, he's wearing a ski mask, and—oh, my God!—"
He was cut off by the sound of gunfire, weirdly hollow—pop
pop, pop pop pop—across the phone line.

"It's Contrell," I said. "He's doing it."

We leapt up and raced out of the office. Barnaby Toll was on
dispatch. I told him to send every cruiser on duty to the high
school. We sprinted out to the parking lot, dove into my car, and
hit the flashers and the siren as we peeled out.

It made a good show, but the real show had already started.

Chapter Nine

CITIZEN'S ARREST

It turned out that Ed kept all the money from his drug deals and petty thefts in a steamer trunk buried in the sand near Second Bend. "Like a pirate," Lonnie said.

"Yeah, well, those fucking pirates knew what they were doing. Delavane can't put this dough in the bank, he can't fence the jewelry on-island, and keeping the stuff at home is too risky. It makes so much sense that Toland started hiding his drug money there, too. It's an easy score. And tomorrow night we're going to take it all."

—From Todd Fraker's deleted blog

Billy Delavane and Mitchell Stone were standing twenty feet up on a staging plank, replacing a rotten window casing on a Surfside Road hospital-housing saltbox when Mitch noticed the boy with the duffel bag.

He touched Billy's shoulder. "Did you hear that?"

"What?"

"That clanking."

"I heard the staging creak, I heard your hammer, and some-body's got WACK playing around the corner, but—"

Mitch held up a hand to silence him. "Just look. Down there, the kid on the bike with the duffel bag."

Billy squinted. "I see him. What about him?"

"Who brings a duffel bag to school? I had one just like that when I shipped out for Afghanistan. Where's he going this morning?"

"What are you saying?"

"He's got a gun in there, Billy. Probably some kind of assault rifle. With extra magazines. That's what I heard clanking."

"How could you possibly know that?"

Mitch gave him a humorless little smile. "That's a long story. And it's mostly classified."

"Debbie's in there."

"So is Ricky."

"What do we do?"

Mitch unclipped his tool belt and set it down on the plank. "What we always did. I take the lead. You back me up."

"Okay, only shouldn't we call—"

But Mitch was already halfway down the ladder. He jumped the last few feet and started jogging easily up the sidewalk. By the time Billy had dumped his tools and scrambled down, Mitch was dodging through the stalled traffic, angling for the main entrance of the high school. Billy put on a little speed to catch up. Someone honked at them. Then they were sprinting across the wide pavilion, under the overhang, through the glass doors, and inside.

The scene was nightmarish—utterly unreal, sickeningly familiar. Billy's first thought, his animal impulse, was to turn and flee. But Mitch must have sensed it; Billy felt the iron grip of his friend's fingers on his forearm. And the gritty whisper, "Hang in there, buddy."

Two dozen students were flat on the floor of the big lobby. Through the glass panels that walled off the administrative offices, he saw secretaries and a janitor cowering. Bissell's door was closed. Maybe he'd had the presence of mind to dial 911. Billy had read somewhere that in an emergency the body went into self-destructive overdrive—people's hands shook so badly they couldn't even poke the digits into their phones. Sometimes they dialed 411 by mistake.

Billy threw a thought like a football at the superintendent, tucked away behind the doors and partitions that would allow him a momentary sense of security, a hard, short screen pass, mind to mind.

Take it easy, Mr. Bissell. Get it together. Breathe.

Twenty feet ahead of them, standing in front of the glassed-in basketball court, a scrawny, pimple-faced kid held what even Billy could tell was an AR-15 assault rifle with its slim barrel extending from the wider cylinder and the evil horn of its ammunition clip jutting down a weapon of war. In an ordinary American small-town high school, it was as frightening as a bomb, a vest of dynamite wrapped around the torso.

Billy could feel his pulse spiking.

"Bring me every spic in this fucking school!" the kid shouted. "Every one of 'em. I want 'em standing in front of me right now, or I start killing everyone!"

To punctuate the threat, he tipped the rifle up to squeeze off five shots into the ceiling. The recoil knocked him back a step and spun him in a half circle. He stumbled against the glass wall of the gym and leveled the barrel again. "Do it now!"

Billy had time to think, *I hope no one's upstairs.*

Then he heard the first sirens.

So Bissell had made the call! Or someone had. There had to be a thousand cell phones in this place. It didn't matter.

Help was on the way.

Mitch started walking toward the kid, slow careful steps, like a firefighter moving across a compromised floor into the smoke, toward the flame. Billy wanted to call out, to stop Mitch, but his voice snagged in his throat.

The kid spun the rifle, pointing it at Mitch's chest. Mitch raised his hands.

Outside, the sirens were getting louder. There were more of them. Three? Four? The chilling thought slithered through Billy—*What if the cops panic the kid, tip the situation out of control?* They were close to the line already.

"Are you going to shoot me?" Mitch asked quietly, taking another step closer. "I'm no cop. I was banging nails across the street ten minutes ago. I'm no Hispanic. I'm German Irish, both sides. I was a Marine, two tours in Afghanistan. MOSCOM— you know what that is? You do, don't you? Marine Corps Special Operations Command. The Raiders. Was your dad in the Corps? I bet he was."

"He was in the Army."

"Sorry to hear that, kid."

"He hates you fucking jarheads. He says you're not even a real branch of the military. Just part of the Navy."

Mitch grinned. "Yeah. The men's department."

"He could kick your ass."

"Maybe. Where did he serve? Panama?"

"Seventh Infantry Division. Operation Blue Spoon. He beat you Devil Dogs there."

"He deployed first, that's all. Marines cleaned up the mess."

Mitch was just a few feet away from the kid now. Outside, the sirens stopped. The sudden silence meant the cops would be storming inside any second. Would the kid freak out?

But Mitch had the boy's undivided attention.

"I've seen men lose their shit in combat, kid. I saw a boy not much older than you machine-gun a camel. He just shredded the fucker. He caught a movement in the corner of his eye and cut loose. My best friend over there shot at a ten-year-old girl, thought she was carrying an IED. It was a frying pan she picked up from a bombed-out café. She was taking it home to her mom. He winged the kid and hit the pan. Kid recovered, but one of the ricochets killed our bomb dog. A little Kelpie named Rags. Forty-two missions, saved our ass a dozen times, and Jimmy takes him out with a stray round for no reason but nerves. He was hugging that dog in the dirt, sobbing like a baby. You kill a kid today, that'll be a thousand times worse. You never come back from that shit, kid. Trust me."

There it was—the clatter of the cops charging into the lobby. Mitch shouted over his shoulder. "Stay back."

The voice behind Billy answered. "It's Chief Kennis. I have ten officers with me."

"Tell them to stand down!"

Kennis gave the order.

Mitch took another step toward the kid, and Billy could sense something about to snap, like the moment before that German shepherd had bitten him, years ago. Saturday morning, the customers out for the day, the big dog guarding the house, tracking his every move, every muscle flexed to a violent stillness. Billy watched Mitch, undivided attention shrilling behind his eyes, waiting for the moment.

"Pack it in, kid. Nothing's happened, yet. You can still salvage this. Put the gun down, and we can talk. That's all you have to do, just—"

Mitch's left hand lashed out like a striking snake. He knocked the rifle aside, twisted his wrist to grab the barrel. The kid squeezed the trigger as the gun dipped toward the floor, and

Mitch sent him stumbling into the glass wall with a single back-fist strike to the nose.

Mitch had the rifle now—the kid was stunned and bleeding. But it wasn't over. Some dumb macho football type was on his feet charging the kid. Mitch wrapped him up with one arm, but the move put his back to the shooter, and Billy saw the boy yanking a gun from his waistband. Billy was charging before his conscious mind had even registered the movement or recognized the weapon. He tackled the kid just above the knees. The big automatic discharged into the glass wall, shattering it, and they hit the linoleum in an avalanche of shards, deafened by the shot. Below him, the kid's sweater was stained with blood. Billy smelled wet wool, fear, sweat, and the stink of cordite.

"Ham will get you for this," the kid snarled at him.

Then the cops were grabbing the boy and dragging him away.

Mitch helped Billy up. "Nice work, buddy. You saved my ass back there."

"Gotta have backup."

Mitch grinned. "Fuckin' A."

Mitch caught sight of his ward—was that the right word?—Ricky Muller, and jogged over to help the kid up. The boy looked dazed but unharmed—just like everyone else. Mitch had managed to close the incident down without injuries, but Billy was still reeling. The white-water wall of events, a classic big-wave wipeout, was still tumbling him along, as he clawed for the surface, gasping and sputtering when he got his head clear, his nervous system trying to play catch-up, failing and overloading. A three-wave hold-down was nothing compared to this.

But Mitch was fine. A closeout set at Mavericks might drown Mitch, but here? He was in his element, relaxed and calm as he shook hands with the police chief.

"That was a risky move, Mr. Stone," Kennis was saying. "That could have gone sideways in a heartbeat."

"Yeah, well. It's like Louis Pasteur liked to say—"

Kennis finished for him. "Fortune favors the prepared mind."

"Something like that."

"I need you to come into the station after work today to give a complete deposition on what happened here this morning."

"A debriefing."

"If you like."

Mitch made a small but unironic salute. "Yes, sir. I'll text you my number, also. It might come in handy someday. Speaking of work...Billy?"

"Give me a second."

"Sure thing. See you out there."

Mitch moved off through the crowds of tense but listless police and baffled students.

Kennis clasped Billy's shoulder. "You okay?"

"Yeah, I guess. I don't know."

"You did great back there. You're a hero."

Billy felt a crooked smile crack his face. "My dad always used to say that about people. 'He has to be the hero! Look. I put up all that crown molding!' That's what you're supposed to do! Anybody would have done that.'"

He felt Kennis's kindly stare—sunlight breaking through clouds on an autumn day, unexpectedly warm on his face. "You think anyone would have done what you did?"

"Well, I mean..."

"You think any of the police officers here would have had the presence of mind to tackle that boy? While he was holding a loaded gun?"

"My dad would have."

"But he wasn't here, Billy. You were."

"Thanks, Chief."

"No. Thank you."

"Listen, about these cops…" Billy looked around nervously.

"What?"

"The kid said something to me when I took him down. 'Ham will get you for this.' That's Ham Tyler, gotta be."

"You know him?"

"We went to high school together."

Kennis sighed. "Of course you did."

"Nasty little prick. He got suspended for spraying a Star of David on Vicky Fleishman's locker. I bet he had something to do with this shit show, too."

Kennis frowned. "I'll be talking to him. As soon as I get back to the station."

"Good. You know his pedigree, though, Chief. So be careful."

"Sometimes being careful is the worst possible tactic, Billy. You proved that today—you and your friend."

Billy made a weighing-the-scales gesture, seesawing his two open palms. "Town politics? Kid with a gun? I don't know."

Kennis smiled. "I'll keep it in mind."

Billy liked the chief; they had history. The man had taken his side when Billy was falsely accused of a series of bombings a few years before. Kennis was a straight shooter, but he was an off-islander. He didn't really understand Nantucket, and he probably never would. Getting Hamilton Tyler off the police force would be like pulling an embedded tick from the inside of your ear, tricky and painful—and you couldn't do it alone. But you couldn't just leave it, either, and let it pump babesiosis and Lyme disease, ehrlichiosis and God-knows-what infections they hadn't even discovered yet into your body.

Ham Bone, they used to call him. He was poison, but some

random, hearsay evidence connecting him to a school shooting wouldn't dislodge him.

Billy could imagine the conversation:

"Some crazy kid dropped my name? So what? Maybe he hoped I'd stick up for him. Maybe he thinks I have some grudge against Delavane. The guy's an asshole, but I couldn't care less. I've talked to him, like, twice since high school. He thinks my uncle messed with him on some DUI twenty years ago, that could be it, though how that Contrell kid knows about it, you got me. Maybe they're pals. Maybe Delavane put him up to the shooting. Fuck do I know? His brother's in the slammer for life, the dad was a nut job, so who knows? This shit runs in the family. DNA is destiny, man. Science proves it."

No, to take down Ham Bone Tyler, they were going to need real evidence, facts he couldn't argue his way out of. And nobody was going to snoop around trying to find it. Boner— another nickname, derived from the first—hadn't committed any crimes yet, and if he was planning to do so, that wasn't police business. The police showed up after the fact. No knock on them; that was their job. And it made sense. You start arresting people for what you think they're planning to do, you might as well starting building the Gulag.

Billy understood that.

If anyone was going to investigate Ham Bone, it would have to be a regular person, working on their own. You could hire a detective—there was a good one on the island now—but Billy had the native islander's hatred for spending money, especially giving it to someone else for a job you could easily do yourself. You rewired your own lamps, changed your own oil, snaked your own toilets. That was common sense. That self-reliant Quaker practicality explained why Billy Delavane, without mentioning it to anyone, even Mitch Stone, and especially not to the police chief, started following Ham Tyler the next morning.

He called in sick, but he didn't fool Pat Folger. The wiry old contractor had launched his own adventures into vigilantism a few years before, when his son got hooked on opioids.

"Do what you have to do, kid," Pat told him. "Just stay safe."

Ham was easy to follow, it turned out, lodged firmly in his own world, no doubt starring in his own cable-ready movie— *Ham Tyler: Crime Patrol*, perhaps, or just *Danger Cop*. He cruised the island, pulled people over for minor infractions, mostly Hispanic people, disappeared into the new fortress police station for paperwork or a quick workout—then back home to his family's paint-peeling ruin of a house in Tom Nevers. Billy owned quite a few properties in similar condition, though set in far better locations—Eel Point Road, Polpis Harbor, Long Pond, Squam—and he grudgingly admired Ham for not selling out and collecting the million or so dollars his crumbling homestead could have reaped in the island's overheated real estate market. Billy occasionally sold an acre here or there, himself, to pay the taxes on the rest of his family's holdings. He had donated some harbor beachfront to the Land Bank, but that was it. Real islanders held on, at least until the next generation cashed out. He thought of the Larrabee place in Cisco—a hoarder's labyrinth of broken cars and trucks, piled tires and leaking carburetors strewn about in the weeds—the acres of automotive rubble now cleared for one more multimillion-dollar subdivision. The Larrabee property had always been slightly disturbing, but it was old Nantucket, a rusting kingdom of objects saved for the moment they might be needed on a scrap of sand too far away from the rest of America to allow the luxury of relying on mainland strangers. The Larrabees' property was an oddball remnant of Billy's childhood, and he hated to lose it. So, good for you, Ham Bone. Hang in there. Replace a few windowsills and repair that roof so your kids can afford to live here, if you ever have any.

Billy sat in his truck and estimated the renovation costs for the Tyler house. He worked out the dimensions of a stairway he was supposed to be building for Pat Folger, and in the course of that solitary week, he learned one of the primary, inescapable realities of police work—done correctly, it's mind-numbingly tedious. And his mind wasn't the only body part that started to lose all feeling. He had never sat so long in any vehicle doing nothing, paying attention to an unused driveway or a closed front door. It was like a staring contest with a stuffed deer head, as he had seen his father attempt once in a drunken stupor.

His father blinked first.

But Billy kept his eyes open and peed into a jar and lived on granola bars and bottled water, and three days into the vigil, he finally got his reward.

He had followed Ham from home to the Chicken Box and slipped into the seedy mid-island bar behind his quarry. At five thirty in the afternoon, no one was drinking but the hard-core regulars. John Fogerty sang "Run Through the Jungle" over the chatter of conversation and the clink of pool balls. A silent TV showed guys in suits talking about the new football season.

Billy almost fled. Everyone knew him here. Someone would call out to him, maybe even the bartender, who had done a stint as a plasterer years ago. What was his name? Danny something. He'd been up on those crazy stilts spreading the blue diamond halfway across a forty-foot living room when he paused and told Billy, "This is a little too much like work."

Well, pulling beers for his old pals had to be easier. As for the fine points of cocktail mixology, he wouldn't get much demand for that skill set at the Chicken Box.

Billy ducked his head and continued inside. This was crazy. He should have just waited in his car. No one had recognized him yet, but—

Ham paid for his beer and headed toward the bathroom. As he walked, he pulled his cell phone out of his pocket. Going into the bathroom to make a phone call? This could be it.

Danny glanced up and grinned. "Hey—"

Billy threw out a flat palm to silence him. It only bought a second, but that was enough.

"Hey, Billy, what's goin' on?"

Ham was already out of sight.

"Later."

"But—"

"Shhh."

Billy moved fast, head down. He stopped at the swinging door to the men's room. Would Ham use a stall? Probably, but, if not—

Billy pushed the door open an inch.

Empty.

But he could hear Ham's voice behind the metal partition.

Billy slipped inside.

"Anybody there? Hello? No, no, I thought I heard something, that's all. Yeah? Well, I have a right to be jumpy! This isn't exactly my thing, all right? Which, I was thinking—you should maybe stick around for a while. You know—after. We could use a guy like you. Like a hired gun."

Billy moved closer. Anyone could walk in at any time. He needed to get into one of the stalls, but that was impossible. Ham would hear him and shut the phone call down instantly. No, he had to stand here, play the odds and hope. He breathed shallowly, through his mouth. The tile walls amplified every sound.

Ham went on: "If I learned anything last week, it's that you can't do ethnic cleansing with kids and punks and amateurs. Sure, sure, but the Hitler Youth got 'em early, man. You gotta get 'em early. Some sixteen-year-old with a bug up his ass...forget it. And speaking of cleansing—you should see the way these fuckin' people live. Makes you puke. Anyway, what I'm saying—there's this surf-bum nail banger doing the neighborhood watch dance, fucking things up. Dude's been a prick since high school. Oh, yeah, we go way back. Anyway, I was thinking...one well-placed round to the back of the head, and—"

Billy felt an actual chill go down his spine, a trill of fever. His fists were clenching at his sides. He relaxed them and drew in a silent shuddering breath, listening. There were steps outside the door.

They moved on.

"—Okay. Okay, I get it! Be cool. I was just—fine, whatever. I didn't mean that. No, no, I was just saying—Good, fine, great. Okay. I can handle this asshole myself anyway. What? Don't sweat it. I took care of that already...what do you care? Anyone can do it. Check it out on YouTube or wikiHow, or who the fuck knows where, anywhere, just go online...yeah, that's what I'm saying. But, anyway, it's done. The what? What the fuck is a dactylogram?"

What was a dactylogram? What the hell were they talking about? Billy cursed himself. Why didn't he have a tape player, or at least a pencil? A carpenter without a pencil! What did Pat always say? "You're a soldier going into battle without your weapon!" Was the pen really mightier than the sword? Maybe this afternoon it would have been. Billy would just have to remember.

"Jesus, sorry, Einstein. I don't have a dictionary stuffed up my ass. Okay, okay, so I got it, all right? Don't worry about that stuff. That's my end. Okay, whatever, fine—I broke into the house and used a chunk of Play-Doh. What difference does that make? From the school, okay? The elementary school, yeah. I grabbed it when I was in there checking out the new alarm system before the school year. No one was around, don't worry. I'm telling you, nobody saw shit! Nobody sees shit, that's the great thing about people. You told me that yourself, remember? That line about Clark Kent fooling 'em with the glasses. And you were right. Anyway…oh, yeah, so I got—what? No, no…well, I thought I heard somebody moving around in the house, but it must have been the wind or something. Or maybe the dog, they have a dog. I was in and out fast. I used the chloroform, like you told me. That spic musta felt like he had a bad night in Tijuana when he woke up next morning. So anyway…you don't need any fancy equipment. All you do is, you freeze the putty, get a batch of gelatin, nice thick gelatin—you have to microwave it a few times to get the bubbles out. Then you pour it on, refreeze the whole thing, and you're done. Fuck you! You asked me! Sorry to waste your precious time. Yeah, well, this is the part I care about, okay?"

Billy chanted to himself: Play-Doh, gelatin, chloroform. Play-Doh, gelatin, chloroform. Some Hispanic guy's house. Someone with a dog. Fuck—everybody had a dog.

Ham was still going: "Do your thing—just make sure that my guy goes down for it. I sent you the picture. She's gonna be off-island for the day. I checked with the Hy-Line. She has a reservation on the three o'clock fast ferry back. You just follow her off the boat. No, no, no—that's what I'm trying to tell you. She has an office on North Water Street and the rental house, and sometimes she house-sits for people, too. She could wind up anywhere, and you can't afford to be waiting around in the wrong place. People notice strangers around here. You got a narrow window and it closes fast. Wait till she's inside, so you can leave—right, right, sorry. I'm used to dealing with retards around here. You know what to do. Just do it. You're welcome." There was a pause. Then: "Asshole."

They were done. This was the moment!

Billy lunged toward the stalls, unlatched the one next to Ham's, and pushed in just as the other door opened.

"Who is that?"

Billy lowered his voice. "Unngh."

"You okay in there?"

"Unngh, yeah."

"Don't forget the mercy flush, skipper."

Then he was gone.

Billy waited ten minutes and then ten minutes more. Ham was shooting pool when Billy finally eased out of the men's room, across to the door, and outside.

He took a long breath of the chilly night air—autumn was finally coming—skirted the dirt parking lot, and climbed into his truck. He pulled out, cruised into the rotary, and let it fling him like an Olympian's discus, true and level, due east to Quidnet and the Stone family house, perched above the pond.

He had urgent questions, and only Mitchell Stone could answer them.

The house on Sesachacha Road looked like a museum of the 1970s, with the Danish Modern furniture and fake-wood floor-to-ceiling paneling untouched for decades. The hooked rugs on the scuffed strip oak floors, the glass-top coffee tables, the knotty-pine kitchen cabinets beside the avocado-green refrigerator and rusting four-burner gas stove teetering on the sloping pebble-pattern linoleum, the white-glass dome light fixtures on the cracked plaster ceilings, bought straight from the old Sears outlet store, prized because they were the cheapest ones Bessie Stone could find… It all brought Billy back to his childhood, the days of roaming the island with Mitch and Mike Henderson, building forts in the national forest, surfing the autumn swells, driving battered SUVs on Coatue, raking the first scallops when family fishing season started.

That was a different Nantucket, a smaller Nantucket.

Billy missed it. Fuck it. Nostalgia was like boozing—it felt good, but the next morning nothing was different except you had a wicked hangover. It was like Mitch always said—"People who live in the present stay alive."

In the present, dirty cops were planning murders with off-island hired guns, and Billy was one of the targets. Who were the others? And why?

Inside the old house, Mitch and his sister, Susie, were cooking dinner, while Ricky worked on his homework at the kitchen table. The food looked good—pan-fried arctic char and new potatoes, mesclun greens and tomatoes from Bartlett's. Vicky Fleishman was sipping a glass of red wine, supervising. It was good to see them together again. It felt like the old days—except for those early streaks of gray in Vicky's hair, Susie's heavy-framed glasses, and Mitch's proprietary comfort in a kitchen where he had always felt like a hostage or a prisoner. And, of course, the kid. They all had kids now.

The parents were gone, though. The ghosts of Joe and Bessie Stone had been scrubbed away—no more framed paint-by-number watercolors on the wall, and the gun cabinet that used to hold Winchester and Weatherby hunting rifles now housed Susie's collection of Nicholas Mosse pottery. The fresh coat of pale off-white paint on the kitchen walls made the room seem twice as big as it used to be, and the smell of the pan-seared fish, garlic, and olive oil beat the aromas of canned peas and stale bacon that Billy remembered from the old days.

"Hey, Billy," Mitch said as he flipped the char. "You want some dinner? We've got plenty."

"There's beer in the fridge," Vicky added.

Ricky looked up. "Hey, Mr. Delavane."

"Hey, hi. No, no—I didn't mean to interrupt. I just—I need to talk to Mitch for a couple of minutes."

Mitch picked up a fork and stabbed one of the red potatoes in the pot of boiling water, then turned to Vicky. "We're five minutes away. Can you take over?"

"Go talk to Billy." She lifted her head to him. "You sure you won't stay?"

"I wish I could."

"You okay, Billy?" Susie asked.

"I'm fine. I'm good. This won't take long."

In the living room, Mitch stood at the picture window while Billy paced the carpet describing Ham Tyler's phone call.

When he was done, Mitch sat down in a leather armchair beside the cold fireplace. He pulled his fingertips down over his face and then back across his temples, thinking. Billy took a seat on the matching couch that faced the hearth to wait.

Mitch expelled a long breath. "Okay, first of all, it's obvious Ham Bone is hooked up with the Contrell kid. They're up to their asses in some white supremacy bullshit, which is why Ham Bone wants to pin this murder they're planning on Sebastian Cruz. That's what the Play-Doh and the gelatin stuff was all about. Making a fake fingerprint. A dactylogram's a fingerprint, for what it's worth, if you're a dumb guy and you want to use a big word to sound smart. All Ham has to do is get Cruz out of the way with no alibi while his hit man takes out the woman. Two birds with one stone. Which is doable, by the way, if the birds are close enough together." He caught Billy's confused look. "Killing two birds with one stone. I'm saying it can be done. You bounce the rock off the first one's beak, like a bank shot in pool."

He wasn't sure Mitch was serious, but Billy believed him. If anyone could pull off a crazy trick like that, it was Mitch Stone. "The question is—who's the woman?"

"Rental house, office in town, house-sitting gigs. Obviously a local. You tell me. I've been away for a while. The good news is the hitter obviously has no interest in coming after you. You gotta watch out for Ham Bone, though. But, I mean, you know…Ham Bone."

"Yeah. So what do I do?"

"Call it in to the cops. Anonymous tip. Stay out of it, but get them the information. Then you've done your duty and you're not involved. And watch your back. More to the point… check your house and your car for drugs. And lock everything. I know that's not the Nantucket way, but it would be the easiest thing in the world for Ham to plant a bag of weed in your glove compartment, pull you over, and call it in, just like his uncle—remember?"

"Jesus Christ. Toad Tyler. The original state police brownshirt."

Mitch shrugged. "Keep an eye out."

Vicky called from the kitchen. "Dinner!"

Billy hugged the women, squeezed Ricky's shoulder, grabbed a new potato off Mitch's plate, and left them to their meal.

A few minutes later, he pulled off Polpis Road onto the grass beside the bike path and called the NPD crime tip line. He recited Ham's phone call as best he could, put his truck in gear, and drove home to his beach shack in Madaket, thinking he had done well.

In fact, he had made two serious mistakes. The first one was not pushing through the computer menu to speak with a live human being. Hamilton Tyler was monitoring the tip line, and he deleted Billy's call the moment it ended. That only delayed the message—deleted calls could be retrieved if the sabotage was detected. But delay was crucial in this case, marking in minutes and seconds the difference between life and death.

The second mistake was worse. He failed to watch his back. He put off acting on Mitch's dire precautions until the morning. He was feeling relaxed and resolved when he climbed out of his truck and started for his little house, lulled by the low boom of the surf and the prospect of a good night's sleep.

He never made it to the door.

Chapter Ten

STALKERS

Mark Toland stepped out of the nimbus of shadow, into the spot-lit glare. He flipped a coin to Haden, who caught it reflexively. "Thanks for the magic silver dollar," he said. "Worked like a charm. Didn't it, Mr. Peanut?"

—From Todd Fraker's deleted blog

As we reconstructed the incident later, Roy Elkins met the three o'clock Hy-Line fast ferry at Straight Wharf and followed Marcia Stoddard home to her cottage on Bank Street in the Codfish Park section of 'Sconset.

First, he followed her on foot to the town parking lot, and he must have had to scramble when he realized she was heading for her car. We have to assume his own vehicle was nearby, most likely at the harbor Stop & Shop, where he was lucky to find a space even in the early fall. I could visualize him watching as she unlocked her battered old Subaru, racing back for his own ride, picking her up on Orange Street, probably a few cars back, tracking around the rotary and east on Milestone Road. There was a fair ration of luck involved—the devil's luck because Roy

Elkins was as close to the devil as anyone I've ever known. Circumstances just break well for bad people, it seems...until they don't. The most intelligent and cunning bad people make mistakes, and Roy made a catastrophic one that day, for himself and for Marcia Stoddard, whose only crime was bearing a superficial resemblance to my fiancée.

He must have felt things were going well as he rolled on after watching her pull into her tiny driveway. He probably parked on Beach Street and walked back uphill around the corner to Marcia's house. It had to be a short walk—the next-door neighbor heard the shot something like two minutes after she heard Marcia's car pull in. This was Edie Kyle, aged sixty. Her husband, Arthur, had driven into town, so no vehicle indicated a human presence in the house. Roy most likely thought the little street was deserted, another lucky break.

Did they speak after he entered the cottage? Perhaps a few words, but this was an efficient gangland-style execution: two in the chest and one in the head.

Roy had fled by the time the frantic, whispered 911 call was transferred to my cell. I dropped Jane off at the Darling Street house and tore out to 'Sconset, lights flashing and siren blaring. I got to Marcia's door in a record-breaking twelve minutes, leaving a string of panicked drivers in cars scattered across the grass verge of Milestone Road behind me.

I stepped into Marcia's house. The last time I'd been there, she was under suspicion for murder, having quit her long-standing job as production designer for the Nantucket Theatre Lab, and she'd been planning to leave the island for good—embattled, bitter, already in exile.

Since then, she had been cleared of the murder charge, gotten her job back, and rejoined the island community with a heartwarming flurry of activity—sets and costumes for

Sebastian Cruz's play *Fundamental Attribution Error*, enthusiastic contributions to the annual flower show and Arts Week—she designed the posters and the programs, with a lovely playbill for a dramatization of Gertrude and Hanna Monaghan's lives at Greater Light, complete with a cover that duplicated the hand-forged art deco iron gates of the old house. Rumor had it she had even found a boyfriend—the new technical director, fresh off the boat from some regional theater in Indiana. All in all, Marcia Stoddard was having her own personal renaissance.

And the grim fact was, she should have left the island while she had the chance. If she had fled in despair and disgrace three months before, she'd be alive right now. Miserable and angry, sad and bereft.

But alive.

Instead, she was lying on her living room floor, in a growing puddle of blood. The wide-eyed stare of shock and terror on her face was pitiful, tragic, infuriating. This was the flood I had joined the police force to fight, with my puny sandbags always overwhelmed by the muddy water. I turned away, understanding why people instinctively cover the faces of the dead.

I pulled myself together. Brooding and self-recrimination would help no one. This killer had to be stopped. That was my job.

I addressed the rest of the house, from the RISD diploma on the wall to the drift of mail on the floor below the slot in the front door. Then I looked at Marcia again, and I understood what had really happened here.

The execution-style killing was the new signature of Roy Elkins—every murder he had committed since breaking out of jail in California had been performed with the same three-shot precision. I saw no shell casings, but he always collected them. He had come here to kill Jane, but he had followed the wrong woman off the boat. And how long would it have taken for him to realize his mistake? Marcia's name was everywhere in the little house—on the wall, on the floor. He wouldn't have wasted time. He had to find Jane, and the most efficient way to do that was through me. Roy had been a private detective as well as a homicide cop. He had access to all the databases. A quick scroll through any one of them would turn up my address—even the *Inquirer and Mirror* website. They'd done a puff piece about our family and toured the Darling Street house.

I ran out to my cruiser, hitting 911. I got Barnaby Toll on the line and told him to send every unit to the house. But I didn't trust them to get there fast enough.

I called Dimo Tabachev—he and Boiko were guarding the house, the first and last line of defense at this moment.

Voicemail.

I called Haden Krakauer.

Voicemail.

I jabbed the ignition button and ripped out of Marcia's drive-way, dry-skidding around the turns onto Beach Street and up the hill under the pedestrian bridge to the top of Milestone Road. I opened it up on the long, straight run into town, calling Jane as I drove.

Pick up, pick up, pick up.

"Henry?"

I kept my voice calm against the surge of relief. "You have to get out of the house. Grab the kids. Go out the back door. Take Dimo and Boiko. Go to the Horners' next door. I have units on the way, but they might not get there in time."

"Roy Elkins."

"He killed the wrong woman, and he's coming for you."

"Roy?" She wasn't talking to me.

"Jane—"

He was in the house.

"Roy? Mr. Elkins? Don't do this. I don't know you, I never did anything to you. But we can talk about it, we can work it out. Maybe I can help if you can let me try to—"

I could imagine her edging closer, plotting her moves. She had been studying tai chi with a local devotee named Chris Feeney. I prayed Jane wouldn't make a rash move now, but what choice did she have?

"Roy! No!"

Shots rang out. Her phone dropped and disconnected.

By the time I got to the house, Jesse Coleman and Quentin Swann were stringing yellow tape, Quentin happy to be outside and off the booking desk, Jesse happy to still be on the force. He had screwed up, but that was a few years ago, and I believe in second chances.

I got my own second chance a few seconds later.

My delay pinning Roy Elkins as Marcia's killer and those frozen moments while I deciphered his real intention weren't fatal, after all. Jane wasn't dead, and neither were the Tabachev brothers.

Only Roy Elkins was dead, taken down by the one guardian angel I didn't expect. Her presence was inevitable, though, once I thought about it, her demeanor as cool and unflappable as always.

She walked out of the front door, the same slim, sharp-eyed live wire of controlled energy, brushing past my chief detectives Kyle Donnelly and Charlie Boyce as if they were just two more bystanders, which they might as well have been. There were some new frown lines between Franny Tate's eyes. The time at Homeland Security had aged her a little.

She ducked under the yellow tape to give me a quick hug.

"It's over, Hank. All the kids—Tim and Caroline and—Sam, right? Jane says they're at a Whalers game. I assume that's football? They're safe. Elkins is gone. I was waiting for him."

We disengaged. "I should have been."

She touched my arm. I remembered the gesture. "You had Jane protected."

"I thought."

"What were you supposed to do? Guard her yourself twenty-four seven with a cocked Remington 870?"

"Sounds like a plan."

"You had a job to do. Elkins was my job."

"Thanks for that."

"It's true. You don't abandon this town's police force for God knows how long because you think some crazy guy might show up. And besides, Hank…no offense…do you really think you could have gone up against Roy Elkins, one-on-one?"

I shrugged. "No. Not really. But I could have gotten Jane off-island."

"Would she have gone, though? She has a business, too. She's a landscaper, right? I remember you told me that when we saw her walking around that big park a few years ago—"

"Sanford Farm."

"Right. We were debating the bombing case, and we saw Jane with her little boy. You didn't know her then, but you told me she was a landscaper—and a writer."

"And you remembered that."

"Well…she was a good-looking woman, and you were obviously interested, so…and anyway—remembering things is my profession. The point is, Jane wouldn't have wanted to walk out on her job over some vague threat. People flip out when they miss work for jury duty. And this wasn't one morning, and getting released because all the cases got settled without a trial.

This could have been days or even weeks of hiding out, feeling terrified, and going broke."

"I guess."

"Elkins was an anomaly, Hank. He hurt a lot of people. I was the only one of them who could do something about it."

I nodded. "I wouldn't want to have you on my trail."

At that moment, Jane burst out of the door, slipped under the crime scene tape, and threw herself into my arms. She knocked me back a step, and I held tight. "Oh, my God, Henry, he was going to kill me. He was—I couldn't—"

"It's okay. You're okay. It's over."

"It was his eyes. I've never seen eyes like that. They weren't even human. They were like—seagull eyes. That was the scariest thing. Those eyes. You couldn't talk to them. They had no... no feeling. No mercy."

"But you were going to attack him, weren't you? Some tai chi thing? Dim mak? Fa jin? You were trying to lull him while you moved closer."

"It didn't matter. He saw it, he stepped back. He was about to—"

"Shhh."

She shuddered as I held her, and we stood still, with the damp autumn wind pushing at us.

Finally Jane eased away. "She saved me. Who is she?" She took a step toward Franny. "Who are you?"

Franny extended her hand formally. "Frances Tate, deputy assistant director, National Protection and Programs Directorate, Department of Homeland Security."

Jane shook the offered hand. "Well, you certainly have the protection part covered."

"I do my best."

"You did a great job. Thank you."

Franny addressed me. "We'll be taking over the body. It goes to an anthropological research facility, probably the one at the University of Tennessee at Knoxville, after we take the head back to DC. I know that sounds a little ghoulish, but we're always trying to figure out what makes people like Elkins tick, and postmortem forensic brain analysis occasionally turns up something that helps. Anyway, we'll be out of your hair soon, and you can go back to business as usual."

"Keeping the peace in Whoville?"

She shot me a rueful smile. "I guess I'll never live that one down." She answered Jane's baffled look: "Ancient history."

There was a moment of awkward silence. A hearse pulled up from the funeral home commandeered by DHS to store Elkins until he could be airlifted off-island. A small crowd had gathered on Darling Street. Finally, Franny said to me, "I suppose that's it. I'll let you know if we find anything interesting." And to Jane, "You snagged one of the good ones, sister. Treat him right."

Jane echoed Franny's words, and her formal tone. "I'll do my best."

I devoted the rest of the afternoon to paperwork, protocol, and logistics. I arranged for Marcia Stoddard's body to be removed to the funeral home, notified her family—an older brother in Connecticut, an aunt in Maine. I scanned Karen Gifford's email about Billy Delavane's deleted message, and I read the transcript after I sent Kyle Donnelly out with a couple of uniforms to secure Marcia's house for the Barnstable Crime Scene Unit. I wanted the gun Elkins had thrown down after the shooting. When I identified the prints, I'd know which Hispanic individual Ham had targeted for the frame. I was ninety-nine percent sure, but I needed that last one percent confirmed before I confronted Ham Tyler. Franny was happy to let me have the gun. Her investigation was finished, and her unsub was dead.

I got Jane home and settled in with a glass of wine and an episode of *Gardeners' World* on Britbox, figuring that Monty Don could soothe her nerves better than anyone else. And I was right. As England's most beloved horticulturist pushed his wheelbarrow over the graveled paths of Longmeadow, trailed by his two golden retrievers, quietly declaiming an elegy for the summer, I left her smiling.

Chapter Eleven

HIGH SCHOOL REUNION

Then Ed told us what he was going to make us do, and
I said, "But we're not gay!" He laughed at that one. "Of
course you're not gay. This wouldn't be any fun if you
were gay."

—From Todd Fraker's deleted blog

Todd Fraker clenched his fists until his nails cut his palms.
Stigmata—that was perfect. His bloody hands spoke volumes.
He was betrayed, shamed, persecuted, forgotten, and forsaken,
and all his wounds were self-inflicted.

Sincere, trusting little Toddie Fraker taken down again.

He wanted to scream, but he had to stay silent. He shouldn't
be here; he couldn't let himself be seen, couldn't let himself be
captured. He ducked down behind the line of shrubs, opened
his fingers, let his hands shake and dangle at his sides.

The plan had gone perfectly up to now—all the abductions,
even ambushing Haden in the police station parking lot, the
trip to the liquor store to create the "bender" narrative, the
quick sap behind the ear, the drive out to Coatue, clipping him

to the steel bar with the rest of the prisoners, all without a hitch. He had followed the advice of the great Miyamoto Musashi, whose sixteenth-century manual on strategy, *The Book of Five Rings*, Todd had found, dog-eared and coffee-stained, on the paperback shelf in the Bridgewater library and held ever since as his constant companion and guide. Musashi instructed— Suppress the enemy's useful action, allow his useless actions. He had done that perfectly with Haden, letting the man's own weaknesses take him down. It had almost seemed too good to be true.

And it was. For Todd Fraker, at least, it always was.

It was the same with this house. He had chosen it so carefully 9 Darling Street, just across from the Kennis home, with a deep lot that extended all the way to Hiller's Lane, plenty of greenery for concealment, and an easy escape route past the patio with its high-end blue cushioned white wicker, past the clutter of bicycles and surfboards on the grass, beyond the deck, and out the open white gate onto the brick parking apron. From there, it was an easy jog to his parked car on Fair Street—two minutes in and out, owners gone, renters not yet arrived.

But there had been cars parked on the bricks today.

Someone was living in the house! He was trespassing officially, crouched in a flower bed halfway along the side wall of the mansion in full view from the glass door of the basement laundry room. The housekeeper could glance up and see him; anyone looking out a window could see him just as easily. He was exposed, vulnerable, baffled, raging, stuck in place.

He remembered the day his mom's car ran out of motor oil on Pico Boulevard. One minute cruising along, the next minute broken down, engine seized, blocking traffic, going nowhere.

After all the dry runs and rehearsals, he had come to Darling Street today ready to kidnap Jane Stiles, prepared to knock out her comical bodyguards with his flexible rubber blackjack or shoot them if necessary, whatever was necessary, whatever he had to do. He had tensed his spirit as he would tense his stomach, ready for a punch. But it never came.

He was moments away from being discovered. The Kennis house had been invaded; the street was full of cops; nothing made sense. First, the stranger had knocked out the Bulgarians, so easily, so quickly, a couple of blows with the butt of his gun; then the stranger was inside, and the woman appeared—who the hell was she? What was she doing there? Then the gunfire and the sirens. It was like watching his own worst nightmare coming true, except it wasn't happening to him. Someone else had come for Jane, someone else had been shot. The police were swarming Darling Street; the cars were blocking both ends. And there was Jane, with the police chief and the other woman.

Todd turned away. He had to go, he had to move.

He crouched down and scuttled away from Darling Street, crossing the patio, breaking for the hedge. Someone came out onto the back deck, some kid in madras shorts and a white University of Nantucket T-shirt.

"Hey, you! Hey—!"

Todd put on a burst of speed—through the gate, slipping between the two parked SUVs, and gone, sprinting up Hiller's Lane toward Fair Street. He forced himself to slow down. There could be cops around the corner, raw-nerved, hyperalert cops, triggered by the sight of a wild-eyed running man.

A car eased by him as he walked along, trying to catch his breath. Not a cop car, just a car. Ten feet away from the Darling Street incident, life was normal. Todd was part of that life, one more tourist touring the tourist town. He pulled out his phone, pausing to take a picture. What a picturesque little street! There was an anonymous missed call on the screen. He had silenced his phone while he staked out the Kennis house. The call had to be from Sippy.

Sippy!

This was Sippy's fault—it had to be. Sippy had set this craziness in motion somehow. This was the "business" he'd been talking about when Todd met his plane three days ago. Todd wanted to move on with the plan: kidnap Jane Stiles, get out to Coatue, and start the trial. But Sippy had other ideas, other priorities. He always had his own game running.

"What business?" Todd had demanded.

"My business. And no business of yours."

Todd took a guess. "Is this about the Ed Delavane jailbreak?"

"Nice. Very shrewd, Frakes. Yes, it is. But it's a very sensitive situation. Extremely sensitive. I have a lot of balls in the air right now, and neither of us will be happy if I drop one of them. Leave it at that."

There was something terrifying about Sippy when he said that. He had changed. The crazy side of him had calcified somehow. He was stronger. His killing spree had changed him in a chilling but simple and obvious way: he was a killer now—he was willing to kill, he could kill anyone, and he might kill Todd as easily as anyone else.

His last words: "Keep your phone charged. I'll call you from my burner when I'm ready."

And now Sippy had called. Now Sippy was ready.

Todd approached the plane carefully from the far side of the field where he had cut the fence a few days before. Sippy had given him the precise route to avoid the CCTV cameras. "They may have you on film already, Frakes. You don't want to be seen coming here twice. A limp and a fake beard only take you so far." He had duly changed his disguise today, walking normally, sporting a Patriots cap and sunglasses. He hoped that would be good enough.

Sippy was sitting in the pilot's seat of the Cirrus jet, studying the console, when Todd climbed inside. It was cool in the cabin, the air conditioner running against the unseasonable heat of the autumn day outside. The space was cramped but luxurious with a pair of seats set against the back wall, a small table between them and the control panel. Mini fridge, wet bar, dense-weave gray carpet, padded arched tube cocooning them, big Lexan windows showing the empty tarmac, faint smells of leather and jet fuel.

Sippy swiveled around to face his friend. "That was quick."

"What's going on? What did you do?"

"I used the available resources to expedite the desired result."

Todd heard himself shouting. "What are you talking about? What did you do?"

"I got Delavane out of jail. My plan involved some trade-offs. What was your plan?"

"I don't understand this."

Sippy sighed. "I did some quite wide-ranging research. I found an LAPD detective named Roy Elkins whom our police chief arrested several years ago in Los Angeles. Elkins melodramatically swore vengeance on the loved ones of his enemies. That would include our Jane Stiles, which made him a perfect instrument. I gave him an escape plan that involved calling in many favors from across the span of his law enforcement career. People are the best weapon, Frakes. Elkins didn't understand that. He had to be instructed on how exactly to weaponize the people in his life."

"But—you said...he was in jail. How did you even contact him?"

"I made an appointment and arrived at the prison in a six-thousand-dollar charcoal-gray three-piece Brioni suit, six-hundred-dollar Ferragamo cap, toe Oxford shoes, and a twenty-four-hundred-dollar Tom Ford briefcase. No one questioned my authority for a moment. People believe what they see. Mr. Roy Elkins has extensive contacts on both coasts. In exchange for duplicating his escape plan for the benefit of Mr. Delavane, I told him about Ed's buried stash. He helps Ed escape, they share the wealth, and Elkins leaves the country without touching his own bank accounts. His real money is overseas. Everyone gets what they want. Elkins gets to kill Jane, and—"

"Wait, what about me? What about the trial?"

"Jane was never going to testify at your trial. I was never going to let that happen, Frakes."

"But why not? I thought the whole point was that she—"

"I won't let her tell what happened that night. No one will ever know about that. No one. Ever."

"That night? What? You mean the Lock-In?"

"That night is gone; I have plucked it out of history. No one knew but me and Jane, and she's dead. She had to die, so I made sure she did. Simple as that. Our night died with her."

"No, no, this doesn't—"

"Listen to me! The plan was a perfect little machine, Frakes. I set each little set of teeth spinning, locked into the next, like a Ducati gearbox. Sweet. Elkins arranges with our old pal Hamilton Tyler to frame some local wetback that Ham's been jonesing about for years. Full circle—Ham gets rid of this landscaper person he hates so much, Elkins has perfect cover for the murder, and we get Ed Delavane delivered right into our arms. Or should I say our bear trap. That must have hurt."

"But I mean…how does Elkins get away from Nantucket?"

"On this jet. That's the last part of my plan. Directly from here to St. John's Airport in Newfoundland. VIP treatment all the way. We travel like rich people—this jet is just like my lawyer suit. It smooths everything over. Elkins has papers and cash in Montreal.

Once we land, he's on his own. It's a twenty-three-hour trip, including the Port aux Basques ferry across the Gulf of Saint Lawrence. Lovely drive, though. And then he's free and clear. What?"

Todd stared at him. "Jesus Christ."

"What?"

"You have no idea what happened."

"I know exactly what happened. Elkins can tell you the details. He'll be here any minute."

"No, he won't."

"Todd—"

"You tried to steal Jane away from me, and you failed."

"No, I tried to bag Ed Delavane for you, and I succeeded."

"You tried to take my trial away."

"Come on. She's dead. That's all that matters."

"No, it isn't. Not to me."

"Well, you're going to have to adjust your expectations."

A grating moment of silence.

Then: "Remember *The Great Escape*, Sippy? Remember how much we loved that old movie? We wrecked three VHS tapes watching it over and over, back in the day."

"So what?"

"So who got away and who didn't?"

"What difference does that make?"

"Think about it. The guys with the fancy suits and the papers and the train schedules—they all got caught. The guys who got away? They stole a bike, or found a rowboat, or hoboed on a train or whatever—simple shit. Under the radar. Complicated plans fail, Sippy. That's the lesson. There's too many moving parts, too many little gear wheels, like you said. No one can keep track of them all. You out-think yourself with your big brain. Everything depends on everything else, everyone depends on everyone else. But people aren't dependable."

"My plan didn't fail."

"Are you kidding me? Are you fucking high? Your plan went to shit. I was there—I saw it happen. Jane is safe! She's fine. I'm not sure what happened to Elkins, but I'm betting he's dead. Some lady I never saw before nailed him right there in the house. I heard gunshots, and she came out and he didn't."

"No."

"Someone figured out what you were doing. It was that lady, I bet. She looked like a badass."

"You're lying."

"Then where's Elkins? You said he was coming. He should be here by now."

"No! No, no, no, no, no! I won't let this happen."

"It happened. But it's okay. We have Ed; we pulled that one off. Time's running out. The cops will be coming after Ed. People will miss the others. It's a small island, we have to act fast. Regroup, drop back, and punt, like your dad used to say. We can improvise—we can make this work."

Sippy had seemed to be on the verge of tears, his eyes squinting, his mouth turned down, his whole face crumpled. But now he calmed down suddenly. The level, assessing stare, the easy little half smile. It made Todd nervous.

Sippy was in charge again.

"Okay, here's what's going to happen, Frakes. You're going to take Jane despite whatever extra security they have on her, because you can't not do it, you can't keep away. And when you get her to the shack, everyone dies. You, me, Lonnie...Jane, Ed, Haden...all of them, all of us."

"Wait a second, that can't—I set it up with Lonnie, he has a boat there, he's taking it to Hyannis afterward. He has papers and money, a whole new identity. He's getting a fresh start. A second chance—"

"Not anymore."

"I promised him."

"Too bad. Everyone dies, like they should have died in the school fire. Which you failed to set."

"But how—?"

"This plane, Frakes. This Cirrus Vision SF50 single-engine light jet, designed by the good people of Cirrus Aircraft, Duluth, Minnesota, USA. I'm gonna take it up, circle the island, and come down hard right on top of that little shack, and between the impact and the burning jet fuel, there'll be nothing left but the crater, some scorched metal, and the ashes. Then they'll know. Then they'll understand what happened. That's my plan, Mr. Peanut. Simple enough for you?"

"You're insane."

"So are you. So are most people. So what?"

"You're not doing this. I won't let you."

"You can't stop me."

Todd felt Sippy's unearthly calm and confidence like a puncture, small but poisonous, the thorn on a rose. Surprise, pain, anger—and disappointment, the sharp prick of betrayal. Somehow he had his gun in his hand. He pointed it at his friend. "I mean it."

"You have to be kidding. You're going to shoot me now?"

"Stop this. Come with me. We'll take Jane and do what we planned."

"That's over. It's falling apart, Frakes. That little scheme is history."

"It isn't. It doesn't have to be. Just help me. Let's finish it together."

"You trust me?"

"Promise."

"And you'll believe me?"

"Of course I will."

"Fine. I promise. Okay? The trial will go on as intended! Happy now?"

"You mean it?"

"You said you trusted me."

"I do. I have to. I mean…you're Sippy."

"Yes, I am. More than ever."

"We're really going to do this?"

"Put the gun away."

Todd lowered his arm, and the moment the barrel pointed at the floor, Sippy pounced, throwing himself across the six feet of the cabin with a paralyzing animal shriek of rage, cannonballing his head into Todd's stomach. They reeled backward and fell against the passenger seats. Sippy got his hands up and clamped them around Todd's neck. The grip was powerful, relentless, welded. Todd couldn't budge it. He only had one hand to pry the fingers loose. His other hand still clutched the gun.

The gun!

He was blacking out—he had seconds to act. He brought the gun up to Sippy's head, mouthed the word "Sorry," and squeezed the trigger.

The explosion was deafening, ear-puncturing. It catapulted Sippy backward in a spray of blood, dumping him on the gray carpet like a shovel full of dirt. It felt like the recoil had snapped Todd's wrist.

Silence, echoes.

Todd slipped down to the floor, his back against the edge of the passenger seat. He stared at Sippy's cratered temple, blood pulsing from the scorched hole, the face bizarrely intact, still wearing that benign, hideous, invulnerable smile. The cabin stank of cordite and burning hair, and the meaty, stomach-turning reek of blood.

The silence was louder than the gunshot. It felt like someone had jabbed ice picks into Todd's eardrums. He was moaning and keening, but he couldn't hear himself. He was deaf, but the silence roared on, filling his brain like the white noise of a jet engine. The jet, he was in Sippy's jet—how far was it from the terminal building? Had anyone inside heard the shot? Could they hear it? Could they mistake it for something else? A nail gun on a construction project, a car backfire? Did cars even backfire anymore? Was anyone on the tarmac? He'd know soon enough. One 911 call, and the airport would be swarming with cops. They'd surround the jet, storm the cabin, cuff him, and pull him out. He'd kill himself before that happened. He lifted his hand, stared at the gun.

Plenty of bullets left.

The seconds ticked by, the minutes accumulated like snowfall—a dusting, then a sheath, then a carpet deep enough to soak your shoes. Footprints crunching, packing down the soft, white crystals. His mind was coming untethered.

Footprints, leaving footprints.

He sat up. The fight had pulled some muscle in his back, and the pain flared around his ribs. No one had come. He was safe for the moment, but—footprints, he had to cover his footprints. That meant...what did that mean? What could he do?

Focus. Sippy's death had to look like suicide.

That meant wiping the gun, putting it in Sippy's hand, stuffing that cold stiffening finger through the trigger guard—and firing it again. The gun left evidence on you when you shot it. He remembered that. He'd have to fire it again. No one seemed to have heard the first round, but if they had and dismissed it, a second one would set the alarms ringing. He had to take the chance. He couldn't move Sippy, and he had nothing to muffle the sound.

He pushed the lifeless sausage against the trigger. This time the recoil whipped the dead arm up and the gun barrel clapped Todd on the chin. He let out a startled yelp.

Sippy's final blow.

He got to his knees—it seemed like every part of his body was hurting now and stood to inspect his handiwork. Not great, but it was the best he could do.

He stepped to the cabin door, eased it open a crack, and looked out. The airfield was deserted except for a lone pilot walking his checklist around one of the bigger jets, marking a clipboard with a pen. He disappeared around the front of the plane, and Todd lowered the steps, scuttled down, and raised them again. He pushed the hatchway closed and set off on the diagonal route across the tarmac that Sippy had charted to avoid the surveillance cameras.

In less than a minute he was at the cut in the chain-link fence, crouching down to push himself through. He stood on the other side, catching his breath, screened from the road by a grove of stunted pine trees. He had done it—acted boldly, saved his plan, and made his escape. Time was still against him, but he had gained some small advantages. With Sippy gone, there was no one to question or undermine him—Lonnie would always do what he was told. Someone would find Sippy's body soon, along with the evidence of his mission—the journal, the scrapbook, the Jane Stiles novels. Best of all, with Elkins and Sippy both gone—and Lonnie throwing suspicion on the famously inept and drunken Haden Krakauer—everyone would assume Jane was safe.

The culprits were dead!

The danger was past.

Life could go back to normal. They would let their guard down. They would relax. But you never take your guard down.

Musashi said it best—the old samurai had some great words of advice for Police Chief Henry Kennis and his friends:

"When the battle is won, tighten the cords of your helmet."

Chapter Twelve

PENNIES

Think of your life.

Remember the years between 17 and 37—your twenties, your thirties, your youth, your prime, the memories you'll take with you to light up the shadows of your old age—first love, marriage, your career taking off, the birth of your children, the glittering priceless illusion of immortality, your body fit and supple, your parents still alive and vigorous, the rich, delicious main course of your precious existence. Now imagine all of that stolen from you. That's what happened to me.

—From Todd Fraker's deleted blog

With the bodies removed, the crime scenes taped off, and the murder weapon in custody, I had more pressing problems to deal with. Haden Krakauer was AWOL, and not just him: a few phone calls made it clear that no one, including Billy Delavane's daughter, his boss, and his good friend Mitchell Stone, had seen hide nor hair of him in the last twenty-four hours.

On top of that, there was no one I trusted at the station to receive Roy Elkins's gun. Monica Terwilliger was gone, also.

What the hell was happening? A mass kidnapping? Some Madequecham Jam rave-up no one had told me about? The Rapture?

I calmed myself down and tried to make sense of these most likely unconnected events. Monica was taking her accumulated personal days to deal with what Barnaby Toll—who had taken her call that morning—reported her describing as a "family emergency."

The station consensus on Haden Krakauer was that the stresses of the last few days had knocked him off the rails, and he had launched on another of his famous benders. Haden's sobriety was a delicate and tentative thing at the best of times. With school shootings and murders turning the island into a mock urban hellscape, he had obviously needed to hide out, and his favorite spot for that was the inside of a bottle, preferably a Smirnoff handle jug. Charlie Boyce had found store video from the Islander: Haden buying booze. A never-repaired software glitch dating from the last winter's power outage had disabled the time and date stamping, but the clerk remembered seeing Haden and a pal there sometime in the last few days.

Kyle Donnelly said, "The last time Haden disappeared, it was about a year before you got here. He woke up in a motel outside New Orleans wearing some fat girl's prom dress, with two hookers playing cribbage and a box of puppies. French bulldog puppies. Must have cost him a fortune. He had no idea how he got there, and the hookers weren't talking."

As for Billy, the note he left on his door two days ago for his daughter, Debbie, said, *Gone surfing. Big swell at Cuttyhunk. The cash is for cabs and food. No parties, please!*

Tiny Cuttyhunk Island, the outermost of the Elizabeth

Islands—less than a mile long, population less than a hundred people—lay anchored between Buzzards Bay and Vineyard Sound. Its main appeal is a single, superb point break with a flat stone bottom that engineered perfect waves on a strong south swell. I'd heard Billy talk about the place for years, and his expeditions there by Boston Whaler were legend in the local surfing community. Debbie was taking care of his pug. She was sixteen and self-reliant, with a thriving babysitting business of her own, and she was used to Billy's sudden surf trips.

So that was that: a phone call on the NPD personnel line, a liquor store sighting, and a note at the Madaket beach shack solved all the mysteries. No loose ends. No red flags. But something still bothered me.

When everyone was gone, I brought up the liquor store CCTV video. The snippet ran four minutes and ten seconds, according to the numerical readout on the bottom right of my computer screen. The time and date information had indeed been zapped out of the liquor store's system. According to Kyle's interview notes, they needed a tech guy to rewrite the JavaScript. But the owner was a jolly redneck Luddite who had never bothered with the upgrade. He laughed it off. "Shit, man, JavaScript? Ain't that the way your handwriting looks after too many cups of coffee?"

But the gap nagged at me. It seemed minor, a relatively small window for speculation—the transaction could have occurred on Wednesday or Thursday, according to the clerk. The woman remembered Haden, and she hadn't been working earlier in the week.

I ran the video again and froze on a frame showing the man with Haden. The guy was wearing a Toscana hoodie—the old, politically incorrect one with the cartoon of the back-end loader hiking up a woman's dress. Locals sneered at the trite tourist outerwear sold at town shops, T-shirts featuring the imaginary "Nantucket University," but a tee from Botticelli & Pohl, a local architecture firm with a cool logo, or a classic from a legendary contractor, like the Bruce Killen Death and Resurrection T-shirt, or an early D. Goodman Fine Painting and Ceramic Tile number from the eighties with its grout-knife swoop was a priceless totem for the wealthy washashores who craved some local cachet. The old-school Toscana sweat was a perfect example of the type. So the guy in the video could have been some slumming one-percenter. But there was only one person I knew personally who owned one of those old Toscana hoodies.

Billy Delavane.

My head was spinning. Could this be possible?

If the tape was made before Billy disappeared on Wednesday, it was all too possible. The bullet points lined up in my mind like someone else's presentation:

Haden and Billy had been feuding for years.

The mother of Billy's daughter was the long-lost love of Haden's life, and Haden had spent endless drunken nights in the officers-club bar in Camp Doha, during his tour in Iraq, plotting out various unhinged revenge plans, including framing Billy for a series of bombings. He brooded about that shit literally for years. And no, he never actually did anything. Someone with a grudge against Haden had listened to all those schemes and come to the island to make it look like Haden was actually carrying them out…in effect framing him for the crime of framing Billy. I still got a migraine thinking about it. But that was history now. Haden never set off a bomb and never tried to frame Billy for anything.

But he wanted to. That was the point—he wanted to.

Dreams of revenge got him through two deployments in Iraq.

And there was more stuff, too. Rancor dating back to high school that neither of them ever talked about. A lot of history festering under the skin like a cedar splinter.

And then: Haden knew Billy's routine. Billy always stocked up on beer and bagged ice before one of his surf trips, and always at the Islander. A swell hitting Cuttyhunk was all the information Haden needed, though on this gossip-ridden little island probably half the people Haden knew were aware of Billy's planned expedition.

So it would have been easy to intercept him at the store.

And now both of them were gone.

I turned off the video.

That was crazy talk. Haden was no criminal. I'd made that point to Franny Tate four years ago when she was investigating the bombings. And lots of Nantucketers collected those old Toscana sweatshirts. It could have been any of two dozen people in that store with him.

And there was something else, some detail slightly askew. I couldn't put my finger on it. I ran the tape yet again, cataloguing all the mostly irrelevant visual information: the hard liquor bottles lined up behind the counter; the March of Dimes collection box next to the cash register; the rack of *Inquirer and Mirror* copies beside a rack of the give-away newspaper, *Yesterday Island*; trays of candy below the counter; cartons of cigarettes lined up behind the video monitor bolted to the wall.

Nothing. I ran it again. Still nothing—except that maddening tickle of disquiet.

I set my harebrained theory about Haden as a mad kidnapper aside and got back to work.

We arrested Hamilton Tyler for attempted murder, conspiracy, and falsifying evidence. When I played him the tip line message from Billy Delavane he had tried to erase, showed him the

gun—clean except for one ostentatiously perfect thumbprint—
and let him read Sebastian Cruz's deposition about being sent
off to the far end of Eel Point Road by a call from the NPD
about stolen leaf-blowers—Sebastian recognized Ham's voice
and wondered why the call had come from a burner cell and not
the main switchboard at the police station—Ham broke down
and confessed. The capper was his burner's number on the call
record of Elkins's iPhone. For a young man who spent most of
his short adult life studying criminals, he was strikingly inept at
imitating them.

Ham's downfall dominated the front page of the *Inquirer
and Mirror* that week. (*The Shoals* had temporarily suspended
publication while David Trezize was off-island.) And the story
even made it into the Boston and Providence papers. I expected
some blowback from the town, but Ham Tyler must have been
more widely disliked than I realized.

I was with Jane the next day when the final mystery was solved
and the last threat eliminated. I had gone to Apex Academy on
Essex Road to pick her up for lunch. One of the girls on her
landscaping crew had dropped her off for a late-morning meeting with Diana Fox. The head teacher was a formidable woman—"a force of nature," someone had called her, comparing her
to various natural disasters, from tornadoes to tsunamis. I was
beginning to suspect sinkhole might be the more appropriate
image.

So I got to the school early, expecting some fireworks, to
provide backup if Jane needed it—the old LAPD Code 9 alert:
officer needs assistance.

The academy dominated the far end of Essex Road off
Bartlett Road, the only structure with vehicles from the "other"
Nantucket parked on the apron and at the curbside nearby—
Range Rovers; BMW X5s; giant, new four-door Jeep Wranglers

from the new dealership; and the inevitable MINI Cooper Countryman convertible.

Apex was clearly the preferred alternative school for the year-round residents who had the money to choose. Spanish was taught in the school but most likely not spoken in any of the students' homes.

Inside, walking past a bulletin board that featured a *Moby Dick* reading group, rehearsals for the school production of *Marat/Sade* (seriously?), trips to the Boston Museum of Science and Plimoth Plantation, along with notifications for fundraising dinners at the Pearl, and babysitting services, the first door I reached was Diana Fox's office.

There was no secretary at the desk in the anteroom, and the inner door was open.

I slipped inside to eavesdrop.

Jane's voice: "—a completely unacceptable response!"

"I can't help that. I have a problem with praise."

"Then get over it! Kids need praise! You're not a ballet master or a drill instructor. You're a teacher."

"What a lovely way to put it. Ballet and master and drill instructor! I think of myself as a combination of both. Instilling grace and discipline—and the will to fight."

"Kids need kindness."

"Kids abuse kindness! Particularly little boys. Just last week I assigned them to do a capsule review of a summer reading book. A capsule review! To make their lives a little easier and give them a fun assignment. But also to teach concision. Sam chose *James and the Giant Peach* by Roald Dahl."

"I know."

"Then perhaps you remember the *four words* he chose to use for his full book report."

Jane laughed. "Jim met a bug."

"That is ludicrous!"

"It's concise."

"It's disrespectful!"

"It's funny. Funny stuff is often disrespectful. You would have picked up on that if you had a sense of humor."

"I have a perfectly functional sense of humor! And I do not appreciate these ad hominem attacks. We are discussing your son, not me, and I strongly suggest you start him on a course of Adderall."

"Excuse me?"

"I'm very much afraid he suffers from attention deficit disorder."

"Based on what?"

"Based on obvious syndrome-conforming behavioral symptomology. Lack of attention, fidgeting, doodling, daydreaming in class."

"Did it ever occur to you that he's bored?"

"Excuse me?"

"Bored—not interested. You're boring, Ms. Fox! Sam is responding the way any healthy kid responds when he's bored. Get him interested, and see what happens! I've been reading to Sam from *1984* every night. Last night we spent two hours discussing *The Theory and Practice of Oligarchical Collectivism.*"

"What does that have to do with *1984*?"

"Are you kidding me? It's Emmanuel Goldstein's book, the bible of the Resistance—the book within the book. It's meta-text, Diana. Ask Sam sometime; he loves meta-text. He'll talk about it for hours. Because he's interested."

A sniff. "The Resistance. That's appropriate. Perhaps he views his own disruptive behavior in that same grandiose light."

"What disruptive behavior?"

"Well, for one thing, he insists on drawing pictures of me for the amusement of his classmates, placing my head on top of various animal bodies. Ridiculous animals! A kangaroo, a giraffe, and a penguin. I am not a penguin!"

"Did you discuss the drawings?"

"I confiscated them."

"Those drawings are constitutionally protected free speech—and private property. You had no right to do that."

"I am not a penguin!"

"He wasn't saying that. He was saying you look like a penguin."

"I demand an apology."

"And I want those drawings back. Along with Sam's book of riddles. You know, I was looking through that book the other day, and I found one riddle that applied perfectly to you. It goes like this—How do you draw a line and then, without touching it, make it longer?"

"This is absurd."

"The answer is, you draw another, shorter line next to it. Then it's the longer line. I would say that sums up your teaching philosophy perfectly. Make yourself feel bigger by making other people feel small."

"This is all beside the point. The question is, what are you going to do about this situation?"

"Something I've wanted to do for a long time."

"Oh, yes? And what might that be?"

"I'm getting Sam away from here and putting him in the public school—where he should have been in the first place."

"He'll never get a decent education there."

"I did. So did all my friends."

"Well, things have changed and not for the better. I hope your little boy can speak Spanish. That's the lingua franca at Cyrus Pierce right now."

"Jesus Christ."

"Don't roll your eyes at me! It's true. We're being overrun by these people!"

I heard Jane push her chair back. "That's what the Wampanoag Indians said three hundred and sixty years ago—when Thomas Macy and the Quakers showed up. The difference is, the Indians were right—and you're just a bigot. You should read *1984* sometime. Orwell has a lot to say about people like you. Check it out. And take notes. I may come back and give you a famous Diana Fox ten-page pop quiz. You wouldn't want to flunk it."

Jane came out a few seconds later, holding Sam's book in one hand and his drawings in the other. She seemed amazingly calm.

I gave her a hug. "How did it go?"

"Let's get out of here."

When we were outside in the cool, windy sunshine, she said, "How much did you hear?"

"Most of it. The end of it. You're really putting Sam into Cyrus Pierce?"

"If they'll take him."

"I think they have to take him."

I was parked on the curb. As we climbed into my cruiser, I said, "Joe couldn't make the meeting?" Joe was her ex-husband.

She shrugged. "He's kind of opted out of this whole thing. He's a good dad—Sammy loves him. But he's not that great at the real-life stuff…school and taxes and child support. It's fine. Really. That's the great thing about divorce. I don't have to resent Joe for being Joe any more, or expect him to take care of me or Sam. I can take care of us."

I reached across to squeeze her knee. "And now you have a little extra help."

She grinned. "Can you arrest Diana Fox?"

"Not yet. But I can cook you dinner and take Sam to Little League."

She leaned over to kiss my cheek. "That sounds good enough for Nantucket."

"I love it when you set the bar low."

I pulled out, did a two-point turn, and headed for Bartlett Road.

"We never should have put Sam in that school," Jane said after a while. "We were snobs. I hate to admit it, but I was a snob. A big, stupid snob."

"Sam will be fine. And I don't know much about Apex Academy or Diana Fox, but I can tell you one thing. She definitely looks like a penguin."

We were halfway home when I got the call from Charlie Boyce. He'd identified the pilot of a Cirrus Vision who'd been found dead in the cockpit of his plane that morning. The death had been provisionally ruled a suicide, but the man in the private jet wasn't the bipolar dot-com millionaire or guilt-besotted Wall Street corporate raider whom one might have expected driving the airport road and glancing at the array of multimillion-dollar private aircraft parked on the tarmac. As some wag pointed out later, it was a telling detail that the Cirrus Vision was the cheapest private jet you could buy, and this one was preowned—a used model that probably sold for under a million dollars. That detail made locals smile because the wealthy aviator was, in fact, a local Nantucket boy from one of the stingiest families on the island.

And Jane had known him since high school.

The Bascombs were "tight as ticks" in local argot, borderline hoarders who never threw anything away and never spent a dime when a penny could get them a crappy substitute. Jim "Sippy" Bascomb's mother famously boiled and reused her dental floss, a small, specific lunacy that spoke volumes for the off-kilter thrift of the whole pinched, squinting family.

Jim was an only child, and he "pulled a Larrabee" when his mother finally died, except the Bascombs owned ten times more property than the Larrabees—or the Tylers—and in much better locations. Only the Delavanes could boast comparable holdings.

Unlike Billy Delavane or Ham Tyler, Sippy had unloaded everything as fast as he could. There were Realtors pacing out the main house on the day of his mother's memorial service, and you could see surveyors' tripods and orange spray paint on more than two hundred acres of prime Nantucket land by the next week. Sippy could have sold all that real estate to the Land Bank or the Conservation Foundation and made an ample five or six million dollars instead of the fifty he supposedly cleared.

When David Trezize asked him about that at the time, Sippy's answer was succinct: "I owe this island nothing."

By all accounts, Sippy was a mean, ugly, bitter little boy who grew up to be a mean, ugly, bitter little man, and everyone was glad to see him go when he finally left.

Jane was especially glad. She was the first fifteen-year-old she had ever heard of with a stalker, and Sippy had remained a vaguely troubling presence right until he sold his family's property and disappeared in the early summer of 2010. She knew the dead flowers she received on her birthday every year came from him, and she suspected the MV keyed into every car she drove was Sippy's work, also. Jane had been a big Whalers booster in the old days with a proud, strident, irrational contempt for Nantucket's sister island. Sippy always sat with the Martha's Vineyard fans at the big rivalry football games and had actually been caught spray-painting the MV initials on the gym wall. Keying Jane's car was the next logical step in his bizarre love-hate relationship with the island and the girl who had somehow come to represent it for him.

Then it got worse.

During the annual Lock-In, in which the senior class spent the night in the empty high school, Sippy had hunted her through the dark halls and classrooms. "It was like some kind of low-budget horror movie," Jane told me at dinner after the body in the private jet had been positively identified. "He tried to rape me, but he couldn't…it didn't work."

I just stared at her. I had never heard this story before. "Did you fight him off?"

"No, just the opposite."

"I'm not sure—"

"I had this idea that going along with him—turning it into some kind of bizarre romantic interlude?—might work better than struggling with him. Sippy wasn't ready for that; he didn't want that. It's all power and control for people like him. So I did something a little crazy. I took his face in my hands and I kissed him."

"Jesus."

"It was a big risk, but I didn't have too many options at that point. Anyway, I guessed right. And it worked. The kiss knocked him right off the rails. He got his pants off, but he couldn't do anything. It was his big moment, his dream come true, or it should have been. But he didn't know how to respond…and he didn't. He couldn't. He had thrown me on a table. I was lying there, and he was standing in front of me, limp and furious and mute, and I think he was actually starting to cry when Billy showed up."

"Late to the rescue?"

"I don't know. Not necessarily. Sippy seemed really crazy at that moment. I don't know what he might have done. I don't even like to think about it."

"But Billy showed up. What did he do?"

"He didn't have to do anything. When he gets mad, he gets super calm, and that's ten times scarier than someone yelling. He just sort of appeared out of the shadows and said, 'That's enough of that, Jim.' It seemed to freak Sippy out, Billy using his real name, like he was saying I know who you really are. But it was kind of, I don't know—respectful?—also. This was the two of them man to man. Like Billy was holding him to some code of behavior. Whatever it was, it worked. Sippy had picked the lock on one of the gates. We went outside for a smoke. That's when we found Todd Fraker trying to burn the place down."

"Quite a night."

"Billy had his phone in his pocket. He managed to hit 911 by touch, and the police and the fire department came. They took Todd away, and that was pretty much that."

"Close call."

"Several of them. But it all turned into a lot of nothing."

"Maybe for you. Not for Sippy. Or Todd. One of them has been killing your look-alikes for the last ten years, and the other one spent the last two decades in the looney bin."

Jane wound up using the Lock-In for one of her books, and Sippy was the obvious model for the mopey, delusional killer who kicked off the mystery in the haunted-house corridors of the deserted high school in *Pimney's Point*. But she never wrote about what really happened on the night of the Lock-In. She never reported it to the police. It had been their secret ever since.

Sippy never gave up, though. He turned into a cyberbully at the end with constant friend requests and a creepy Instagram account that featured shots of Jane taken without her knowledge, complete with snarky, conflicted captions. A shot of her pushing a lawn mower while her two El Salvadoran crew members blew leaves and edged the lawn: "The Queen among the Peons." A picture of her fully dressed, picking storm-beached sea clams from the beach at Surfside: "Venus among the Quahog shells." The saddest one was from a reading she gave at the Atheneum. He snapped the picture during the Q&A. Jane was smiling at some comment from the audience. It was actually a good picture—she looked alert and relaxed and happy.

Sippy's one-word caption: "Heartbreaker."

Then he was gone, and all his social media accounts were closed. After a few years, various theories surfaced—he had joined some bizarre cult, retired to a compound in Myanmar or the Canary Islands, died of a drug overdose, killed himself.

What no one managed to guess was that Sippy had finally snapped. His passport had an Australian visa that matched the date of the Bondi look-alike murder. Other visas matched the locations of the other killings.

On top of all that, there was another copy of *Beyond Brant Point Light* in the jet along with some fetishistic Jane Stiles memorabilia, including her long-lost Lamy fountain pen, inscribed by her father, and her favorite winter hat from the old days, a gray woolly thing with a pom-pom that had gone missing back in high school.

Very dark, very creepy, but the consensus was we'd dodged a bullet. On the eve of his ultimate crime, something in him had collapsed, and he'd taken his own life instead. Killing Jane herself would have concluded the whole purpose he'd built for his existence. Maybe that made him realize how hollow that existence had actually become. Anyway, he'd chosen to end it almost as soon as he arrived at his old stomping ground. All in all, the story of Sippy Bascomb's self-inflicted demise was neat and well constructed, clear and comforting, complete with poetic justice and happy ending.

There was just one loose end still dangling—the CCTV footage from the General Aviation office that showed someone, face tilted down and obscured by a Patriots cap and wraparound sunglasses on the tarmac near Sippy's jet around the time of death. And three days before his death, another guy, roughly the same height but with a heavy beard and a noticeable limp, had been caught on camera near the plane. The images were blurred and fragmentary, stitched between camera setups, seeming to take advantage of gaps in the coverage. The same person? And if so, who?

My first thought was Todd Fraker, but Lonnie shot that theory down. Todd was out of Bridgewater, but he remained closely watched and heavily medicated—safely tucked away in a Boston halfway house, where he had been given a low-level janitorial job and had to sign in twice a day.

Jane doubted the connection between the two random tarmac pedestrians, anyway. Security at the General Aviation area of the airport wasn't exactly military grade, and they often caught lookie-loos trying to get a close-up view or taking selfies beside one of the big private jets. You could park in the GA lot and walk right out onto the airstrip. Plus, maintenance crews were also there all the time, along with all the other owners, and their guests.

We were still discussing it over dinner. Jane had gathered mussels at the jetties that morning at Bill Sandole's special spot before her meeting with Diana Fox. My mom had given directions, and I prepared a simple *moules meuniere*—one of the many dishes I'd learned to cook from watching her in the kitchen when I was a kid. "Quick and easy!" she said gaily, adding a little more Pinot Grigio to the pot. It was her kitchen battle cry, and I had adopted it myself, rarely cooking a meal that took more than twenty minutes. In her healthier days, we had bandied around the idea of writing a "half-hour meals" cookbook, but we never got around to it.

The Parkinson's had affected her mind in peculiar ways. "The past is coming for all of you," Mom said that evening over Häagen-Dazs bars and coffee. I wasn't sure what to make of her oracular tone. She was still sharp, but she could come out with bizarre, cryptic statements, apropos of nothing. A few days before, driving home from the grocery, she had waved a hand airily at the clapboard-and-shingle homes on either side of Pleasant Street and remarked, "All of these people are dead."

"Excuse me?"

"All the people in all the rooms in all the houses. Dead."

I forced a strangled little laugh. "I guess so, Mom. I mean—eventually."

I asked her about it later, but she didn't remember making the comment. I didn't press her. When your septuagenarian mother has a disease no one understands, you have to let some things go.

Her statement this evening sounded a lot less crazy and a lot more disturbing. "What do you mean?" I asked her, nervous about my kids listening. Sam was already upstairs doing his homework. This could easily lurch into the kind of lurid "true crime" chitchat that my ex-wife dreaded.

The standard dinner table topics she imagined—head-wound forensics and spatter patterns—never really came up. Mostly we talked about the irritating math teacher who never gave Carrie her homework back, and the English teacher who hated Tim because he refused to use capital letters. "Tell him you're reading E.E. Cummings," Mom had suggested.

When we did indulge in shoptalk, it ran to discussing how I could get my officers to tidy the break room and debating Jane's theory of "bespoke" versus "found" clues in her jury-rigged mystery plots. She much preferred building her stories around the real-life details I provided and the day-to-day anomalies she noticed that could be seen two ways and trick the reader.

But Mom's comment was nudging us toward the dark side this evening. And it was about to get worse. "Think about it, Hanky. Elkins comes for you, and this Sippy person comes for Jane. And it's still at least possible that someone else was coming for Sippy! Not to mention all these disappearances, people just kind of slipping away lately. I know everyone has a reason, and it all makes sense if you look at each case individually. But taken together... I don't know. Your grandmother always said, ignore the past and it will tiptoe up behind you and slip the piano wire around your neck."

"Mom!"

"She had a difficult childhood."

The kids were staring at her, wide-eyed. Miranda was going to love this.

Jane stepped in. "I've been thinking about this whole business with the plane, Henry. There's no footage of anyone boarding."

"No, but there were no cameras on that side of the plane. So, I mean..."

"Besides, and I hate to say this, suicide is a lot more common than murder—especially around here. Anyway, murderers kill themselves all the time. That 'Facebook killer' and Keith Hernandez committed suicide on the same day! I studied killers' suicide notes for a book I never wound up writing. More of them than you think talk about protecting the world from themselves and their uncontrollable impulses. Like werewolves locking themselves in a cage during the full moon."

"Maybe."

"I hate the way you say maybe. It sounds like 'no way.'"

"Sorry. I just hate loose ends."

"Okay, but think about it. Let's say Sippy was coming here to kill me. Let's say Patriots-cap guy or beard-o, or both of them, really knew him, and even knew about his plan. They stopped him. They killed him. They saved my life. That's a good thing, right?"

"Sure."

But I thought of Chuck Obremski back in LA getting that coke-dealing movie producer out of jail so he could wear a wire with the Russian mobsters. And Hamilton Tyler covering for Sebastian Cruz in Airport Park so he could call him to a non-existent crime scene when Elkins was doing the murder. What had Chuck always said back then?

"All motives are ulterior. All agendas are hidden."

Chuck was a cynic. But he wasn't dumb.

I decided not to push the point any further. I could see I was scaring Jane, and protecting her was more important. I wanted her cautious, not rattled. Panicky people make mistakes.

Tim stepped into the awkward silence, like a model onto the runway. "Debbie and I are back together," he announced.

Carrie expelled a breath just forcefully enough to turn it into a snort of contempt.

I ignored her and spoke to Tim. "What happened?"

"We had a huge fight, and she promised to stop flirting with that new kid, plus I convinced her she was being a total bitch to Judy Gobeler, and she invited Judy to her house for a sleepover and told Carrie not to come. They're not best friends anymore."

"All because of you," Carrie hissed.

"No, all because of you! Because you're so horrible to people. Did you know that Judy plays the tuba?"

"That is so ratchet. A tuba? It's bigger than she is!"

"Ratchet?" I asked.

"God, Dad! Gross, stupid, annoying, okay?"

Tim glared at his sister. "So she's short—that's the problem?"

"She spits when she talks—that's the problem. And shows

her big pink gums when she smiles. Plus she gets her clothes at the seconds shop."

"She has style. She can sing! And she speaks, like, three Slavic languages. Not just Russian—Belarus and Lithuanian, too."

"She should talk in weird languages more often. We wouldn't know what she's saying when she starts blabbing about fashion weirdos from the sixties and her favorite creepy furniture or whatever. And that stupid Mexican music."

"It's called Tejano, and it's really cool."

"Cool, really? Cool? Did she teach you that word?"

"Everyone says cool."

"Everyone who's not."

I used the brief, seething silence between them for a little parental diplomacy. "One day when you're grown up, you two will look back on this constant warfare and wish you'd been a little nicer to each other."

Carrie rolled her eyes. Tim pushed his chair back and stood. "Grow up. That's the key word, Carrie. Grow up! I'm walking the dog. Come on, Bailey."

The Portuguese water dog jumped to his feet, eager for a little action as always.

Mom said to me, "You and your brother were worse." She turned to Carrie. "Fistfights in the living room. They broke one of my favorite chairs once. I'm surprised they didn't kill each other."

"Don't give me any ideas, Grandma."

"Carrie." I shot her a cautionary frown.

"Just kidding, Dad. Sort of. Can I be excused? I have a social studies paper to finish for tomorrow."

We cleared the table and started the dishes. The kids' departure was like stepping into a stone hut, out of the wind. The new silence reverberated with the subsiding echoes of adolescent strife. I felt bad for Jane—what was she getting herself into with this family? Nevertheless, the marriage was still on, and she chatted with Mom about our wedding plans: justice of the peace on the beach at Madequecham, lobster salad sandwiches from the Straight Wharf fish store, Prosecco. A few friends and family. Reception at the old Admiralty Club in Madaket, and a one-night honeymoon at The White Elephant.

When we were finished cleaning up, Jane quizzed Mom about her days working for the Connecticut College Upward Bound program. After her interview, Josephine White had stuck the tiny, raspberry-blond, freckle-faced candidate for assistant program director in a room full of African American inner-city New London high school kids—"Sink or swim"—and then faded back to watch the show.

Mom set about discovering what was on the kids' minds and discovered that they had been hurting themselves during college interviews because they habitually said "aksed" instead of "asked." They needed some mind trick to help them remember the proper pronunciation. Mom thought about it for a second and then said, "Repeat after me—everyone! Say ass kisser." Bewildered giggles and some outright laughter greeted this bizarre request. Little white ladies weren't supposed to swear. But Mom remained stern, albeit with a twinkle in her eye. "Come on, say it. After me: ass kisser." They had no idea where this was going, and I could see that Jane didn't either as Mom recounted the story. "So finally they all said it. And I told them—just leave off the 'isser'. Ask–isser."

Jane said, "Wow."

Mom flashed an impish grin. "It worked! I got the job. And six of those kids got into college."

I was back at my own job the next day dealing with DHS, the FBI, the LAPD, and the California Department of Corrections over the Elkins interstate rampage, Franny's officer- involved shooting, and the Ed Delavane prison break. I had posted a BOLO and alerted the Steamship Authority and the airport TSA personnel, in case he was foolish enough to head back to Nantucket. I expedited the Marcia Stoddard autopsy and personally took Hamilton Tyler's confession. There was also a load of paperwork pertaining to project security for the proposed sewer project, various shellfish bylaw infractions, and new Selectmen's rules for the use of mopeds on the state highway, otherwise known as Milestone Road.

By two in the afternoon, I was ready to deal with my own business. I met Dimo and Boiko Tabachev at Siam to Go near the airport for a late lunch. They had been so crushed at their failure to protect Jane from Roy Elkins, they had offered to quit, offered to give me my money back. I tried to console them— Roy had been one of the most dangerous men on the planet, without scruples or reservations, a human-guided missile that would have taken anyone by surprise.

"Except for the government lady," Boiko said softly.

"The government lady is plenty dangerous herself—and she knew exactly what she was dealing with. Roy was hunting Jane, but Franny was hunting Roy. That's the difference. She had the element of surprise."

"Maybe so," Dimo said. "But we have idea for you. We add to the team."

"Our friend Angel," Boiko added.

"That will be more safe for you. Look at Boiko. Big and scary, yes?"

I nodded. "Definitely."

"He scares me! But Angel scares him."

Angel lived up to Dimo's description—six foot four, probably two hundred and forty pounds of hard muscle with a wide, flat face and a military brush cut. He had been standing at the counter at the far end of the restaurant, a little apart from the others, when I walked into the warm air and the smell of soy sauce and ginger.

Dimo, standing beside him now as Boiko paid for their take-out orders, tipped an arm toward the big man, palm out, and crossed his body with the other arm so they swept together, parallel in a gesture that said, "Voilà!"

Angel extended his massive arm, and I shook his hand. It felt like some dense chunk of polished wood. A spectacular grin split the giant's face. "Do not worry! I shake hands very gentle."

"Good to know."

"Angel Vaslev."

"Henry Kennis. Good to meet you."

"Likewise. Dimo says I work for you, protect your woman, yes?"

"For a while. I'm not sure how long the job will last."

"Does not matter, I work for nothing. I have big disability payment from Bulgarian government."

I looked him over. "You're disabled?"

Another chrome-glare grin. "No. I lie!"

Dimo stepped in. "Angel work for Voenna Politsiya, the military police. He was wounded in big gunfight with men stealing electronic materials from Navy for black market."

"Shot and disabled!" Angel clarified.

"He visit United States to be with family. He recovers. Money keeps coming. No one knows!"

"Everyone happy," Angel added. "Government takes care of Angel—feels good! Angel takes care of Angel—feels better! And you get free bodyguard for woman. Best of all."

"Are all Bulgarians criminals?" I asked, half joking.

"We are not criminals! We are free enterprise men! Like America."

"Angel strong," Boiko said, handing the giant a pair of wooden chopsticks from a jug of them on the countertop. "Show him, Angel."

The big man took the two chopsticks, gently separated them then laid them across his fist, with his middle finger curled over them. He clenched his hand into a fist with a grimace of concentration, and after a second or two the pieces of wood cracked and broke, sticking up on either side of his thick finger. "People who hurt your woman, I snap like chopsticks," he said.

I winced. "Hopefully, that won't be necessary."

When they left with their food, I took apart a pair of chopsticks and tried Angel's trick with one of them. All I did was hurt my fingers. I was impressed, but better than the man's brute strength was the fact that he'd been an MP. He knew police procedures and tactical planning. He could stake out a house and, despite his little show, take down a suspect without serious injury. That was essential. If this hoodie person was a real threat, I wanted him—or her—alive and well and sitting in one of my interrogation rooms, not DRT (Dead Right There, as we used to say in the LAPD) because of an overeager bodyguard.

I admit I had more or less come around to Jane's way of thinking by the next morning, a spectacular early autumn display of peerless blue skies and dry cool air, with a light breeze out of the north sifting the first leaves off the big honey locust, ash, and silver maple trees that shaded Darling Street. The bright, dazzling town seemed the least likely spot in the world for evil plans and nefarious behavior.

Jane drove the kids to school, and I had one more cup of coffee before I stepped out of the house into the sharp Atlantic sunlight.

Dimo saw me and snapped a mock salute. "Ready for our new day of vigilance, boss."

I nodded to him. "Just stay out of sight."

It was a tedious morning until my appointment with Karen Gifford. I spent the best hours of the day finishing up Haden's performance ratings on the summer specials in my overlarge, overheated office, worrying about his whereabouts and listening to the sounds of construction from the over-the-top fire station being built next door. I couldn't imagine the plague of arson or the terrorist attack that could justify this new fortress, which could easily serve North Providence or South Boston. It reminded me of Jane's rueful description of Nantucket: "A city at sea."

I called Haden one more time but still got bounced to voice-mail. Where the hell was he? Could he have really fallen off the wagon? Was he still with the elusive hoodie person? Had he been kidnapped by the hoodie person or killed by the hoodie person? If the person was in fact Billy Delavane, had Haden kidnapped him? Or were they just launched on Billy's surfing safari together? Haden had surfed as a kid, though he hadn't been near the water in years.

I yanked myself out of the speculation spiral. Still, the thought persisted: even on days off or sick days, Haden had always answered his phone or at least picked up his messages often enough to get back to me promptly.

I set my phone on the desk and took up the next evaluation. Haden was a big boy. He could take care of himself. If he was sleeping off a bender, I should just let him sleep. If he was surfing, good for him. If he had snapped, which he hadn't, there wasn't much I could do about it right now.

But I kept one eye on the silent black rectangle as I worked.

Karen Gifford came into my office without knocking at a few minutes before noon. She was a lovely girl, but she looked terrible at that moment, her face pulled down into lines of fatigue and worry, her hair a tangled mess.

"Karen?"

"I went to Monica Terwilliger's house this morning. I was worried."

"Is Monica okay?"

"She's gone. I found this on her pillow."

She strode to my desk and set a single penny down on the blotter.

"That's a good sign, isn't it? Like leaving a note saying you're coming back. Mike Henderson found one on Cindy's pillow."

"David Trezize is gone, too. He's off-island, supposedly."

"No penny there."

"Not on the pillow. But I looked around a little. He has a pair of penny loafers. One of the pennies was pried out of the shoe. I found it on the floor of his closet. And there was one on the floor next to Haden Krakauer's bed, too. I just came from there."

I sat forward. "What are you saying?"

She stared at me. "You know exactly what I'm saying."

"Someone has come back here and they're…kidnapping people, and leaving the penny as a calling card. Or, alternatively… this is just a crazy conspiracy theory. Everyone is accounted for, and people come and go all the time."

"What about the pennies?"

"People are careless with them—it's the one coin you probably won't bother to pick up if you drop it. Besides…the only person who might have been hatching a crazy plan like that was found dead in his own private jet. If it was happening, it's over."

She considered that. "Maybe, Chief. But you ought to talk to Jane about this. She knew all these people growing up. If she sees the big picture, she might have an answer for you, or see some pattern you missed because, you know…"

"I'm a washashore."

"Basically."

"I'll call her right now."

I picked up my phone and hit the speed dial.

"Hi, this is Jane. Leave me a message. It's not necessary any-more since my phone has your number and the time of your call. But it's friendly, and that counts for something."

I set the phone down. "Voicemail. My life is ruled by voicemail."

"Maybe she left her phone somewhere. I do that all the time."

"Yeah, but she doesn't." We stared at each other. "I'm starting to freak out a little now, Karen. Do me a favor, come back to the house with me. In case I need..."

"Backup?"

"Or just another pair of eyes."

"What about your bodyguard guys? There's three of them there, right?"

"Right." I called Dimo.

He picked up. "Yes, boss?"

"Everything okay over there?"

"Everything good. I make coffee run."

"So you're not there?"

"I'm at Fast Forward."

"Get back." I stood up. "There's only two of them there now."

Karen jumped to her feet. "Let's go."

We were in my cruiser, turning onto Old South Road with the flashers pushing the traffic aside, when the incongruous jaunty "Me and Julio Down by the Schoolyard" guitars broke the silence. I dug the phone out of my pocket and glanced at the screen.

"It's my mom." I ignored Karen's aghast, wide-eyed stare. "Mom?"

"Henry, there's a man in the house. I think he's done some-thing to those Bulgarian boys. He has a gun—he's looking for Jane."

"Hang up and hide. Get out of sight. Do it now. I'm on my way."

Karen picked up the radio handset and cocked her head in quick question. I nodded, hit the siren, and stomped the gas.

"Officer needs assistance," Karen shouted into the commo. "Possible 10-17 at number 10 Darling Street, number one zero Darling Street, all units respond." 10-17 was the "shots fired" code. "Repeat 10-17 at 10 Darling Street."

She disconnected with a grimace of stymied rage. There was nothing she could do now but sit tight. I tore down Pleasant Street past the Stop & Shop, sirens screaming full blast, fear and guilt closing my throat. Somehow, I had put my mother in the crosshairs of this lunatic, and Jane, too. Jesus Christ, Jane! Why had I ever listened to her? Thank God the kids were safe in school, as long as another shooter didn't pop up. The world was insane.

I jabbed Dimo's number into the phone, swerving to avoid a woman rolling her baby carriage in the street.

He picked up before I heard it ring. "They're dead," he wailed, so loud that Karen could hear him. "They are shot—he has kill them. Boiko! Oh, God, Boiko!"

I disconnected, blew through the Five Corners intersection, skidded onto Silver Street, took the hard left, and gunned it the wrong way up Pine Street. We were less than thirty seconds out. I could hear other sirens.

Karen was squeezing her own throat. "What is happening? What is going on?"

I had no answer for her. I cranked the right onto Darling Street, screaming to a stop in front of my house. We were the first to arrive. I could near Dimo wailing somewhere off to the side. I dashed out of the car, took the front steps in two strides, and pushed inside.

My mother was standing in the hall, leaning on her walker, supernaturally calm. "They're gone, Henry. He took her away."

I turned to Karen. "Get my mother a glass of water and sit her down in the living room. Call an EMT unit. I want her checked out."

I moved carefully past them up the stairs and along the corridor to our bedroom. I could see signs of a struggle—the overturned console table, the shattered lamp—but the gun must have cut it short.

I kicked open the bedroom door. "Jane?!"

She was gone. Mom was right about that.

And there was a penny on her pillow.

Chapter Thirteen

JUDGMENT AT SNAKE HOLLOW

Billy said, "You don't know what's going to happen. Anything can happen. Someone could die from smoke inhalation in there, or fall and hit their head, or get third degree burns. Then you're looking at felony assault or even second degree murder, along with destruction of property and arson. You don't want that. We won't turn you in. No one has to know. The gas will evaporate. It'll be like nothing happened."

Jane said, "You're not a criminal. You're better than this."

I ignored Billy. I spoke only to her. I said, "Run away with me."

—From Todd Fraker's deleted blog

Todd Fraker was running out of time.

He felt every second passing as he studied the five men and three women handcuffed to the steel bar in his family's shack on Coatue, thinking of Mark Twain's famous remark that truth was stranger than fiction. Well, Todd had written the fiction, and twenty years later he'd turned it into the truth, so he had earned the right to disagree. Truth wasn't stranger than fiction. It was bigger and smaller and better and worse.

Most of all, it was much, much harder to control.

So many problems and glitches and complications. Nothing proceeded according to plan. You had to improvise. In "Nuremberg II," his protagonist assembled the culprits of his childhood ordeals in a Romanian castle with all the time in the world to enact the ceremonies of punishment and retribution. A castle in Romania! He couldn't even find Romania on a map—then or now. He was stuck with a shack on Coatue. The watch on his wrist was a fuse, burning and sputtering toward the detonation.

Gathering his personal war criminals here on Nantucket under the noses of their friends and their families and the local police had been a logistical nightmare.

But doable. He had done it.

Not alone, of course—he realized that. His best friend and his half brother had helped. Of course they had. But Sippy was gone. Ultimately, he couldn't be trusted. Ultimately, there was no one you could really trust but your family. That was the fact, the one tie that bound you forever. He and Lonnie were brothers. Nothing else mattered. But Lonnie was stuck running interference with the police. Todd was alone with his captives. They were hungry and thirsty, they needed to relieve themselves, and every trip to the porta-potty in the other shack was a risk and a liability.

Plus, Ed Delavane was in rough shape. Sippy had purchased four vintage antique bear traps from the 1960s on Etsy. Todd had surrounded Ed's treasure trove with them, and the ambush had worked, but Ed was badly hurt. It had been almost impossible to open the trap to free his leg, and now the big man was hobbled and suffering extreme pain, going into shock with an open fracture of the shin bone.

Todd had done the basics—tied a rough tourniquet, elevated the feet, eased Ed onto his side, covered him with a blanket… but without access to oxygen and antibiotics and intravenous fluids, there was nothing more he could do. He had to finish the trial and the execution while Ed was still aware enough to know what was happening to him, before infection and delirium set in. Plus, he only had one gun left in his arsenal, and it was Lonnie's old Police Special .38 with no stopping power and a rusty barrel.

Everything was unraveling. But it had all started so well.

Taking his victims had been easy, and reading each of them the inventory of their crimes had lifted some oppressive burden from him. It was a physical pleasure, like pulling off heavy, sweat-drenched clothes on a summer day and plunging into the ocean. Their whining defenses had been so predictable, but that was a good thing. Like his mother had always said about the romance novels she loved to read—"Sure they're predictable! As predictable as the next Godiva chocolate."

Todd's favorite plea was that his victims wanted to put the past behind them and "move on."

"Well," Todd had told Mark Toland, "this is how I'm moving on."

Of course that wasn't strictly true, or at least not in the way they understood it. Todd wasn't going anywhere. He had reached his destination. The last body dangling from the noose would be his own. Why did mass shooters shoot themselves at the end of their killing sprees? People always asked that. But the answer was obvious.

They stopped because they were done.

No second chances, no second acts. No cash-grab sequels, no coming out of retirement for one last tour, no final six-week engagement in Vegas for the losers and the drunks.

You finish. The lights go out. And you walk off the stage for the last time.

Or you step off the gallows.

That's why he had lined up nine lengths of rope, not eight, with a loop for the gibbet hook on one end and the noose on the other.

You choose your own ending. Nobody else.

Only Ed Delavane and Jane Stiles were left to interrogate and convict. Now that he finally had her, the hangings could begin.

He crossed the rough-plank floor and kicked Delavane awake. The others were weak and starving and dehydrated, but Delavane's grunt of pain got their attention. Had Todd cracked one of the big man's ribs? He hoped so. Nothing hurt quite like a cracked rib, except a broken one, so aim the next kick well!

Delavane looked up. "Fuck do you want?"

His face was contorted with pain but also rage and contempt. An intolerable look. The urge to kick him and keep on kicking him until there was nothing left to kick twisted through Todd like a cramp. Get control. Walk it out.

When he spoke, he was calm. "Thanks for asking, Ed. I want to talk to you…or, more accurately, I want to begin your direct examination."

"Right. We're all on trial. So where's my lawyer?"

"You'll have to fill that role yourself. Just like all the others. But I must remind you…a man who acts as his own lawyer has a fool for a client."

"So get on with it, you little freak. My leg's getting infected, and I need a doctor."

"Not for long."

"The fuck is that supposed to mean?"

"I'm asking the questions, Ed. And I want to talk about what happened in high school."

"Nothing happened in high school."

"Do you remember what you called me?"

"No. Why should I?"

"Mr. Peanut. And James Bascomb was Fish Face."

"I didn't make up those names."

"No, but you took credit for them. And you never let them go."

"So I called you names! So what?"

"It means nothing to you."

"It don't mean much, Mr. Peanut."

Todd kicked him again. Bull's-eye on the cracked rib. The howl of pain was almost unbearably sweet. When the grunting and moaning died down, Todd continued. "Do you remember forcing me to shower in the girls' bathroom?"

"You ratted me out for cheating."

"You tricked me into playing heads-or-tails for my clothes with a trick silver dollar."

"Hey Mr. P., I've been here for the last three days. So has everyone else. We all know your sad story. Toland had the idea, and your friend Krakauer over there supplied the coin."

"But you goaded them into it."

"Yeah. So what?"

"Then you almost killed Sip—Jim Bascomb—"

"Fish Face. Right. He had a little asthma attack in our family's storage barn."

"And then you made us sodomize each other."

"After you tried to rip me off."

Haden Krakauer had been sitting in the corner facing the wall. Now he turned.

"That's what he did? Oh, my God, that's what happened? You never told me... I never knew..."

"Well, now you know. And that's why you're here, Judas. You sold us out just so this fucking ape and his pals would like you.

And it didn't even work. They despised you more than ever after that! You betrayed me and Sippy—you destroyed our lives FOR NOTHING!" Todd turned back to Delavane. "So what do you think about those days, Ed? Any regrets?"

"I don't think about those days. And I don't regret shit."

"Not even now?"

"I was thinking of killing both of you that night and chucking your bodies into the sound for fish food. I let you live. I regret that."

"No remorse. You know, judges consider leniency when they sense remorse."

"Come on. We were just fuckin' around. Colleges have frat houses. The initiations are ten times worse than anything we did. And guys love it. They do it to the next guys. They don't whine about it and start lynching people twenty years later."

"Are you fucking kidding me? I was harassed. I was humiliated. I was tortured."

"Come on! We were fuckin' around, that's all. Kids' stuff."

"So did anyone ever fuck around with you?"

"Nobody's that stupid."

"How about your dad?"

"My dad was a great guy. He was a war hero, okay? Thirteenth Marine Expeditionary Unit. Navy Cross, two Silver Stars, and a Purple Heart."

"Wow."

"Yeah."

"Marine dads are tough."

"So what?"

"So maybe your dad was a little too tough on you."

"He kicked the crap out of me. My childhood was a fuckin' boot camp, and I'm grateful for that. Okay? He taught me values. I have values because of him."

"Attack weak people because they're weak. That's a value?"

"Push weak people to make them strong. That's the value."

"So you were doing me a favor?"

"Fuckin' right, I was. You cracked, that's all. Most guys get stronger. They turn out okay, they get married, have a bunch of kids. Hard-working family guys. Pillars of the fuckin' community."

"So bullying is good."

"Bullying. Fuckin' pussy word. You had some tough times, and you couldn't handle them. Boo hoo. Things are tough in the real world out there, too, Peanut. Life is tough. You learned that early. Unlike most of these spoiled brat punks we went to school with. Too bad you couldn't handle it."

Todd stared at him for a long moment. "Well, that was a tragically inept defense, Mr. Delavane. Suicidally inept. The verdict is guilty, and the sentence is death."

Ed started to say something, lurching forward until the pain in his crushed shin bone yanked him back like a dog at the end of a chain. Todd retreated involuntarily. Even in his weakened state, Delavane was a dangerous animal, not that much different from the bears the trap had been intended for. But bears were innocent. They killed to eat or defend themselves. There was a simplicity about them, a beauty, a nobility.

Delavane was the opposite in every way: tangled with complex human pathologies, ugly and debased.

Todd cleared his throat. "You will be hanged, like all the other convicted defendants here. But first, we have one final villain to stand her turn in the dock."

He strolled up the line of crouching, miserable prisoners manacled to the bar he had bolted into the wall of the shack, wearing the same filthy clothes for days, half-starved, broken and whimpering. The place smelled like the monkey house at the zoo. Todd had boarded up the windows. He didn't want ventilation. The cool breeze from the Sound would make his jail too comfortable. He wanted his prisoners to stifle and suffocate. He wanted them to learn every physical detail of their punishment, to grasp their sins and his retribution on the skin and in the sweat glands before they died. Most of all, he wanted to break their egos, shatter their invincible self-regard. That's what Sippy with his big brain and his check-the-boxes outsourced execution plan hadn't understood. Merely killing these people? That would have been meaningless. They had to die with their brains full of their own guilt and self-hatred, their fear and remorse, the way the rooms in a burning house are filled with smoke.

He thought again of the school—the great burning that Jane and Ed's do-gooder brother had prevented. Todd had convinced the jowls and jackets at the Bridgewater medical board that he was a different person from that adolescent arsonist, that he could never even contemplate such an act of madness again.

But he was contemplating it now. A splash of gasoline in each of their laps, their wide eyes staring at the match glowing between his fingers…but he had no gasoline on hand, not even in the generator, which he had emptied showing Mark Toland's vile, incriminating home movies—the awful party, the unendurable night on the beach here, the arrest at the school, all of it.

Hard to mount a defense in the face of that evidence!

One picture was worth a thousand words, wasn't that the phrase? How about hundreds of thousands of pictures, flickering past at twenty-eight frames a second? There weren't enough words in the language to make that exchange.

So, anyway, he had burned off all his gasoline. But that was fine. That was better. Hanging was the appropriate punishment backed by hundreds of years of judicial precedent and authority.

These monsters would die with all the proper legal trappings and formalities, and Todd would remain in control at all times. He would maintain his dignity. He would maintain the dignity of these proceedings.

"Jane Stiles."

She looked up. She was still disoriented. She hadn't had time to assimilate her situation the way the others had. She was still in denial, still in shock. But she had listened to Ed Delavane's testimony. She knew what was going on, and she must have sensed that she was next.

"Todd—"

"Jane Stiles, your trial has begun. At long last you will have to answer for your crimes. I would put you under oath, but you have nothing to swear upon, no loyalties and no beliefs."

"That's not true. How can you say that? You don't even know me and—"

"I loved you."

"You didn't. You couldn't. You barely knew me."

"We were fated to be together."

She squeezed her eyes shut. "I don't know what that means, what you think that means. How could we be fated to be together? We've spent our lives apart."

"But we're here! Don't you see that? Fate manifests itself. It unfolds! This is the proof. This shack, this beach, this day. It was fated from our first meeting. On the ferry."

"I walked in on you puking, that's all. It was an accident—a coincidence. You liked the way I looked and filled in the blanks."

"You don't believe in love at first sight?"

"No. I don't know. I suppose so. Maybe."

"And what happens at that moment? When the lovers first see each other?"

"I don't... How could I possibly—why are you asking me this?"

"Because I think that moment is sacred. It's all we can ever know of God. And because you violated it. You crushed it like a bug. Like, like...like I was some kind of water bug on your face. I reached out. I offered you everything."

She met his furious gaze with a calmness that silenced him. "Todd, listen to me. No one is going to be grateful if you offer them something they don't want."

"You saved me that night, the night of the party. You got me out of that house, you got me away from those people. We crossed the water together! We were alone under the stars, just the two of us. You made me believe we had a connection. You let me dream. And then you woke me up in hell. I've been there ever since. Twenty years of hell. Because of you!"

"I had nothing to do with it! I can't help the way you—"

"You refused to accept our fate! You led me on! I was a steer in a cattle chute—you herded me right into the slaughterhouse. German butchers wear a cup around their necks to drink the first blood when they cut the cow's throat. Oooh, you must have wanted to drink mine that night. Pumping out hot from the jugular."

"Todd, stop! You don't mean that. You can't mean any of this. You had a crush on a girl. So do a million other boys every day. They move on. Didn't anyone ever tell you there are other fish in the sea?"

"Yes. Yes, they did. I made a joke about it. Would you like to hear my joke? It's very literary. We're both writers, so it can be our private joke."

She shut her eyes. "What is it?"

"They say there are other fish in the sea, and I say, 'That's what people told Ahab.'"

"So, I'm your white whale?"

"You took my leg! So I hunt you down and I harpoon you, and we go down to the bottom of the sea together. Get it?"

"Todd, look. You're a free man. They let you out of Bridgewater. That's an accomplishment. You proved yourself. You've served your time. You're still young. Nothing final has happened here yet. Ed won't press charges. We can call it an accident. We can call this whole crazy trial a game. No one even has to know about it. Let us go. You can start over. You have the best years of your life—"

"What about Sippy?"

"What?"

"What did you do to Sippy that night? At the Lock-In? He never told me. He never told anyone. Only you know what happened. And he wanted to kill you, to make sure you'd never tell. But things are different now. Sippy's dead, and you're on trial for your life. What did you do to him?"

"Nothing."

"WHAT HAPPENED? Don't lie to me."

"Nothing happened. He tried to rape me, but I cooperated and he couldn't...perform."

"Why would you do that?"

"I was trying to shift things, to make it a shared moment between two people instead of one person wielding power over another."

"And you knew."

"Knew? Knew what?"

"You knew the effect that would have. You used your female judo! You stole his power and turned it against him. You ruined him for life."

"I accepted him."

"You tricked him! You knew what would happen!"

Her look was cool and level. "I took a calculated risk."

"You neutered him!"

"I pitied him."

He mimicked her earlier didactic tone: "No one will be grateful if you give them something they don't want. No one wants your pity! You castrated him with your pity! You should have used garden shears. It would have been kinder."

"I'm not the villain, Todd. I'm a good person. I tried to help Sippy afterward. I told him about Dr. Abruzzese at the Counseling Center. I could have turned Sippy in, but I felt bad for him, and I didn't. Now I wish I had. I should have. We wouldn't be here now. You needed him, you and Lonnie. You couldn't have pulled this off by yourselves."

"And thus concludes the testimony phase of our proceedings. Jury summations will be waived due to time constraints. The prosecution rests, and the defense abstains. Sentencing has been determined in advance. Let the executions begin."

Todd pulled the handcuff key out of his pocket and threw it to Billy Delavane. It landed in the raw planking between his feet.

"Uncuff yourself and your brother. You're the executioner today."

"Todd—"

He turned at the sound of Jane's voice. "You had your turn to speak." Back to Billy: "Get your legs under you, walk over, and uncuff your brother. If you think I won't shoot you, you're a bigger fool than I thought."

Todd moved back toward the door of the shack. He knew enough about guns to know they could be taken away if someone got too close. Distance was your friend. Bullets travel faster than people.

Billy uncuffed his brother and helped the hulking bully to stand. They were both stiff and feeble. It felt good to see them so diminished.

"Re-cuff him—hands behind his back."

Billy did it.

"Now, single file to the door. Ed first. Move!"

It happened as Ed was crossing into the sunlight. He stumbled, Todd impulsively stepped in to help, and Billy seized the moment. He jumped Todd, and they struggled for a few seconds until Todd connected to Billy's forehead with the butt of the gun and sent him reeling backward.

The fight was over. Todd was in control again.

But Billy had flipped the handcuff key to Mark Toland, and Toland had managed to open his shackles and Cindy's, then flip the key back toward the door while Todd and Billy struggled. It was the right move. Todd was hyperalert, nerves jacked to circuit overload. His first words proved it. "The key! Where's the key?"

"I—it's… I dropped it."

"Pick it up. Throw it to me."

Billy obeyed, and Todd slipped it back into his pocket. They moved out toward the viewing platform. Lonnie had built the post and crossbeam for the noose so that it lay flat and lifted easily on two big hinges, braced with a pair of folding brackets. Todd had set it up that morning and hung the first noose from the hook.

He was ready.

Ed and Billy took the stairs slowly, like old men, securing both feet on each tread before moving upward. Todd edged toward the door of the shack, feeling paranoid and outnumbered. But the situation was stable; the others were still huddled there, now stunned and disbelieving. Well, they'd believe it soon. They'd believe everything soon. The brothers reached the top of the platform.

"Stand him on the trap door! Fit the noose around his neck!"

Billy did it.

"Now pull the lever!"

Billy put his hand to the switch and then seemed to come out of his trance. He dropped his arm to his side.

"No."

"What? What did you say?"

"I won't do it."

"I'll shoot you."

"Maybe."

They still had no respect for him! It was infuriating. "I'll give you five seconds. Five. Four. Three…"

Billy stood absolutely still, watching him. He must have thought Todd was bluffing. After all these years, after all this work and planning, he thought Todd was going to chicken out like the night of the Lock-In, like all the other nights and days when they had laughed at him and sneered at him and tried to turn him into nothing.

"…Two. One. Last chance."

Still Billy didn't move. Todd took his stance, aimed the big gun, and squeezed the trigger. The shot boomed out over the water. The bullet caught Billy in the leg, spun him around, and toppled him off the platform. It sounded like he broke something—his arm? his wrist?—when he hit the sand.

Todd grabbed the lever. "Any last words?"

Ed gave him a crooked grin. "Fuck you."

Todd pulled the lever, and the big man dropped out of sight. The rope went taut with a shuddering crack and twisted as Delavane thrashed against the noose, his windpipe crushed by the raw hemp, strangling under his own weight.

Finally the rope went still.

Todd pulled out the Bowie knife he had purchased and sharpened for this purpose only and cut the rope. The bulky corpse dropped to the sand with a gruesome thud. Todd set the knife down beside the open trap. He was going to need it again soon. He lifted the rope off the hook, dropped it, and attached the next one, the special one he had prepared for Jane Stiles.

Inside the shack, he could feel the dislocated horror, the utter shock of his captives. Some part of them had refused to believe he was actually going to carry out the executions. Now it was different. Now they knew they were going to die. They were paralyzed, mute, shaking, gasping. Terwilliger was sobbing. It looked like her face was melting.

How do you like your Mr. Peanut now, bitches?

His voice was raw, high-pitched, and strange in his own ears when he spoke. "You're next, Jane."

Her calm voice startled him. "I have a proposition for you."

What could she possibly offer him now? But he was curious. "What?"

"I want a rematch."

"I don't understand."

"The heads-or-tails game, Todd. Fair and square this time. Your coin. But when it comes up tails, you let one of the others go free."

"Why would I do that? I could make you strip at gunpoint."

"But that's not you, Todd. You're not Sippy. You're the opposite of Sippy. You want me to do this freely. You want me to choose it. You want a game that's not rigged with a player who'll play to the end, no cheating. Ed's gone. You don't care about the others anyway. Not the way you care about me. This is the chance you've been waiting for since that night on the beach. Take it."

"You're just stalling for time."

"What if I am?"

"Another calculated risk."

"For both of us."

"You wouldn't do it."

"I will. But you have to promise. You have to keep your side of the bargain."

"Why trust me?"

"I know you, Todd. You can't lie to me. Maybe to the others but not to me."

They stared at each other, unblinking.

At last he nodded. "All right."

"But not in here. Outside, where it's just the two of us."

He threw her the key. She uncuffed herself, stood stiffly, and handed it back. He stepped out into the freshening breeze, and he missed the quick nod she gave to Mark Toland.

Billy Delavane was groaning in the dune grass, his brother, Ed, a heap on the sand below the gallows, but Todd ignored them. He had other things on his mind: fifteen throws, just like last time. How many items of clothing was she wearing? How many captives were left inside? Four, five counting Billy, six counting Jane herself.

Sandals, no socks, pants, underwear, sweater over a T-shirt; she never wore a bra.

Five garments, six captives, fifteen throws.

His head was spinning. Jane had knocked the situation out of control, derailed his perfect tidy train, but he didn't care. He was glad; the thrill in his blood was almost unbearable. His head was filled with some vast organic symphony, a thousand birds tweeting their territory, a million cicadas ruling the night.

He had come home for this. He hadn't known it; he could never have guessed it, but this was what he wanted most. And Jane knew it, she had always known it, she knew him better than he knew himself. What more proof did he need?

They walked twenty feet into the dune grass. All he had in his pocket was a penny, but that was perfect, too—the penny you threw off the side of the ferry to make sure you'd come back to Nantucket someday, to make sure you'd come home, like the pennies he'd left behind when he took his captives, like the penny he had actually thrown on that last boat ride to Hyannis twenty years ago.

Jane lost the first two throws.

She had kicked off her sandals. She was pulling off her sweater—then Todd heard the soft thump behind him. It was Cindy Henderson. She was free somehow! His mind rejected the thought. It was impossible—she was handcuffed to a steel bar! This could not be happening.

But it was.

Cindy had slipped in the sand and toppled against the door of the shack. That was the sound he had heard. Before Todd could react, Mark Toland appeared in the doorway, took Cindy's hand, and helped her up. They stumbled away, down the beach, toward Great Point and civilization. Todd fumbled his gun out, squeezed off a shot, but they were already out of range.

A moment later they were gone.

Chapter Fourteen

HIGH HOPES

The doctors said talking about what happened to me in high school would help. It didn't. The halfway-house people said that writing about what happened to me in high school would help. It hasn't. The time for words is over. It's time for action now.

COMMENT:

Interesting blog. Go to Fish Face and Mr Peanut (ffandpnut.blogspot.com) for our reunion.

ANSWER:

Contact me at the old AOL email.

COMMENT:

First delete this account. I'll be deleting mine within the next hour. Your blog did its job. We found each other. What we do next is private.

—From Todd Fraker's deleted blog

I stood in our bedroom holding the penny that announced Jane's kidnapping, the thoughts going off in my head like fire-crackers, sharp, fast, and loud, jumping on the string.

This penny, all the other ones, Karen Gifford's theory, Jane's proposed book about the connected rock-and-roll murders, her actual book *Beyond Brant Point Light*, so weirdly prescient, life imitating art, art imitating life, truth stranger than fiction, fiction telling the truth—lying to tell the truth, as my dad used to say...

Before I had even formulated what I knew I was thinking, I was bounding out of the room, leaping up the attic stairs two at a time. Lonnie Fraker was standing behind me shouting something, but it was just noise.

Tim had brought the "Nuremberg II" story home, happy to put the whole incident behind him and stuffed it back in the box near the vent at the far end of the narrow space under the roof, now with a cautious red ink *B-* on the top right-hand corner of the title page. I clambered into the attic and scuttled forward in a crouch, moving across the squares of curling plywood laid over the studs. It was hot up here, a dry, combustible heat that matched my mood exactly.

I reached the box and opened the flaps. The story was sitting on top of the jumbled papers and notebooks, cassette tapes and CDs, photographs, and an old wallet. We'd go through every scrap of junk later. Right now, all I wanted was a name.

The original title page was tucked below the sheaf of papers sitting on a manila file-folder marked *Report Cards*. I pulled out the sheet and stared at it, gut-punched but not surprised. This was on me. I should have followed up; I should have checked this earlier. But I was as eager to be done with the whole messy affair as Tim. So I ignored it, failed to identify the perpetrator, the UNSUB—the Unknown Subject—perched like a spider at the top of my own house, sitting here all the time.

Todd Fraker. It had to be him.

Todd Fraker killed James Bascomb and kidnapped Jane and all the others.

I said the name aloud.

Lonnie's high, nasal voice chirped at my back. He must have followed me up the stairs. "It can't be him, Chief. I told you. He's at High Hopes—the halfway house in Medford?"

"He must have escaped."

"They'd have called me. But forget that. Miles would have called the state police, and they would have called you. Anyway, I talked to Todd on Saturday. Saturday morning. With the meds they have him on, I don't think he could kill a fucking cockroach."

I absorbed the information. "What's the number? Who runs the place?"

"The resident administrator is Miles DeSalvo. Decent guy. I have him on speed dial."

Lonnie pulled out his iPhone, swiped the screen, touched it once, and handed it to me. It was already ringing at the other end.

"High Hopes. Building a better world, one life at a time. Can I help you?"

"Miles DeSalvo, please."

"Speaking."

"This is Chief Henry Kennis, from the Nantucket PD. I'm calling about one of your patients—"

"Clients."

"Right. One of your clients. The name is Todd Fraker."

"Is there a problem? Todd's been doing really well since we started him on Abilify and cut down on his Ativan."

"I'm actually just trying to determine his current whereabouts, Mr. DeSalvo. And—"

"Dr. DeSalvo."

"You're a medical doctor?"

"I have a doctoral degree in social work, Chief Kennis. I hold a BA from Wheelock and a DSW from the University of

Chicago. The program's psychiatric staff manages the pharma-ceutical treatment protocols."

I shifted to jargon. "And Todd Fraker is currently in residence at the halfway house?"

"We like to call it the *whole*-way house."

Breathe, Henry. Relax. Yelling at this guy would get me nowhere. "Is Todd Fraker living there? That's all I need to know, Dr. DeSalvo. This is an emergency. People's lives are at stake. We need to determine this individual's whereabouts ASAP."

"He's here. Of course he's here! At this point in time he could not manage outside of a controlled care environment. That being said, I have to tell you…this is not a mandated workday for Todd, so he's sleeping in. Which does not mean he's lazy, by the way! Sleep is a vital dimension of Todd's healing process. Insomnia has been an ongoing element in his psychopathology, and every minute of deep REM slumber is golden for him. But I can wake him if you like. He may sound a bit foggy."

"No, that's fine. Let him sleep. Thanks for your help."

I disconnected and handed the phone back to Lonnie. "Shit. Now what?"

"Well, I grew up on this island, Chief. I know the people. I know the history. I know where the bodies are buried. I mean—there are no bodies, obviously. Except for that skeleton Pat Folger found in the moors last Christmas. Whatsisname, Coddington. And we dug a grave for Billy Delavane's dog out in the moors back in fifth grade. That probably doesn't count, though."

The impatience was climbing my spine like insects. The attic was sweltering. I grabbed his arm. "Lonnie, what are you trying to say?"

He tugged his arm free. "You're not going to like it."

"Just tell me."

"Todd was part of a group—the dead guy in the plane, Sippy Bascomb, he was one of them. And so was your assistant chief."

I stared at him. The sun emerged from a cloud, and the hard light through the fan window made the attic hotter. We were baking up here. I flashed on the liquor store video—Haden and Billy before both of them vanished into thin air. "Haden Krakauer..."

"They were pals, him and Todd and Sippy. They were losers. And Haden loved that story Todd wrote—the geek revenge story. They were always over at my house, once Todd moved in—after his mom died, we adopted him. I heard Haden raving about that story all the time back then. 'A private Nuremberg trial! Someone should really do that!'—he said that all the time. 'Someone could pull it off if they had the money and the brains.' Well, think about it. Haden had the brains. And Sippy had the money. Sip sold this island out but good when he finally left. They put in thirty new houses on the Bascomb family property. Thirty families, every one of them with at least four cars. Because traffic wasn't shitty enough on Old South Road."

"Jesus."

Lonnie lifted his hands, palm out. "Where there's smoke there's fire."

"What is that supposed to mean?"

"That guy is squirrelly, Chief. He's an oddball. He's a drunk. He likes birds more than people. The kind of guy...you find out he has a bunch of dead hookers in his basement, you're like... hmmm, makes sense."

"Except the people who really kill the hookers, everyone's, like, 'I can't believe it, he always seemed so nice and normal.'"

Another hand-lift. "I'm just sayin'."

I silently crunched the numbers, running everything I knew about Haden through this new algorithm of doubt. And that video, that cold, indifferent visual indictment captured on camera. Lonnie was charging ahead. "Haden disappears, and it looks like he's been kidnapped. But—surprise! He's the kidnapper."

"Haden was last seen at the Islander, buying beer with someone in a gray Toscana hoodie. The kind Billy Delavane wears."

"And he's gone, too. Coincidence?"

"He left a note for his daughter."

"Written at gunpoint?"

"Maybe. If it was, whoever was holding the gun had to know Billy's family setup. His routines, and his favorite surf spots. This was no stranger."

Lonnie shrugged. "Except maybe we're all strangers, you know?"

"Yeah. Maybe we are."

We stood in the airless furnace heat for a few seconds. Then I pulled out my phone and called Charlie Boyce to start tracking down anything we had on Haden Krakauer, including all known real estate holdings where he might have stashed the victims. A second after we disconnected, the guitar opening of "Me and Julio Down by the Schoolyard" seemed to jump from my phone. The ringtone sounded gratingly jaunty, starkly out of place in that haunted attic.

I recognized the low-pitched scratchy voice on the other end of the line—Carl Borelli, the State Police forensics investigator, always sounded like he was about to clear his throat, though he never did.

"Sorry for the delay, Henry. You're good to go."

He was talking about Bascomb's plane. The CSI people had been swarming it for the last two days. "Is there anything left to see?"

He laughed. "Oh, yeah. We left everything in place except the body. Of course there's ninhydrin and bichromate everywhere.

That's gonna be a helluva cleanup job for somebody. What the fuck, Bascomb don't care anymore."

"And you didn't use benzidine."

"No, no, don't worry about it. Best fingerprint powder ever, by the way. FYI. But, ooooh, it causes cancer supposedly, so that's all she wrote. You have to go on the dark web to get that stuff now. Not that I ever would."

"Sure, of course not."

"Everything good causes cancer, you ever notice that?"

I pushed on. "Find anything interesting?"

"It's what we didn't find. Apparent suicide, holding a Sig Sauer 1911 in his paw. But there's no note."

"GSR?" If Bascomb had really killed himself with a Sig Sauer, there'd be gunshot residue visible as far up as his elbow.

"Yeah, but the funny thing is, he's still holding the gun. Normally, you see muscular release before rigor sets in. And there's another shot. Could be some kind of test, make sure the gun was working, whatever."

"But more likely that shot was done to plant the residue, after the fact."

"Yeah. These crooks today spend too much time watching TV. *CSI Wherever-the-Fuck.*"

"So, what do you think? Murder?"

"Probably."

"Any CCTV footage?"

"We're still looking, but so far we got nothing but those fuzzy screen grabs. They show a guy in a ball cap. Head down, turned away, moving sideways. This guy might suck at staging a suicide, but he's pretty smart about dodging the surveillance cameras."

I couldn't help thinking: Haden Krakauer had helped install this surveillance system a few years ago. He was a tech geek, a hacker, and a tinkerer. He had to know where the airport's blind spots were.

He could have built them in himself.

"Thanks, Carl. Keep me posted."

I closed the phone and turned back to Lonnie. "I have to go. Karen Gifford should look this stuff over. I'll send someone to pick it up."

"Why bother?"

"Why not? Todd was in the middle of whatever happened back then. He and Haden were pals. If there's something we can use, Karen will find it."

Lonnie seemed about to say something.

"What?"

"It's just...this is family business, you know? Private stuff."

"No one's going to print it in the paper, Lonnie. But if Todd left some clue up here, we have to find it."

"Sure, right. Yeah. Of course we do. Sorry. We should both get back to work. The clock is ticking."

"Yeah."

I called in to the station and sent Randy Ray with Karen to pick up the box from my attic along with anything else she noticed that might be important. She had a good eye—better than mine—when it came to the details of island life.

I was in my cruiser starting up Old South Road when my phone rang again. I struggled to work it out of my hip pocket, but it went silent before I managed to get it loose. I glanced at the screen as I slowed behind a line of cars waiting for the red flashing lights of a school bus. Classes ended at 2:20; it must be almost 3. A glance at the car's digital clock confirmed it: 2:51.

The call was from Jackson Blum.

I hadn't heard from the owner of Nantucket's biggest

sporting goods store since he'd spent the night in jail the previous Christmas Eve. It was quite an ordeal for our local Scrooge, but the man he had supposedly killed twenty years before turned out to have been a suicide; and Blum's gay son, Martin, survived his own yuletide suicide attempt. Blum hadn't known any of that as he sat on the cement bed in my jail cell through the long, cheerless night contemplating life in prison and the dire consequences of his homophobic rage.

Interestingly, his redemption had stuck. He had turned into quite a decent guy, welcoming Martin back into the family, volunteering at the food pantry, teaching an AP business class at the high school, paying for the cookouts at Whalers games... and actually smiling at other human beings from time to time.

Remarkable.

"How can I help you, Mr. Blum?"

"I'm helping you, son. I have my drone in the air right now doing flyovers of the whole island—Tuckernuck and Muskeget, too."

"I'm not sure..."

"We're looking for the missing people, Chief. I know, it's police business. But this is Nantucket, not Los Angeles. Word gets around."

"But how exactly did you even—"

"Martin and Connor were here for the weekend, and this reporter, Joshua Talbot? Martin grew up with him. He works for *The Shoals*, covers local sports and town business. I suspect David Trezize is grooming him to take over the paper someday. Anyway, Josh started talking about Trezize investigating these disappearances, you know—why now? Were they all connected? He knew every one of the missing people. Sure, it's a small town and coincidences happen...but this seemed a little extreme.

"So Trezize starts poking around, asking questions. Then he disappears! Josh starts looking into it and gets nowhere. It occurred to him that you'd have to stow the people somewhere, and not in a house they might recognize if they escaped. Maybe some of those cheap prefab sheds? Or one of those military surplus tents? But with all the hedges and walls, and with so many rich residents still on-island, it was hard to snoop and tough even knowing where to start.

"So I offered my drone for aerial photography. Josh has been curating the screenshots. But he needs your email so he can send the file."

"Wow. Thank you, Mr. Blum. But I don't want—"

"I know. Not a word to anyone! And nothing in the paper until the situation is resolved."

"No problem. This could really help."

"I know what you're thinking. Why doesn't the NPD have a drone? Well, I'm donating this one as soon as my new state-of-the-art drone gets delivered—it's all carbon fiber with much better image stabilization and lift capacity."

I had to smile. Despite his generosity, Blum couldn't help bragging about his new toy and making sure I understood we were getting his hand-me-down.

"Well, thanks again, Mr. Blum. My email is AckChief@gmail .com."

"I'll pass it on. Good luck and good hunting."

Out at the airport, Byron Lovell and Bob Coffin were lounging outside the small, sleek jet. Both of them were absorbed with their phones, which they stuffed into their pockets with comical haste when I pulled up. A strip of yellow crime scene tape blocked the open door over the plane's wing.

I climbed out of my cruiser and walked up to the two uniforms. "Boys."

"Hey, Chief," they said in unison.

"Anything happening?"

Byron snorted. "We only get posted when nothing's happening. When everything's happened already. I mean—who's gonna show up now? Ghosts?"

Bob nodded. "We could start a haunted private jets of Nantucket tour."

The plane's door, just in front of the wing, was open, with fold-down stairs up to the cabin: two pilot seats side by side facing a set of screens, one seat in the back with tracks and fasteners for several more, dark-gray leather and plastic, white fabric on the arched ceiling. Black dust covered everything like ash after a fire, and the interior stank of cigarettes, the chemical tang of ninhydrin and the underlying lingering musk of decomposition. Bascomb's body had been in situ for a day or two, and they'd never get the smell out of the seats and the padding. The new owner would have to gut it, right down to the metal struts.

I would have found the cramped space claustrophobic in any case, but I clamped down the urge to rush my search. *Go slow, breathe through your mouth.*

This was far from my first murder scene, but you never get used to it. The two detectives I'd known in my career who had seemed to relish these death rooms were both dead themselves now—by their own hands. Franny Tate's old boss at Homeland Security had been the most recent one. He'd blown his brains out in my office to avoid spending the rest of his life in a maximum security prison cell. But Al Hurewitz, my first partner in the LAPD, had eaten his gun in his kitchen on a Saturday afternoon and left his friends the exact type of crime scene that had driven him to suicide in the first place.

No note—and no need for one.

Enough. I set my morbid thoughts aside, pulled on a pair of latex gloves, and got to work.

I pulled the jet's flight log from under the pilot's seat. Bascomb's itinerary matched perfectly with the locations of the Jane-look-alike murders, including his last port of call in Sydney, Australia. I flipped through the pages, but there were no revealing scribbles in the margins, just standard FAA notations—aircraft make and model, aircraft ID number, points of departure and arrival, all of it in aviation codes—numbers and letters that meant nothing to me, apart from the obvious airport codes like SYD. The "memoranda" pages held repair details and refueling records, nothing interesting beyond the fact that jet fuel was insanely expensive and jet engine mechanics didn't make much more an hour than the kid who changed my oil on Nantucket.

The log held flight routes and ground condition notations, times but no dates. Bascomb must have stopped in Sydney for a while, though—there was a postcard tucked into the flap of the notebook, addressed to J. Bascomb at a local post box. The card was invisible, tucked into the end pocket of the log, and it hadn't been dusted for prints. The state police had obviously missed it.

Score one for the home team.

I held the card by the edges. The front showed a standard aerial photograph of Nantucket—green crescent floating on the blue sea. There was no return address on the other side, just a short message, "Greetings from Snake Hollow," and a crude smiley face. No signature.

Snake Hollow. I felt a faint chord chiming at the back of my mind, like a name I couldn't quite recall in a barroom debate. Who was the rat-faced guy who came back from two sets down to beat McEnroe in the 1984 French Open? Anton something? Egon something. In ten seconds, Google could spit out the name Ivan Lendl. I almost reached for my phone, but Google couldn't help me here. This reference was private.

I slipped the postcard into a glassine evidence baggie, tucked it into my jacket pocket, and continued the search.

A large cardboard box dominated the tight floor space behind the pilot's seat. Covered with black powder, it had obviously been dusted, dumped, pawed through, and catalogued by half a dozen people before me.

My own inventory:

A Ruger .45 and two boxes of ARX ammunition.

Two pairs of handcuffs and a ball-gag.

A complete library of Madeline Clark paperback mysteries.

Two copies of a *Vanity Fair* magazine from 2014 with an article about Jane Stiles.

A ring-binder scrapbook full of other clippings.

A Xerox of Todd Fraker's inescapable "Nuremberg II" manuscript.

A Dell laptop—harder to open than a Nantucket quahog, secured by some complex password no one had even tried to crack.

A pocket moleskine notebook, with two pages of scribbles:

> *Strategies: schemes and dreams until you act.*
> *Korzypski: the map and the territory.*
> *Blue line on the map, river gorge on the ground. See for*
>   *yourself.*
> *Roy Elkins: takes the bait?*
> *Face to face. See the eyes.*
> *Give what he wants, get what you need.*
> *Research: Ed Delavane, post high school: military records,*
>   *newspaper stories, police reports.*
> *Paydirt: October 18th 2002. Bar fight, Madison Wisconsin,*
> *Delavane: football scholarship*

Elkins: Attending Criminal Justice Certification program.
Argument, brawl. Ed arrested. Elkins bailed out.
Bar fight—bully-bonding?
Elkins' graduation pics: Delavane there. Big hugs.
After Iraq: Facebook friends.
Elkins wants Jane, needs Delavane. Money
Delavane needs Elkins to escape
Match making
Honey trap.
Bear trap? Cost? Vendors?
Elkins, Jane: outsource the dirty work. Why not.
Alibi research. Blackmail? Check browser history
The key: People gone for other reasons.
Plausible distractions.
Mr. Peanut: "Smoke and mirrors!"
With enough smoke, you don't need mirrors.
Mirrors are for seeing yourself later.

I stood with the moleskin in my hand for a minute or two. It answered some questions and raised others. So Bascomb had dug up a connection between Roy Elkins and Ed Delavane, masterminded both jail breaks, and then left the actual killings to his stand-ins. The entries explained the strategy—and some of his tactical thinking, as well—the diversions that covered the kidnappings. And the hardware. Jesus Christ—a bear trap, seriously?

But who was "Mr. Peanut"?

And whose alibi was Bascomb planning to secure with blackmail?

I set the questions and the notebook aside and kept digging.

At the bottom of the box, I found some scraps of clear plastic shrink wrap. My first thought having struggled with enough of them over the years: DVDs. One of them had part of a label: "Commentary by Director Ma." Matthew Vaughan? Martin Scorsese?

No. Obviously not.

Director Mark Toland. If he had been taken, then Cindy Henderson was gone, also. They had been together when they disappeared. My stomach clenched, a swift cramp of frustrated rage. I could feel the time passing, each second hitting like a sledgehammer on a spike. Where were they?

The rest of the cabin was empty. I stood hunched over for a second, paralyzed, brain empty. They put out oil well fires with explosives—the blast literally blows the fire away from the fuel it's burning. That was me in Bascomb's jet—blank and extinguished, anchored in the smoky reverberations of his crazy plan.

Then I remembered: the luggage compartment. If there was a suitcase stowed back there, the crime scene techs would have sorted through it already, and if they'd found something, Carl Borelli would have told me. But the thought of it got me moving, and at that moment, what I needed most was to move.

I climbed out the hatch door and walked around the wing to the baggage compartment. It was empty except for a gray vinyl Yeti duffel bag dredged in ninhydrin, like everything else. I hauled it out, set it on the wing, and unzipped it. My surgical gloves were black by now. I peeled them off and pulled on my last pair.

"Nothing to see there," Byron called out.

"More guys been pawing through that case than Casey Anthony's underwear drawer," Bob added.

"Shut up, both of you."

They could see I was serious, and they backed off a few steps and turned to face the airport building across the tarmac.

I started pulling out the contents of the duffel and setting them on the wing beside me: generic clothes, socks, a pair of well-worn Top-Siders, a high-end electric toothbrush, a hairbrush, some pens, a phone charger, another Maddie Clark mystery…

And, on the lapel of a classic Nantucket blue blazer, a New York Giants Super Bowl pin from 1986.

Something else the Staties had missed.

It caught my eye because Jane had talked about it, described Ed Delavane gloating about it. She had wanted to give it to her dad back in the day, but Ed had delighted in refusing, even though he was a diehard Patriots fan. And there was something else—Haden telling me Ed had buried all sorts of valuables somewhere on the island when he was a kid, like some teenage Blackbeard the pirate.

Stuff like this pin. Sippy must have raided the stash and taken it. That meant he knew where the treasure was buried and where Ed was heading when he got out of jail. He also knew what the pin meant to Jane. Of course he did…he was obsessed with her…they grew up together.

So what was the pin supposed to represent? What was its function in Bascomb's plan?

Totem? Taunt? Tribute?

Grave marker?

Whatever he had meant to do with it, those plans died with him. But I had a direction now. I had to find Ed's stash. Ed Delavane was headed there—it was the bait for Sippy's trap, the center point, the nexus. My gut told me Jane and the others were there already, captive and in mortal danger.

And the same question clawed at me, a feral cat thrashing in my hands.

Where was it? Where were they?

Haden had let the information slip, he knew—he had been

part of Sippy's crew of losers. So Lonnie Fraker's instinct had proved right, for once—Haden was holding them at the spot on the treasure map marked with the X.

It had to be on his own property. He wouldn't be safe anywhere else. I thought of Haden's shabby house in 'Sconset—too familiar, too public, sitting right there on Morey Lane, too central. But the Krakauer family owned another house out in Squam, a ramshackle nineteenth-century mansion, crumbling into disrepair, perched on a bluff overlooking the Atlantic, as remote and inaccessible as a piece of property could be and still be on the island.

X marks the spot.

I pushed myself off the wing, thinking hard.

I called Charlie Boyce and Kyle Donnelly, told them to swing out to the airport and pick up Bob and Byron. The best foot soldier on the roster was Sam Dixon. I told him to get out to the airport pronto.

"I'm in the middle of a domestic altercation here, Chief."

I heard shouting in the background. "They're going to have to work this one out for themselves"

"Ned Hollis is with me."

"Good, bring him."

My next call was to Peter Salros at the Coast Guard station. At twenty-six, Pete was the youngest commanding officer they'd ever stationed on Nantucket. It was obvious why—I had barely started to explain the situation when he said, "I'll have two cutters and four RHIBs ready to launch in twenty minutes. I know the house. Twenty-five-foot rusting flagpole with a Wharf Rat Club pennant. We navigate by it."

Those Rigid Hull Inflatables could slide right up onto the beach. Pete had the picture. I nodded, though he couldn't see me. "Everyone armed, but—"

"No trigger-happy redneck-cowboy testosterone cases."

"Right."

"Just smart, fearless, level-headed Coasties who know how to follow orders but take the initiative in a jam."

"Right."

I could hear the smile in his voice. "We can rustle up a few of those."

"See you out there."

My next call was to Lonnie Fraker. I wanted the state police involved with this bust—no jurisdictional rivalries, no red tape, no hassles or delays. Besides, I was betting Lonnie knew the house, and I was right.

"There's an eight-foot hedge that runs right down to the beach on the east side of the property," he told me after I laid out my plan. "Someone's gonna have to cut through it. You go around and you're in plain sight from the deck. I have a good pair of loppers in my garage, and my place is on the way."

The rest was straightforward—one group charging from Squam Road, another coming at the place from the west, and, of course, the Coast Guard taking the beach and cutting off any escape by water. We had superior numbers and the element of surprise on our side—a slam dunk.

My old boss and mentor, Chuck Obremski, who among other accomplishments had earned a degree in Culinary Management from the Cordon Bleu school in his hometown of Atlanta, always said a good raid should be prepared and timed like a five-course meal with everything, from the lamb shanks that had been brining for five hours to the baby peas that needed to boil for just three minutes, ready to plate at exactly the same moment.

Chuck would have approved our assault on the Krakauer house—Lonnie's troops breaking the lock on the bulkhead and pounding upstairs from the basement while the Coast Guard boys swarmed up the beach and I kicked open the front door as my detectives burst in from the side entrance on the deck. There was only one problem.

The house was empty.

We stood there in the yawning deserted living room, the furniture covered by heavy canvas drop cloths, panting and disoriented. For some reason I thought of Billy Delavane's pug Dervish chasing a rabbit right into the flooded cranberry bog. Billy had to wade in to save the little dog. We were just treading water.

Charlie holstered his Glock. "Shit. Now what?"

I had no answer for him. None of them said it, and none of them needed to, but I had called this one wrong, wasted precious time and resources. And my friends were still in danger. We stood in silence for a few seconds, and then my phone chimed with a text message.

Saved by the bell.

I checked my phone—Josh Talbot. He had sent me the screenshots from Blum's aerial surveillance.

"Check these out," I said. "Anything look suspicious?" Lonnie, my two detectives, and Pete Salros gathered around me as I swiped through the pictures.

One by one we were able to identify and dismiss every suspicious-looking structure. The new shed was a landscaper's equipment storage, that would be Sebastian Cruz—I had helped him set it up. Kyle Donnelly and Charlie Boyce identified the new tents. They belonged to a pair of washashore entrepreneurs—one an auto-body repair guy, Cliff Jepson, the other a medical marijuana grow house operated Charlie's cousin Gary. One giant tent was just a tented house—I remembered the permit application to fumigate the place for termites. The other tent—a massive white one—had been set up for Lena Perry's wedding, which Jane and I had been planning to attend in what now seemed like a different lifetime.

I swiped again and saw a skeletal structure. From the air, it looked like it was made out of toothpicks, perching in the dune grass and brambles of Coatue.

"That's our viewing platform," Lonnie said. "So people can see what the panorama from the widow's walk will be like, when they build their house."

Kyle was shocked. "You're selling the land on Coatue?"

Lonnie blew out a disgusted breath. "Don't get me started. The family's been fighting about that parcel for five years. The cousins who don't even live here and never gave a shit about the island want to sell to some billionaire. My parents want to sell it to the Land Bank for lots less money, obviously, and I want to keep it in the family. No one can agree, and no one can afford to buy anyone else out…it's like the Darling Street house. Or half the properties on this island. Families going to war with each other, and when someone wins the war, they get to go to war with a Conservation Commission and the HDC and the abutters—that's what we call neighbors around here, Henry. Abutters, that's the legal term—because we only talk to each other in court."

I seemed to have touched a nerve. "So who built the viewing platform?"

"That was the compromise—list it, show it, make the cousins happy. Someone told me the platform was falling down. It was built like crap in the first place. I hadn't been out there in months, since before they put the platform up. I don't even like to think about it. Still, whatever—I drove out yesterday and yeah, there is some rot and rust, and it needs work, and we're all gonna have to pay for it, even though most of us never wanted it in the first place. Families and property. They go together like ice cream and hot beef gravy. You can choke it down…you're grateful, I guess. I mean, it's better than starving—you need to eat it. But who wants to?"

Quite a soliloquy—I don't think I had ever heard Lonnie speak so articulately, or even say that much at one time, in all the years I'd known him. I thought of my mother's favorite quote from *Hamlet* the Dane's mother critiquing the actress overplaying her grief in *The Murder of Gonzago*: "The lady doth protest too much, methinks." I assumed Lonnie was simply dodging the truth—he really did want to sell the Coatue property, just as he had been pushing the family to sell the Darling Street house before we moved in. It was fine to profit from those giant real estate transactions, but you had to deplore them publicly if you wanted to maintain your old-school island credibility.

Anyway, I was only half listening to him, using the pause his diatribe created to plan out my next move.

I was ready to go before he finished. "I need a state police helicopter."

Lonnie stared at me blankly. "It's—what? Why?"

I turned to Charlie. "That halfway house, High Hopes, it's outside of Boston, right?"

He nodded. "Medford. You take the Green Line to Lechmere and transfer to a bus—takes about forty-five minutes." He caught my startled look and explained, "I went to B.U., and my girlfriend went to Tufts. The good news is it's only about ten minutes by car. Maybe fifteen from the airport if the traffic's okay." He grinned. "Or if you have a siren."

Lonnie still didn't get it. "High Hopes?"

"There's only one person who can help us now—one person who knew Sippy and Haden and all the victims, who just might have the answers to every question on this case—the guy who literally wrote the book on it, twenty years before it happened. Well, the short story, anyway. I need to talk to Todd Fraker."

Lonnie frowned. "The choppers could be a problem."

"Why?"

"One's out in western Mass doing drug intervention in the Pioneer Valley. The other one's down for scheduled maintenance. We're grounded. Nantucket's the last priority, with the Coast Guard doing the medevac runs."

I turned to Pete Salros.

He knew what was coming. "That would be unauthorized civilian use of military aircraft, Chief. You'd have to clear it through the head of Station."

"That would be you."

"You make a request like that, you have to hope the CO is one of those smart, fearless level-headed Coasties we were talking about before, who knows how to follow orders—but takes the initiative in a jam."

"And that would be you?"

"Fuckin' A right, that would be me. Let's go."

Half an hour later we were in the air over Nantucket Sound in a Coast Guard Sikorsky HH-60 Jayhawk, heading for Boston, with a state police cruiser on the tarmac at Logan waiting to take us to the Medford halfway house and Todd Fraker. It was the fastest possible route, short of rappelling down from the chopper to the High Hopes roof in a military-style fast-rope extraction. I should have taken some solace in that.

But I couldn't shake the feeling we were already too late.

Chapter Fifteen

DOMINOES

So we meet again. Old people fear the internet. And they should.

How else could this reunion happen? And what terrible consequences will befall our enemies because of it? I suspect this is the first comment you've ever gotten on your blog, or any blog. You cry into the night without even an echo returned to you. Well, my friend, that long silence has ended.

—From Sippy Bascomb's deleted blog

As the big Sikorsky banked over the island and the sun flared on the surface of the ponds, I pulled out my phone and logged on to Haden Krakauer's Instagram feed. It was an idle gesture, a moment of web-surfing through a lull in the action. There was nothing else to do for the moment, as the big blades chopped the air, and the island gave way to Nantucket Sound below us. I had the idea that I might be able to scavenge a scrap of information from Haden's social media accounts. A selfie with the mystery hoodie person? An image of the spot where he was keeping his victims? Careless, self-besotted criminals often posted pictures of themselves in the act of burglarizing a house or robbing a convenience store. If Haden was drinking, anything was possible.

It was worth a look.

I scrolled through endless pictures of birds and trees, moors and bogs, rosa rugosa and milkwort. I skipped by the only important item, but something made me backtrack. I remembered the day Haden had taken the photo at the airport park after the attack on Sebastian Cruz. Lonnie Fraker had driven up, and a green snake had slithered out of the bed of his pickup. Lonnie told us he'd been fishing in Quidnet. I had sensed a flicker of tension, an off-balance moment when he confessed to that lapse in his work ethic. He hated to be caught having fun. He liked to say, "My idea of a good time? Overtime!" Of course the Staties paid time and a half, and Lonnie liked the money, too.

I stared at the picture of the green snake. What had Haden said to him in the park? "Guess we know where you've been today."

How? And why?

Haden's caption held the answer:

Smooth green snake, Opheodrys vernalis. Habitat, Coatue. Found nowhere else on the island—except Lonnie Fraker's truck!

It all came together at that moment, all the facts and details that had somehow not collided, crashing into each other like the traffic pileup I had witnessed years ago in LA—a vintage Porsche stopping for a dog crossing the street, car after car behind it jamming the brakes, missing rear-ender after rear-ender by inches—until the natural-gas tanker plowed into the last one and sent all the cars slamming into each other, front to back, front to back, bang bang bang, like giant dominoes.

Dominoes. I found the liquor store video, froze it at the

newspaper rack. The picture above the fold showed a surfer at Madequecham riding the hurricane swell.

That was the latest issue. I knew it because the week before had featured the girls' lacrosse team posing ahead of the new season. Carrie had been thinking about trying out for the team, and the kids had been fighting about the "losers' gallery" photograph over dinner.

The paper came out on Thursday. Billy Delavane was gone by the day before. He couldn't be the man in the hoodie, and Haden hadn't kidnapped him. In fact, the man in the hoodie had very likely kidnapped Haden.

It was all coming faster now.

I pulled up Cindy Henderson's diary page:

That drive out to Snake Hollow, why would I hide that? No one's going to read this. And why would I even want to go back there, especially with Mark? It was perfect, we almost got stuck in the sand just like the old days. Flat cactus souvenirs, quoting Eliot, Hollow Men in their local habitat. All the echoes. Mark said remember rowing against the tide? He was laughing but it was one of the scariest days of my life.

Eliot, that poem: "Here we go round the prickly pear at five o'clock in the morning." Haden had shots of the Coatue prickly pear plants on his Instagram also.

I had my own pictures. I found the screen grabs of the drone photographs—the viewing stand on the Coatue property. I spread the picture with my fingertips for maximum enlargement, and then I saw it, the faint square etched into the middle of the platform: a trap door. And outlining the edge of the platform, a three-sided square of heavy beams. Were those hinges at the feet? Raised vertical, it would become a gibbet. I wasn't looking at a viewing stand at all.

I was looking at a gallows.

Todd Fraker was at Snake Hollow, he was "Mr. Peanut"— probably some sort of high school nickname or slur. The villains must have had a falling out—Bascomb was a stone killer, but Todd wanted the elaborate ritual of his deranged "Nuremberg" trial, obviously an obsession since he'd written that disturbed short story in high school. They never should have let him out of Bridgewater. Someone would have to pay for that lapse of judgment.

Meanwhile, Lonnie was up to his own neck in Todd's psychotic vendetta, running interference for his half brother. That meant throwing suspicion on Haden Krakauer, who was innocent, more than innocent. He was one more victim waiting for his turn in the noose. I had believed the worst of my assistant chief too easily, but my own suspicions of Haden's and Lonnie's sly deceptions had combined with my stubborn respect for the uniform, my fundamental trust in the state police, and Lonnie had used all of that, weaponized it, with shocking skill.

But I still didn't understand—why? Why throw his life away for Todd's psychotic crusade? It couldn't be just loyalty to his half brother. Lonnie must have had some dark grudges of his own. I couldn't imagine what they might be, and I had no time to speculate.

Meanwhile, I did clear up one more minor mystery: the vanishing porta-potty. Lonnie stole it; he must have been delivering it to Snake Hollow when he got the call out to the airport park.

I thought of Miles DeSalvo, the administrator at High Hopes. He was guilty, too. Another co-conspirator—though perhaps not a willing one.

I pulled Bascomb's moleskin out of my pocket.

Alibi research. Blackmail? Check browser history

Of course: Bascomb had been blackmailing this guy with something from his internet searches. I took a breath, letting the engine roar vibrate through me.

There was no need to go to Boston anymore.

I leaned forward and shouted to the pilot. "Turn back to Nantucket! Get this bird on the ground ASAP."

He stared a question at me then shrugged and started into a long banking turn toward the airport. I needed to get away from the engine noise and put my feet on the ground.

I had a rescue to organize.

——

At that moment, or close to it—her computer had actually chimed just as the state-police Sikorsky was taking off from Nantucket Airport—Karen Gifford found solid proof for Henry's case.

Her search had started a few days before, when Francis Tate of Homeland Security stopped the Roy Elkins attack. Karen had taken the woman aside for a few seconds. "Can you recover a deleted blog? I mean—the government. Homeland Security. Can you do that?"

"Sure. All they really delete is the start index. It's like trying to find a book in the library when someone's taken the card out of the catalogue. The book is still on the shelf."

"But impossible to locate."

"Well—difficult. You do a search tied to a few key words looking for orphaned files...books without that reference card.

You'd have to work all the platforms—Blogger, Wordpress, Hibu…"

"That would take forever."

The woman smiled. "That depends on how powerful your computers are. Don't try these tricks at home."

"You could do it fast?"

A curious squint. "What exactly do you want done?"

Karen told her.

And two days later, Francis Tate and her powerful Homeland Security computers had finished the job.

It had all started with a theory—the disappearances that had plagued the island were connected and rooted in the past. All the vanished people were the same age—odd coincidence—and they had all spent some part of their childhoods on Nantucket. They were part of the NHS graduating class of 2003. She had known most of them—or at least known of them. She was a freshman that year, so she might as well have been living in a different universe.

She started poking around in the archives, refreshing her memory—police reports, newspaper stories, school records, old issues of the school newspaper, *Veritas*. She came upon a late-spring editorial by David Trezize, one of the two editors that year, written after the Columbine shootings and ominously titled "Are We Next?" She had no recollection of it, but she had been too much of a journalism snob in those days to even glance at the student rag. She read it now, though.

This was how David's editorial began:

"We read about the Columbine shootings, we watch the aftermath on television, and we think, "That would never happen here." We feel superior. We feel very relieved. Most of all, we feel lucky. The problem is, we're wrong. It's going to happen here, and we're not ready for it…"

Karen had sighed when she read that. It had taken almost twenty years, but David was right. The mainland pandemic of gun violence had finally reached her hometown. David described the situation with the analogy borrowed from a friend's father, who painted houses:

> "Never leave a pile of rags with linseed oil or stain on them. It takes a while, but they're gonna catch fire. It's called spontaneous combustion. A lot of too much bad stuff in one place with nowhere to go, and all them chemical reactions reacting on each other in that tight little space, and it looks like nothing until it all lights up.
> Works that way with people, too."

David started there and proceeded to inventory the separate rags that might lead to a Columbine-like conflagration on Nantucket. Chief among them was a blog posted by a kid named Todd Fraker called *Law of the High School Jungle*. She remembered him as the pathetic misfit who had tried to burn down the school during his senior year Lock-In.

Todd had used Bolt.com, a teen social networking service, shut down since 2006. But once a blogger always a blogger. Karen searched for a new blog with Todd's name or "high school" or "jungle" in the title and found nothing. Either it had never existed, or it had been taken down.

Hence the challenge she had presented to Francis Tate.

Karen knew the searchers had a few advantages, the main one being a conveniently narrow window of opportunity. If Todd had created and deleted a blog, it could only have happened in the eighteen months since his release from Bridgewater State Hospital. There was no access to computers there for even the most privileged inmates. Frances Tate had assured Karen that if the blog had ever been live, the Homeland Security software could find it. They no longer needed a court order or a warrant, and, in any case, most blogging platforms were happy to cooperate with any reasonable request. They left it at that, and Karen settled back to wait.

Now the waiting was over. The Homeland Security email contained screenshots of the entire blog.

It was called *The High School Military Tribunal*.

URL: hstribunal.blogspot.com

Karen stared at the screen of her computer feeling a feverish chill of dread, a queasy reluctance to take a first step into that darkness. She shook it off. She was a professional law enforcement officer. She had done good work, and the fruit of her labors was laid out and waiting for her. She wrapped those comforting facts around her like a blanket, opened the file, and started to read.

She was a fast reader. Still, she had barely finished when she looked up to see her desk surrounded by two FBI special agents, a Barnstable SWAT team leader, and five state police troopers in full regalia.

The taller FBI man flashed his badge.

"We need to find Edward Delavane."

———

I made my first call from the tarmac, walking toward the terminal building. I hit the cop-shop speed dial and got Kyle Donnelly on the line.

"Chief?"

"Find Lonnie Fraker. Check his house and activate the GPS tracker in his cruiser. Check his gym, check the Chicken Box, take as many men as you need."

"Hold on, he just called. He's coming in to the station. He wants to pitch in with the Haden Krakauer search. Some cottage near an osprey nest in Madaket? Near Long Pond. Krakauer might be hiding out there. It's all dirt roads, but Lonnie knows the way."

One more diversion. Lonnie was good, and he wouldn't give up until he had bought his half-brother every minute and second he possibly could. I knew exactly where Haden Krakauer was, but I didn't have time to go into it with my junior detective.

"Lock him up. Mirandize him, charge him with conspiracy to commit murder, aiding and abetting a known felon, accessory to kidnapping, aggravated assault, voluntary manslaughter—"

"Wait a second! What's going on?"

"Just do it. I want him in a holding cell. Now."

The next call was to the state police in Medford: arrest Miles DeSalvo—conspiracy, aiding and abetting. "And try to get a warrant to search the hard drive on his computer. There's some nasty stuff on there, and someone's been blackmailing him with it."

Next call: State Attorney General Dave Carmichael in Boston.

He picked up on the first ring, gruff and jovial, no secretary, no assistant. "You finally coming to work for me, Kennis?"

"I need your help, Dave. It's an emergency."

A quick, sober silence, then: "Shoot."

I explained the situation. He added the occasional "Holy shit!" or "What the fuck?" and, when I was finished, a quiet "Damn. What can I do?"

"It's what I don't want you to do, Dave. I'm putting together a rescue team—just me and a couple of people I trust. We have to act fast. But if we send in an assault force, we could have a Branch Davidian situation on our hands. This guy is armed. He's violent and unstable, and he's holding people I love out there."

"Okay. Here's the deal. Set up your raid, I'll call the governor, we'll get the full STOP team mobilization backing you up. We'll coordinate out of the State Police HQ on Nantucket."

The Special Tactical Operations teams, with their M4 carbines, sniper rifles, and BearCat armored vehicles, were exactly the kind of paramilitary full-court press I wanted to avoid.

"Listen, Dave…if this guy thinks the National Guard is closing in on him—"

"I get it."

"Plus, that section of the island is remote. There are no roads; you can only access it by over-sand vehicle or boat."

"Or by air."

"No way. You can't put state police choppers up there. The guy will freak out. It has to be ATVs from Wauwinet and boats at the Head of the Harbor, but everyone keeps their distance."

"Okay, okay. But I want choppers in reserve for the cleanup."

There was a long silence after that. I had a call-waiting message from Karen Gifford. I ignored it. More silence. I thought Dave's call had dropped. He was hesitant when he spoke again. "You have the people for this, Henry? I mean…a bunch of inexperienced local yokel Keystone Kops gearing up and charging that beach…I don't know."

"I have the people, Dave. And none of them are cops."

Unless you counted a pair of hard-asses who had beaten the Bulgarian Voenna Politsiya and a thug-pounding spy who had quit the CIA.

I made the last calls.

Mitchell Stone and Dimo Tabachev got to the airport ten minutes later.

My team was ready.

———

Later, the chief would tell her that she had "batted .500" on that fateful day, but Karen Gifford took no comfort in those baseball statistics. She thought of her father's daunting words on her first unrequited crush: "You feel a hundred percent for this boy, honey—but that's still only half of the equation. And fifty percent is a failing grade."

It was the same with police work: one smart move, one foolish one.

And it all added up to failure.

She did the right thing, sending the FBI to the Delavane house on Tuckernuck, though she knew she was taking a terrible risk. If someone died on Coatue because she had diverted the Feds, it would be the end of her career. But she also knew, just as Chief Kennis did, that a massive law enforcement assault on the slim, scalloped barrier peninsula was even more likely to end in tragedy. And this wasn't some archived news story from New Mexico or the Philippines or Waco, Texas.

Those were her friends out there. Those were her people. Once the shooting started, it wouldn't stop before some of them were dead.

So—she made the right call, as it turned out. But she was rattled and upset, and when Lonnie Fraker came into the station and Kyle told her to take him down to holding, there was no explanation, and the chief's phone went to voicemail.

Lonnie explained it, calmly and logically, as they rode down in the elevator.

"It's just a miscommunication, Karen. Todd's my brother. I thought he was still at the High Hopes halfway house. I guess he must have ditched the place and come here, but there was no way I could have known that. Then all hell breaks loose, and I guess I'm considered some kind of accessory, at least for the moment."

"I read Todd's blog, Lonnie. I know you hold Mark Toland responsible for your stepmother's death."

"Please. My stepmother was an *addict*. She did that to herself. No one forced her to gobble the Oxy. Mark Toland wasn't some diabolical drug dealer who tricked her into an overdose... though I guess, at the time, I wanted to believe that. I wanted to blame him. Kids need to blame someone, Karen. I was angry and confused. But kids grow up. Sometimes they channel that anger and confusion in a good way, and they grow up to be policemen. Or women. Police officers. That's us, Karen. This is our real family, and we have to stick together."

"I still have to arrest you."

"Which is fine. Everything will get sorted out. But I need a favor. I have to grab ten minutes face-to-face with Colton Hewes if he's going to be taking command in my absence. There are papers and documents, warrants and subpoenas we have to go over, protocols he never learned, personnel problems I don't want to discuss on the phone...it's going to be a heavy load for the kid, and I don't want the station to fall apart while I'm gone."

"I don't know. Kyle told me—"

"Kyle's a by-the-book guy. That's why he'll still be a junior detective when you're running this place. Handcuff me, that's okay. Whatever makes you comfortable. We'll be back here in half an hour, and my cop shop will be up and running for the duration of this craziness. It's a win-win."

So, she had agreed.

That was her first mistake.

And then she had cuffed Lonnie's hands in front of him, not behind his back—to minimize the embarrassing "perp walk" optics of his brief return to the state police headquarters on North Liberty Street. That was her second mistake.

She never got the chance to make a third.

It happened as they crossed West Chester Street, driving up North Liberty toward Cliff Road. They were alone—no other cars, no pedestrians. Karen sensed a movement beside her and then the impact of Lonnie's elbow, just below her ear.

She would never remember the attack, of course. The last thing she recalled was braking for a family on bikes at the corner of Main and Gardner streets. She woke up in the grass less than fifty feet from the State Police HQ, propped against someone's fence, the handcuffs on the grass beside her.

They found her cruiser in a Polpis Road driveway a few hours later, when the owners called in the theft of their Jeep. The SUV had its 2020 over-sand sticker, along with its required rope and shovel. The family had been planning a beach picnic at Great Point. The island suddenly seemed like a big place to the baffled summer person. "Our car could be anywhere!" he whined at Barnaby Toll, who picked up the call on the complaint line.

Karen Gifford knew the exact location of the man's Grand Cherokee, but all she could do about it was pray to the God who had often failed her.

And trust her boss, who had never let her down.

Chapter Sixteen

CALCULATED RISKS

In 1986 the New York Giants beat the Denver Broncos in Super Bowl XXI. Ed's father purchased a commemorative pin as a memento. For Jane, football was the best way to spend time with her own father, and she wanted that Super Bowl pin for him. Ed knew she wanted it.

He told me: "If you can find it in the barn, it's yours."

The Delavane family storage barn was a cave of black mold, and he locked me in. He stood outside in the fresh air, holding the Super Bowl pin in his hand.

"Guess I had it after all. And right in my pocket!"

—From Sippy Bascomb's deleted blog

When Lonnie Fraker saw Cindy Henderson limping along the narrow sand track between Coskata Pond and the Atlantic, he thought everyone had escaped from Todd Fraker's kangaroo court, and he felt a shameful gust of relief.

Maybe it was all over.

Then the chagrin, the bitter frustration rushed in, like a spike of cold water into a tooth cavity. Was Toland free also? Would Lonnie never get his revenge?

He thought of the glib lies he had used on Karen Gifford. They sounded so reasonable. How much better his life would have been if he could have ever managed to believe them. Yes, his stepmother, the lovely, open-hearted, sad, funny, damaged Janice Mohler, the only adult in his young life who had truly cared about him, truly seen him, truly accepted him for what he was, had some clinical problem like an "addictive personality." She was weak. That wasn't her fault! But her weakness had drawn the predators like Mark Toland.

They had been happy to destroy her.

For money.

Mark Toland wasn't just spoiled and careless and corrupt. He embodied everything wrong with Nantucket and the country and the world. He was the face of evil, the smug, smiling face of the devil, and Lonnie had sworn long ago to have his day of reckoning with that glib destroyer.

Nothing else mattered anymore except his half brother, but Todd was doomed now, too—that was obvious. Kennis was on to them, he had to be—the law was closing in, the trap was set. The intricate machine that Jim Bascomb had built was falling apart like all their other stupid, delusional schemes—Sippy's quest for that useless Super Bowl pin, their plan to rob Ed Delavane, Todd's attempt to burn down the school—all of it. Nothing worked, they never won, they always lost.

They were losers.

Had they lost again? That was Lonnie's one hope now. Todd had waited too long, the executions hadn't begun, the whole shaggy spectacle could be shut down like the fireworks on a foggy Fourth of July. His thoughts were a jumble. Maybe he should just run, refine the lies he had spun for Karen Gifford, leave Todd to his fate. Todd and his fate! But he couldn't have meant this. No, no, no, Lonnie had to find him, warn him, stop him, cook up some explanation for the police, make it all right somehow.

He jammed on the gas and almost spun out. That would be perfect! Stuck in a patch of sand he'd driven a thousand times, waiting for a tow while his world collapsed around him.

Then Cindy saw the Jeep. She veered toward him, staggering through the dune grass, waving and shouting. Her hair was tangled, her face filthy and tear-streaked. But she looked so happy, so relieved. And where was Toland? No doubt he'd left her behind, scampering like a scared rodent to safety. Only a fool would think that coward would let an injured woman slow his escape.

Cindy had stopped moving. She was staring at the car, and she finally realized it was Lonnie Fraker behind the wheel.

The look of absolute horror and fear that contorted her face at that moment, like fingers mauling a lump of dough! It snapped him. He was the villain? He was the bad guy? God, he hated her, her and all the rest of them.

His Glock was on the seat beside him, the passenger window open. He jammed the brakes, scooped up the gun, and aimed it at her running form. She was close enough to see it now, and she lurched to a stop.

"No, please—please don't—"

It would be so easy to burst that squealing face into pulp! One shot! That's all it would take. One shot. He shuddered. His hand was a frozen claw.

In despair, hating himself, hating his weakness and his lack of will as much as he hated her, he turned the gun vertical and emptied it into the roof of the Jeep.

BLAM BLAM BLAM BLAM BLAM BLAM BLAM BLAM!

The shots deafened him. Cindy's mouth was moving—she was saying something, but he couldn't hear her or even himself when he tore his throat calling out, "Run! Run back to town, run to your husband, get out of here!"

She must have heard him, though, or read his lips, because she turned back toward Great Point and stumbled off through the sand.

———

Jane Stiles had a sudden, vivid memory of an accidental free climb in a Williamstown quarry, the summer when she had just turned twenty. It was accidental because she had followed her fearless, brilliant younger sister, Lark, up from the steepening grass and shale-crumbled slope and into the first simple hand and footholds.

The situation had changed so fast.

She suddenly realized she was high enough on the wall for the fall to hurt her, with no way back down and her sister's sneakers disappearing above her. Acrophobia, dizziness, shortness of breath grabbed her…and then vanished. Her mind rejected the panic. She went cold. Her world shrank to the next lip of rock for her fingers to grasp, the next seam where she could lodge her foot. She never looked down, and she never looked up beyond the next few inches of stone. The granite face reduced itself to an abstraction, a series of problems to solve, equations of balance and tensile strength, ridges and protrusions, weight and gravity, sight and breath.

It was only when she pulled herself over the edge onto the weedy grass and safety that her body had started to shake. She had learned a vital fact that afternoon, discovered a hidden resource in her own steely composure.

She was going to need that strength today.

She stood with this madman on a deserted strip of sand next

to the gallows he had built, and she knew that she had only her own mind, her own ingenuity, to save herself. Help was coming, Henry was on his way, she knew it, she could feel it.

But she had to stay alive until he got there.

"Up the stairs," Todd said. "The good news is, I won't hand-cuff you. You'll be able to grab the rope and try to save yourself. The bad news is I greased it, so your hands will slip, and you can try to pull yourself up and feel the way I felt that day in gym class."

"No, wait—we have seven more throws left, and I still have my underwear on."

"It doesn't matter. Toland and Cindy escaped. You freed the others already, so you have nothing left to play for."

"What about my freedom?"

He laughed—an ugly little bark. "You think I'd throw all this away, do all this for nothing, let you walk just for...just to see you... No. No, this ends now."

She grabbed for the last thin ledge and pulled herself up. "What about fate?"

"Fate?"

"You said we were fated to be together. If you really believe that, you'll flip the coin again. Because you know you're going to win."

"You think fate is bullshit."

"But you don't! Prove me wrong. Faith is just talk if you're not willing to test it. An astrologer friend of mine pestered me for months to get my birth time so she could do my chart. I got my birth certificate, but all it had was the date. She told me if I gave her three major life turning points she could calculate the exact hour and minute when I was born. Then I remembered my family's OB was still alive, and he'd have the information in his notes. I told her I could check with him. It would be a great experiment—let her do her calculations and see how close she came. The look on her face at that moment was the perfect refutation of astrology forever. I could see she knew it was bullshit, too. That's the look I'm seeing on your face right now."

"No!"

"Then flip the coin."

The silence between them was a downed power line twisting in the road, spitting sparks. They stared at each other, a bizarre contest. Jane refused to even blink.

Finally, Todd looked down. "One throw."

"For everything."

"Yes."

He flipped the coin, caught it, flattened it between his palm and his forearm. He held it there for five, ten, twenty seconds, then lifted his hand. His lopsided grin told her everything. She was going to die, struggling with a greased rope, naked.

Or maybe not.

She slipped her panties off with no more embarrassment than she might feel undressing in front of a dog. But Todd was mesmerized, stunned. This was her moment. She was never going to get another one. She had been studying tai chi for almost two years. Now was the time to use it.

She leapt at Todd while windmilling her arms in the "cloud-hands" form and caught his arm while she slid her leg behind his and pushed. He toppled backward, the gun flew out of his hands, and she followed him down. Tactical mistake: now they were grappling, and she had given him the advantage. He outweighed her by fifty pounds, and his adrenalized rage would keep him from feeling any blow she might land. Not that she was going to be landing any blows—almost instantly he had rolled her over, with his knees pinning her arms.

It was over almost before it began. His weight bit into her biceps.

What had Chris Feeney told her? "Be careful. You've reached a very delicate stage with this martial art. You know just enough to get yourself killed."

But not enough to save herself.

Then she heard the gunshots—six, seven, eight cracks carried on the wind. The police were finally coming! They must have taken out Lonnie Fraker.

Todd seemed to sense what she was thinking. "Don't get your hopes up. That was Lonnie, killing your two friends. Killing them good. Four shots apiece. Two in the chest and two in the head. How does that feel?" He leaned over to pluck his gun from the sand, lurched off her, and got to his feet, holding it steady with both hands. "Up the stairs. Now!"

She stood and walked to the scaffold. The raw planking was rough and hot under her bare feet. Todd followed, four steps behind, out of kicking range. "Stand on the trap door."

She stepped to the square below the gibbet and felt it give queasily under her feet. Todd slipped the noose around her neck and tightened it. The raw hemp scraped her throat.

"Any last words?"

Did she hear a car engine, over toward Coskata? The police? Or Lonnie Fraker? Todd thought he knew the answer, and she might be able to dig out a last small advantage in that. She cleared her throat to cover the sound, thinking hard.

Last words! He was giving her one more chance. Choosing the right words had always been her specialty, at least when she was sitting in front of her computer, when her detective heroine Maddie Clark was doing the talking. In real life, the perfect answer usually came hours or days or even years too late.

Not today, though. Today she needed the perfect words now.

No, not *words*.

One word.

"Are you a virgin, Todd?"

"Am I—what?"

"You are. You were a loner in high school—then they sent you to Bridgewater. You never had a chance to be with a woman. It's not your fault. The opportunity passed you by. No—it was stolen from you. They took it away, along with everything else."

"What are you trying to do?"

"We're together, Todd. After all this time, in this crazy mixed-up way, but you proved your point. Your faith paid off, and not just with the coin toss. You got us together here. Don't waste that!"

He turned away from her.

She looked over his shoulder. From this height she had a clear view of the beach and the harbor, all the way to Shimmo, Monomoy, and the spires of town. Three kayaks were gliding up to the beach—three men were easing over the sides, slipping quietly into the water, and pulling the little boats ashore.

She couldn't let him see. "Todd!" He turned back to her.

"It wouldn't be just sex. We could run away together. Lonnie built this gallows, we could blame this whole crazy thing on him—him and Sippy. You were just one more innocent victim. I'll testify for you. So will the others! Monica is a police officer herself! That's important. They'll let you go, we can be together, we can travel. I have money. We could see the world. Not just sex in some Paris hotel, but coffee and the newspaper together in an outdoor café afterward in the spring air, not even needing to talk, with the whole morning ahead of us—"

"No!" He seemed to yank himself out of the trance she was weaving. "How many times do you think you can trick me? How stupid do you think I am? You're engaged to that cop! You liar! I would never run anywhere with you, nowhere, not in one million years. I hate you!"

Before she could answer, he pulled the lever, and she was falling into space.

Chapter Seventeen

ENDGAME

They said I almost died that day in Delavane's barn. They're wrong. I died, and I came back to life. The new Sippy understood that people were bad, and happy endings happened in the middle of the story because smart story-tellers know when to shut up. Maybe that's why I was in the hospital the day your mother overdosed. Maybe I was meant to be there. Our stories are connected. They're one story. Don't let it stop in the middle. You say it's time for action. Let's act together. There's work to do! Let's work together. You want a High School Military Tribunal?

Let's make one. Together.

—From Sippy Bascomb's deleted blog

"No phones, no engines, no cross talk. Three men, three kayaks, three guns. I figure a fifteen-minute paddle—the tide is rising, so once we get past the cut it will carry us up-harbor. That's a break. We hit the shore, Dimo secures the shack, the chief takes the gallows, I neutralize the Frakers. Aim to kill, center mass, or keep that gun packed. No fancy shooting. This is not a movie or a Wild West show. We hit the beach, spread out, and sprint. The shack is twenty yards from the Third Point waterline. That's a twelve-second run on soft sand with no cover. Keep low, stay sharp, and get ready to wing it."

I looked up from Mitch Stone's hastily drawn map. "That's the plan?"

He gave me a cold stare. "That's always the plan, Chief. Things go sideways the second you engage. Set your strategy and stick to it? You wind up dead. Guaranteed. No one winds up dead today, all right? That's the plan."

We were standing in the harbormaster's office on Washington Street. The kayaks were bobbing in the water at the end of the pier. Mike Henderson hovered by the door. He had overheard my phone call with Mitch; they were working on the same job-site, and he tagged along, hoping to join the rescue team. I had to tell him no. Secretly, I think he was relieved. He would have been a liability in combat, and he knew it.

I looked at Dimo Tabachev.

He nodded. "We go. We do."

Mitch touched his shoulder. "This is a rescue mission. The man who killed your brother, Roy Elkins? He's dead already. So is the animal who put him up to it. The man out there killed Sippy Bascomb, himself."

"The newspaper reported that as a suicide," I said.

Mitch gave me a cheerless smile. "But we both know better." He turned back to Dimo. "We cool?"

Dimo nodded. "As cucumber."

"Revenge is like booze. It makes you aggressive—and it makes you sloppy."

Dimo grinned—a flash of his old self. "Plus hangover is bitch!"

"Ain't it the truth? Ready, Chief?"

"Ready."

I almost capsized the narrow little boat lowering myself into it from the dock, but once I was seated comfortably with the double paddle in my hands, I got the feel for it quickly. The little craft was light on the water, and it shot ahead with every stroke. I could feel the tug of the current pushing me toward Monomoy at first, but Mitch was right—soon the pulse of water released us and we were riding the flow away from town, paddling hard north by northeast, Dimo beside me, both of us following Mitch Stone's lead, fighting to keep up. It was hard work. If I was physically exhausted by the time we crossed the water, I'd be no use to anyone. But the adrenaline kicked in, as it always does. The best drugs are the ones we make ourselves right there in the suprarenal glands, conveniently located above a kidney near you.

We had reached the shallows at Third Point when we heard the shots. Had the Staties and the FBI decided to launch their attack? But I trusted Dave Carmichael. Then what? Was Todd Fraker just shooting people now? Had he come totally unhinged? All I could do at that moment was paddle harder.

Three more strokes, and the nose of the boat hit the sand.

When I looked up from dragging my kayak onto the beach, I could see Jane, naked, standing on the gallows platform with the noose around her neck.

Then Fraker yanked his arm down, and she dropped out of sight.

I went insane, as insane as Fraker himself, bellowing as I pounded across the soft sand into the dune grass, skirted the shack past the Delavane brothers, Ed inert and Billy pulling on the belt he had wrapped around his thigh as a makeshift tourniquet. I took the steps to the platform two at a time.

Then Fraker was standing in front of me. I charged into

him, slamming him with my shoulder, and he staggered back two steps, pinwheeling his arms. On the third step, he ran out of platform. He fell, squealing, and I saw his knife lying next to the open trap door. I grabbed it and started sawing through the rope. Jane dangled below me, trying to lift herself, her hands slipping on the greasy rope, over and over, the noose jabbing into her throat each time. Fraker had smeared something on the hemp, some kind of oil, and then left her hands free so she could struggle before she died.

The hate rose up in me like vomit.

Jane cried out: "Henry!"

The hemp was dense, the knife was dull. It seemed to shred one filament at a time.

"Henry! I can't hold on! I—"

Her voice turned into a strangled cry as she lost her grip again and the noose tightened around her neck.

I kept sawing at the rope—I was getting through it. I screamed at Dimo, "Get under the scaffold," but he was already there. Finally, the last sinew of twine shredded, and Jane fell into his arms. He already had his jacket off, and he wrapped her in it.

I bounded down the stairs, jumped the last three steps, my gun in my hand as I hit the ground.

Fraker was on his knees, both ankles broken, helpless and terrified. He wasn't even human, just some bristling animal threat, a rat in your kitchen, a snake on your car seat, something you kill by instinct, in some panicked convulsion of the nerves. But this was a man, a helpless, injured man, and I killed him.

I murdered Todd Fraker.

But he didn't die.

I aimed for his quaking chest and felt a grisly spurt of joy as I squeezed the trigger and put a .45 caliber round into his heart.

The bullet never reached him.

Mitchell Stone broke my wrist with some kind of karate kick. My shot went wide, and I dropped the gun. The pain was excruciating; I was trembling, hyperventilating. I clutched my wrist, swarming globules sparking in front of my eyes. I thought I was going to faint.

But I saw the truth. Mitch had saved Todd, but he had also saved me, pulled me back from the brink in the only way anyone could have. When my vision cleared, I looked up, and Jane had pulled loose from Dimo, charging me, leaping at my chest, throwing her arms around me.

"Oh, my God, Henry…thank God you came, you found me, you—he…I thought—oh, God, I thought I was going to—"

I held her tight, wrapping my good arm around her. "Shhhh. I'm here. It's okay. You're safe. It's over."

As I spoke, Todd got to his feet somehow and launched himself at me. Mitch caught him in mid-air, as a firefighter on the burn-line might catch a sandbag, and lowered him into the dune grass.

That was when Lonnie Fraker showed up, wild-eyed, piling out of a stolen SUV with a gun in his hand.

"LET HIM GO!"

Mitch straightened up and took a step away from Todd.

"Help him up, Todd! I'm getting us out of here."

Todd pushed himself back up onto his knees. "Forget it, Lonnie. We're through."

"No, I just figured it out! We take the boat, but we don't keep it! We hijack one of these sailboats in the Sound and make them take us down the coast. Once we're aboard and we sink the Boston Whaler, we're invisible! It's protective coloration. They can't search every boat on the East Coast."

"I can't even walk. I think I broke both my ankles."

"I'll carry you! It's only fifty feet. Then we're gone."

"You're not thinking. The Coast Guard is on alert by now. They have drones, too. I've seen them. We'd never make it."

By this time I had picked up my gun and was gripping it in my left hand. Jane moved behind me, shivering uncontrollably, huddled into Dimo's jacket. "Put the gun down, Lonnie. Todd is right."

"You're outgunned, friend," Mitch added. His feet were set apart in a classic Weaver stance, his gun cupped in two hands, standing sideways to the target.

"You have no moves left," I added.

"We can take hostages!" Lonnie shouted.

It took a moment for the idea to penetrate the fog, but then Todd's face lit. "Hostages! Yes! You start shooting, the bullets go through those walls and cut those two in there apart. You just have to aim low, angle the shots down, right, Lonnie? You can't miss at this range!" He turned back to me. "Call off the Coasties, we're taking one of those prisoners with us. Maybe...Monica Terwilliger. You won't let her get hurt!" He jammed his hand into his pocket and pulled out the handcuff key. "Take it! Get her out here."

"No."

"Ten seconds, and I start shooting."

I cut my eyes toward Mitch. "Ready?"

He nodded.

"You won't shoot until I start shooting! That's the law! So someone's gonna die. Make the call." No one moved. "Ten. Nine. Eight. Seven. Six. Five. Four."

The shout came from behind him.

"You killed Cindy! I heard the shots, you fucking psycho!"

It was Mark Toland, charging across the dune grass with a jagged scrap of driftwood in his hands, raised like a club. He took on a bizarre stature as he ran, turning huge and primal, a black bear defending its turf, lumbering slowly and yet eating up the distance with those big strides. His wide, darting eyes told the story—his brain had short-circuited, overloading with hate and rage and blood lust.

I understood perfectly.

Lonnie wrenched himself around, his own face twisted with hate, more hate, bigger hate, long-fermented hate, and fired.

The shot took Toland in the chest and knocked him backward, sitting him down hard. Lonnie's second shot flattened him, and Toland was dead before his head hit the sand. The echoes of gunfire boomed out over the water, and Lonnie stood staring, transfixed by the motionless pile of clothes and flesh fifty feet away, half-hidden in the dune grass. Lonnie's wide-open face was transformed at that moment—transfigured, as if he'd seen God, or killed the devil.

Maybe he'd done both.

Then Dimo plowed into him, taking him down hard, and it was finally over.

Five minutes later the cavalry arrived: two boats full of Coast Guard troops, two medevac helicopters, and the Sikorsky Jayhawk that had just flown me to Boston. Pete Salros climbed out as three state police Ford Explorers pulled up. Dave Carmichael himself stepped out of the lead vehicle and walked up to me. An aide scurried behind him with a camera.

He reached out to shake my hand, saw the swollen wrist, and thought better of it. "Good work, Henry."

I just stared at him. "What the hell are you doing here?"

"I was late for my own marriage. I worked through the birth of both my sons. But I never miss a photo-op, and this is one for the history books."

I ignored him. The narrow strip of land felt toxic, radioactive. Using the carnage and human misery of the place for some crass splinter of political gain dumbfounded me.

I hugged Jane and turned to Pete Salros. "Get us the hell out of here."

Chapter Eighteen

"GOOD ENOUGH FOR NANTUCKET"

They airlifted Mark Toland's and Ed Delavane's bodies to the coroner's office in Barnstable and his brother Billy to the new, oversized Nantucket Cottage Hospital, along with the other captives. Apart from Billy's leg and the abrasions on Jane's neck, they suffered little more than cuts, scratches, and dehydration. Cindy Henderson jumped out of the lead state police SUV—they must have picked her up somewhere near Great Point—and watched as the bodies were loaded into the chopper.

She walked hesitantly up to me, reached out to touch me, then withdrew her hand. "He's—gone?"

I nodded.

"I don't feel anything. Why don't I feel anything?"

"You will. Right now, you need to take care of yourself. You need to get yourself checked out at the hospital and then get home to Mike and your little girl. Nothing else matters."

David Trezize had emerged from the shack, rubbing his sore wrist, and stood beside me.

"I know you're going to write about this," I said, "but—"

"Hey, I've known Cindy since before either of us came to

Nantucket, Chief. I'm not going to wreck her marriage for an extra column inch of news story."

Haden limped up to us. "Nice work, Chief. I need a drink. But I'm not going to take one."

"Good to hear."

He would need to know about our suspicions and the raid on his house. But all of that could wait.

After the last helicopter took off, I had orders to give, people to thank, suspects to mirandize and take into custody, interdepartmental rivalries to defuse, and a crime scene to secure. The rest of my afternoon was taken up with getting a cast on my wrist, dealing with the press from New York and Boston. I was short with them, impatient, rattled, and exhausted. Charlie Boyce touched my arm at one point and said gently, "Time to delegate, Chief."

He was right. I left them and their trusted officers to deal with the Fraker brothers and their lawyers, the families of the kidnap victims, and the press corps, which was swelling by the moment. All I wanted to do was track down my family and let them know I was okay. Miranda and Joe Arbogast had the kids in his 'Sconset house.

Miranda's response was typical. "Jesus, Henry, I thought we came to Nantucket to shield our children from shit like this. But it just follows you, wherever you go. We're keeping the kids out here tonight. They need some stability right now."

I gave them each a long hug and headed back to town. Miranda could be a bitch, but she was a good mother, and she'd feed them a good meal and make sure their teeth were brushed before they went to bed.

Jane was waiting for me when I got home with a necklace of gauze wound below her chin. She gave me a long hug and said, "My knight in shining armor."

"Well…nothing so important. Maybe…your squire in blue serge?"

She laughed. "I like that so much better! Less clanking."

But that afternoon on the beach continued to trouble me. I couldn't get to sleep. My mind kept pinballing through the same cones and columns. They dinged and lit up, and I racked up the points until the ball was back on the flippers and I sent it up into the maze again, and again.

And again:

I was no knight. I was no squire. Could I really claim to be better than the criminals I chased, better than Todd and Sippy, better than corrupt cops like Roy Elkins and Ham Tyler?

I still wanted to kill Fraker. I still wished I had.

Not a good feeling. I worked my way through it. The incident on Coatue beach had been a uniquely extreme situation. Who wouldn't give in to their blood lust at a moment like that? What kind of man would I be if I had calmly taken Todd Fraker into custody, as if he was nothing worse than a shoplifter? That would have been bizarre, deviant, dissociative. That would have been the real craziness.

And what if I had killed him? The world would not have been in any way diminished. It was like putting down a rabid dog—a public service.

But that was bullshit, and I knew it.

Where did the killing stop? Who made the decisions?

At three in the morning I gave up trying to sleep and went downstairs. My mom was having a cup of tea at the kitchen table.

She glanced up. "Chamomile tea is good when you can't sleep. I have a pot going."

"Thanks, Mom."

I walked to the counter and poured myself a mug of the pale yellow brew, awkwardly, one-handed. My wrist still ached under the brand-new cast. I sat down at the table across from her. We were silent for a long time, sipping.

She spoke first. "You're only human, Hanky. And none of us are down too long from the trees."

"I would have killed that guy."

"And it's keeping you up at night. That's a good sign."

We sat and sipped. She reached out and put her hand over mine. "No one is just one thing."

When I went back up to bed, Jane was awake. She slipped under my arm when I got under the covers, nuzzled my neck. "Give yourself a break, Chief."

"Not my specialty."

"You want to know what I was feeling? Right then, when you were about to shoot him?"

I lifted my head a little to take in her face, sober and wide awake in the moonlight. "Sure."

"When I heard the gun go off, I was screaming in my mind, 'YES!' And then when I realized what Mitch had done and knew you hadn't killed Todd, I sighed and almost fainted, but it was the same word: YES. I desperately wanted you to kill him at that moment, and I desperately wanted you not to...and Mitch let us have it both ways, both of us. You know? You did it, but it didn't happen. I watched it, but I didn't have to see."

"And now you know I'm a killer."

"And I'm glad."

"You take me as I am?"

An amused little squint. "Well. You're not perfect. But you're good enough for Nantucket."

"So sentimental."

"And I love you."

Then she rolled on top of me and proved it.

On Saturday night, the gallows on Coatue burned, a vivid

torch across the harbor, sending a dense throbbing column of smoke up to the full moon. There was no way to extinguish the blaze, so the fire department just let it burn out. Half the town gathered along the shore to watch, from Dionis to Jetties Beach to the decks of the big houses in Monomoy and Shimmo, Polpis, and Pocomo. The fire was laid carefully and didn't spread. The investigation was cursory and short-lived. No arrests were made. The blaze remains a mystery.

When Jane came home at dawn on Sunday, I said, "Feel better?"

She eased beside me under the covers. "Much."

I sniffed her breath. "Who brought the Jameson's?"

"Billy had a flask."

"And David's not going to write about it?"

"Well—just that it happened."

"Scooped by the *Inquirer and Mirror*. Amazing."

She snuggled against me. "It's over. That's what matters."

I was making pancakes the next morning when Mitch Stone appeared at my door. He stood on the little deck at the top of the front stairs.

"Any idea who might have set that fire last night, Chief?"

I smiled. "We suspect Muslim terrorists. Or possibly, disgruntled immigrants. Those are some bad hombres."

"I was thinking of guerilla real estate brokers. A gallows across the harbor really tanks the property values."

"I'll look into it."

We stood just breathing the morning air for a few seconds. A gardener's truck drove by, with a trailer full of riding lawnmowers. We'd be getting the complaint calls as soon as those big engines started up. Mitch made some joke about roasting marshmallows, but I brushed it aside.

"They told some stories, put out some grass fires, passed

around a flask, and went home. The Staties wanted to know if I was pressing charges against the individual who broke my wrist."

"What did you say?"

"I told them I was going to call your girlfriend, find out what kind of beer you drink, and buy you a case of it."

He shrugged. "I like Kronenbourg. But it's hard to find on Nantucket."

"There's a lot that's hard to find here."

Mitch nodded. "Big Macs, fountain pens, ammunition."

"Among other things."

Mrs. Penniston from number 6 strolled past with her two waddling pugs. Dervish was an Olympic athlete by comparison. Billy Delavane referred to his pug as "the sports model." I couldn't see these two dogs chasing rabbits or deer—or the moon. Dervish had been known to chase the moon when he caught sight of it. I nodded to Mrs. Penniston. She smiled and lifted a hand.

I turned back to Mitch. "So what brings a world traveler like you to Nantucket?"

"What brings an LAPD cop to Nantucket?"

"My ex-wife's family were summer people for years."

"Summer people."

"You say that the way I say 'shoplifters.' So I assume you grew up here."

"You don't assume anything, Chief. After the school shooting, you did your research. You know everything there is to know about me. You know my father was an abusive drunk. You know I was suspended from fifth grade for throwing snowballs at police cars. You pulled my Marine Corps service record. You have my whole life on your computer."

"Until 2009, when you disappear off the face of the earth."

Mitch shrugged. "Well, I'm back."

We studied each other. I could see there was no point in probing any further. Whatever Mitch Stone's secrets were, he was keeping them. In nosy, small-town Nantucket that was actually refreshing. I lifted my wrist from the sling. "Thanks for your help."

"We have a saying in the Marines, Chief. 'Two is one and one is none.' You gotta have backup."

Some kids on bikes rode by on Fair Street, shouting and laughing. When they were gone Mitch said, "You think their parents know what they're up to today?"

"I certainly hope not."

Mitch squinted up at the cloudless early autumn sky. "Beautiful day."

"Yeah. Looks like things are back to normal finally."

"Let's hope."

My kids were still talking about the weekend events when I picked them up from school the next day. Carrie gave me a solemn hug. Her friends were watching, but she didn't seem to care. And she had some news of her own. "I made friends with Judy Gobeler. I apologized."

"That's great."

"She tried out for The Grace Notes. She really can sing."

"There you go."

"She and Debbie are friends again, too, Dad."

"Wow."

"So Judy's not going to come back years from now and try to kill us all."

"Well, that's taking the long view. In the meantime, you needed another soprano."

"And she's letting me borrow her Levi's Wedgie icon jeans."

"So it's all good."

At home, Tim found me starting dinner in the kitchen.

"I was thinking about that poem you wrote, about you and your dad and me and all the generations and everything and the dead guy and the whale."

"Maybe I bit off a little more than I could chew there."

"No, it's a great poem!"

"Well, thanks."

"I wrote one, too. I did it today in Social Studies."

"You couldn't wait for study hall?"

"No! Remember what you told me about poems?"

"Uh…"

"They're like visits from the Royal Family. You said you have to drop everything and go outside to wave, or pay homage or whatever."

"I do remember that. It's true. Poetic Prerogative."

"Right."

"Can I see it?"

"It's not that great. Too many rhymes."

"What's it about?"

"Uh…you. You and me. And maybe Grandpa, too, I don't know. I couldn't get the whale in there, but it feels like he's in there, anyway."

I stuck out a flat palm and beckoned with my fingers. "Show me."

He dug his spiral notebook out of his book bag, opened it to a page of cramped but legible handwriting. Was it in the genes? It looked a little like my own scrawl, and a lot like my father's.

> *My dad is strong and good*
> *At least he knows he should be*
> *He's not a bad man*
> *But he knows he could be*
> *He chooses every day*
> *When he has to choose, he's alone*

We've both always known
But neither of us say
I'm not him
He's not me
I'm free, I'm no clone
But he's everything I'd like to be
When I'm grown.

I handed the notebook back. "Nice. But it's a lot to live up to."

He grinned. "Yeah, Dad. Don't blow it."

They were moving Lonnie Fraker to Barnstable the next afternoon, and I wanted to see him before the transfer. I caught him just after his breakfast and buzzed the cell door open as he sipped the last of his coffee.

"Hey, Lonnie."

"Chief."

He sat down on the hard mattress of his concrete-slab bed, "Never thought I'd wind up in here."

"Then you weren't thinking."

Lonnie shrugged. "No, just feeling."

"I was thinking about something you said to me the other day, in the Darling Street attic, when you made your case against Haden Krakauer. That maybe we're all strangers."

"Maybe we are."

"I thought I knew you."

"I showed you the good stuff. No one shows the bad stuff."

"Well, it's all out now. You and your brother are going away for a long time."

"Don't worry about me, Chief. I'll be fine. And Todd's used to the lockup. He's an institutional man."

I studied him as he drained the last of his coffee. "Why? Why do this? I don't get it."

"Sure you do. I saw you with Toddie. You would have blown his brains out if not for Mitch. You were feeling it, all right."

"So that's it? Just—rage and hate?"

"And a dash of bitters. Gotta have the bitters."

"It's been twenty years, Lonnie."

"Yeah. I thought the feeling would go away, but it didn't. Not for Toddie either. Maybe it never goes away for anybody. I thought the law would take care of those assholes, you know? Justice would prevail! And it seemed that way for a while. You arrested Ed. But he wound up king of the prison like some Mexican drug lord."

"He was happy to escape, though."

"He went for the better deal. Getting his stash and getting away. Ed always went for the better deal. And nothing happened to Toland! He got rewarded! That little movie he made about all of us? It was his ticket to Tinseltown. I mean, come on."

"No one could have proved he killed your stepmother."

"My point exactly. Waiting around for our legal system to do its job...you could wait forever. I thought I was going to." He set his cup down on the floor and leaned back against the cinderblock wall. "You know how they say revenge is a dish best served cold?" I nodded. "Well, that's bullshit. Take it from me. Life is a long, cold night. You want roast chicken, you want beef stew. Comfort food, not some cold dinner. Who eats sushi in a blizzard?"

"Good point."

"I got my meal, Chief. Piping hot the way I wanted it."

"You know, they also say if you want revenge, dig two graves."

"I'll let you dig mine. I'm good with that."

We were quiet for a minute or two, listening to the noises of the booking room, the phones ringing, and the muted conversations. "You still haven't told me," I said finally. "Why get involved with this whole crazy scheme in the first place? Why not just hire a couple of hitters from Southie to take Toland out?"

He smiled. "That's a little cold, Chief. And anyway...Todd is my brother."

"Half brother."

"No such thing. Not with us."

"Okay, but what about all the other people? Jane never hurt you. You had no problem with David Trezize. And Monica Terwilliger?"

"I wasn't going to let anything happen to them."

That was too much for me. I charged forward, lifted him off the bed, and slammed him into the wall. "Jane was hanging from your gallows when we hit the beach!"

His eyes were wild. "I didn't want that! I feel like shit about that!"

I pushed him back down onto the mattress. "No, you don't."

A long silence raged between us, cold and uncrossable as a snowmelt river. We stood on opposite banks, with the white noise and the rapids between us.

Lonnie spoke first. "This was a war, Chief. All right? Civilians die in a war. It's called collateral damage."

"No. It's more than that."

"What are you talking about?"

"I read your brother's blog. High School Military Tribunal dot blogspot dot com. It's on the net—anyone can find it. Sippy Bascomb did."

"Yeah."

"And that's when this whole thing started."

I pulled out my phone, went online, and tapped in the URL for Sippy's blog. I wanted to read the words verbatim. Sippy had to start his own blog just to comment on Todd's, because he went on for so long, and they have a 4,200-character limit. "Here it is. Fish Face and Mr. Peanut dot blogspot dot com. I guess those were the nicknames the mean kids gave them. What did they call you?"

"Pumpkin Head. Squeaky. After Toland spread the word, they left it at faggot, basically."

"Here it is. Listen to this. He's talking about the Nazi government. 'It would have been unthinkable without the agreement of the ordinary people, each ordinary person. Everyone who participated with a secret smile, everyone who could have helped a single Jew and decided it was safer not to, everyone who looked away—they all deserved to be put on trial and convicted along with their overlords.' A little later he tells Todd, 'You understand the culture of cruelty that tormented us. So I respond. You've earned it.' The culture of cruelty. You believed in that, too."

Lonnie looked up at me. "It was real."

"So they all deserved to die? David, Monica, Billy…Cindy and Jane? All of them."

He grabbed his face with his hands and shook his head. "What do you care what I believed? Or Todd or Sippy. You never knew us. And you won. It's over. Let it alone."

"I will. I'm done here."

I called for the cell door to open. I was on the other side, and the bars slid shut again when Lonnie stood up and approached them. "Chief—"

I turned. "What?"

"You can fix this."

"Enough, Lonnie."

"You can tell them I was working undercover, helping you from the inside. That Bulgarian punk won't say a word; he doesn't want to get deported. And Mitch Stone knows how to keep a secret. They'd go along. And it's a good story. I'm the hero. I tipped you off. I saved the day. There's no scandal. The state police look good, everybody's happy. Wait a second! I'm not asking for favors! There's plenty in it for you, Chief. I still know where Ed's stash is buried. You can have it all. Those kids of yours are gonna be going to college soon. That ain't cheap."

I watched him closely, more sad than angry now. "You know, Lonnie…my mother always says liars think everyone is lying, and thieves think everyone's a thief. She's right. You think everyone's just like you. But they're not. Apart from everything else, you've just violated Massachusetts General Law 268A Section Two 'corrupt gifts, offers or promises to influence official acts.' That's another five years on your sentence. Looks like you've found a home."

He had no answer for that, and I left him there, climbed the stairs to the main lobby, and walked out into the bright, cold autumn sunshine. Patty Stokes and Jill Swenson were walking across the parking lot about to start their shift. Two tough, smart young women, one white, one black, first in their classes from the Academy, highest scores on our own aptitude tests, and I heard they had rented a house together off of First Way with a couple of other female officers to save money. They waved happily at me and returned my salute. It felt good to see them at this moment. I badly needed a dose of their high spirits and their optimism. They had a mission, and so did I. We were all struggling toward a better world. We were making progress. It was slow and irregular and incremental. But we were getting there.

That was a good thought to remember.

I married Jane Stiles the next Saturday, after Sam's first full week at Cyrus Pierce, where he had already made two new friends and gotten his first A on a book report. I took the week off and left Haden Krakauer in charge of the cop shop. Jane and I worked on our vows together, organized the reception (Spanky's raw bar and all the booze anyone could drink at the Admiralty Club in Madaket), found rooms for Franny Tate, my brother Phil, Jane's sister and her dad, plus Chuck Obremski, who took some of his bereavement leave from the LAPD to come east for the wedding.

We held the ceremony on the beach at Madequecham under the steep sand cliff in the lee of the sharp north wind with the rest of our families and friends—my ex-wife, Jane's ex-husband, our kids, a few friends like David Trezize and Kathleen Lomax, Mitch Stone and Vicky Fleishman, Mike and Cindy Henderson, Billy Delavane, on crutches, with Karen Gifford—so they really were a couple now!—Sam and Claire Trikilis—with my father's ghost muttering, "All the world does not love a lover. All the world is in fact bored to tears by a lover," and my mother presiding over the ceremony from her wheelchair at the top of the bluff. There was no whale on the beach, but the porpoises in the water put on a fine show for the occasion. Bethany Starbuck, the new town clerk, presided, while Dervish and Bailey chased each other and tussled over pieces of driftwood and an abandoned flip-flop sandal.

I recited my vows first:

"I will clean the toilets when you least expect it, step on the edge of the rug when you vacuum, and always be on the other side when you're making the bed.

"I will bring you flowers for no reason.

"I will read to you from books that are exactly the right amount of boring when you cannot get to sleep.

"I will listen to you working out the plot points of your books and comfort you when you hit page one hundred and nothing makes sense and you want to throw the thing away and remind you that you always feel that way on page one hundred.

"I will swim in the ocean with you late in the afternoon in

the late summer when the tourists have gone back to their rental houses for cocktails, even though the water is cold and the air is chilly.

"I will make your first cup of coffee in the morning and let you add the milk.

"I will let you navigate when I drive off-island and enjoy all instructions, even, 'Oh, my God, turn left, I mean right!'"

"I will hug your son all the time until he's old enough to hate it and then again when he's grown up and doesn't mind again.

"I will not tease you about losing your glasses, even when I find them in one of your boots or the vegetable drawer of the fridge.

"I will edit your books and always say exactly what I think.

"I will tell you that you're beautiful and argue the point like a high-school debate-team star when you disagree.

"I will kiss you when these vows are done just long enough to make everything absolutely clear to everyone.

"I will plan amazing trips to Europe and China and the Maldives with you, and I swear we will take one of those trips before we're too old to enjoy them.

"I will grow old with you. You are my favorite person who doesn't share my DNA.

"I will choose you, every day, forever."

Bethany said, "Jane?"

She took my hands.

"I will laugh at your jokes and smile at your puns and enjoy your plays on words. 'Be it ever so crumpled there's no plate like chrome' isn't exactly funny or even witty, it's just awesome.

"I will watch the *Godfather* movies and *Chinatown* as many times as you like.

"I will scratch your back even when I'm exhausted.

"I will dance with you whenever we hear good music, especially Creedence.

"I will do the dishes after every meal you cook and only have you in the kitchen to keep me company.

"I will fall in love with you again a tiny bit every time you volunteer to pump the gas.

"I will always listen with adoring, undivided attention when you tell me your police stories and thrill at your courage and admire your patience and love your doubts. And then I'll steal all the good parts for my books.

"I will try to be the best stepmother ever to your kids and hope I can hold out long enough for us to be friends.

"I will stupidly break every nice wineglass we ever buy.

"I will accept your compliments with no argument.

"I will kiss you as long and deep as you want in a minute or so in front of all our friends and family, despite the fact that I hate public displays of affection.

"I will walk our fabulous dog alone when you're too busy and will walk him together with you when you're not, and I will show you every great secret walk on the island before we're too old to enjoy them.

"I will grow old with you.

"You are my favorite person over the age of eleven.

"I will choose you, every day, forever."

Bethany pronounced us husband and wife and told me, "You may kiss the bride."

But I was already doing it.

ACKNOWLEDGMENTS

Thanks to Nantucket Chief of Police William Pittman, for putting up with Henry Kennis, to Ginger Andrews for her crucial knowledge of local wildlife, to Annette Rogers and Barbara Peters for the stringency and surgical skill of their editing. And to Larry Page and Sergey Brin, for creating the greatest research tool a writer could ever have. Don't know who they are? Google them.

ABOUT THE AUTHOR

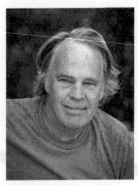

Photo © Cary Hazlegrove

Steven Axelrod holds an MFA in writing from Vermont College of the Fine Arts and, as a former Hollywood screenwriter, is still a member of the Writers Guild of America. A father of two, he lives on Nantucket Island, Massachusetts, where he paints houses and writes.